About the Author

On a personal note, I am married, with two grown children. I have lived in the wine country of Santa Barbara County most of my life, but currently reside in Tucson, Arizona. My business experience is in finance, but my passion is writing.

Flight to Armageddon

William Congdon

Flight to Armageddon

Olympia Publishers
London

www.olympiapublishers.com
OLYMPIA PAPERBACK EDITION

A CIP catalogue record for this title is available from the British Library.

ISBN: 978-1-80074-733-3

First Published in 2022

Olympia Publishers
Tallis House
2 Tallis Street
London
EC4Y 0AB

Printed in Great Britain

Dedication

I would like to dedicate this book to my wife, Mary, for her constant support and encouragement as I worked through the writing process.

Chapter 1

Vladimir Petronovich sat on the deck and sipped his drink as he took in the majestic view of the valley below him. The birds in the trees broke the silence; they scattered when the cabin door squeaked open and slammed shut. Jason McClintock sat down next to Petronovich and placed a tumbler of Glenfiddich on the table. The eighteen-year-old single malt scotch was Jason's drink of choice. Petronovich, with his Russian background, preferred vodka, specifically, Grey Goose.

"Vladi, I'm glad you made the decision to come up here. Montana in the spring can be a bit chilly, but you can't beat the beauty," Jason said as he inhaled the bouquet of his scotch and took a sip.

McClintock had met Petronovich the year before. Petronovich was ex-GRU (Russian Intelligence Agency) and had been brought to the U.S. under contract with the CIA after the Soviet Union fell. He was tasked with using his lethal expertise, without question, if called upon by the Agency. That day came when Jason's brother, Mike, retired FBI Special Agent, used his contacts to check the background on an individual with whom Jason was about to work in South America. Jason, with his Doctorate in Geology from the Colorado School of Mines had been hired by the State Department to assist Uruguay in developing a gold mine in the northern part of the country. Jason was uneasy with his business associate. Mike had unknowingly exposed a sinister CIA rogue operation that had to be stopped. Petronovich was told to eliminate Mike McClintock, and if need be, his family. He couldn't do it. What followed was an unlikely alliance between the McClintock brothers and Petronovich. They followed, exposed, and terminated the individuals that threatened them. The bond that developed between them was stronger than that experienced by most families.

"I told you I always wanted to see Montana," Petronovich said. "I am not disappointed." He glanced over at Jason.

Jason smiled. "Tomorrow, I'm taking you to the mine. I think you'll find it interesting." When Jason mentioned the gold mine, Rosie, Jason's golden retriever jumped up from her bed in the corner of the deck and sat in front of Jason, her tail wagging, as if to say, "Let's go!"

"Not now, Rosie, tomorrow we go," he said. "Now, lie down." With that, Rosie sauntered back to her bed and plopped down. Vladi chuckled and took a sip of his drink just as his cell phone rang.

"Hello, is everything all right, Marina?" asked Petronovich. Marina Mikhailov was one of Petronovich's closest friends from Russia. She had immigrated to the U.S. using standard, but expedited procedures. Her Doctorate in Biochemistry made her highly sought after, which allowed her to cut through much of the red tape.

"Yes, Vladi, I'm fine," Marina said. "No, I'm really not," she sighed. "I'm sorry to bother you, but I need to see you. I have a problem, and I'm not sure where to turn. I don't want to talk about it over the phone. Can I see you the day after tomorrow? I'll fly to Montana," she said.

"I'm sure it will be okay," said Petronovich as he looked

at Jason who nodded in the affirmative. "Fly into Butte. Let me know your flight number and we'll be there to pick you up."

"Thank you so much, Vladi, I'll be in touch soon," Marina said and hung up.

As she sat at her desk, she wrote a detailed letter, explaining the situation in which she found herself. She sealed the envelope and wrote instructions on the outside to open only in the event of her untimely death. Then she placed the smaller envelope inside a manila envelope and addressed it to Vladi's home in Southern California.

"Something must really be bothering her for her to call," Vladi said. "Marina is as level-headed as you can get, and very little flusters her." He stared down at the valley.

"Well, whatever it is," Jason said, "we'll know soon enough. How about if I get the grill started for those two-inch thick T-bones I had cut?" Without waiting for an answer, he rose from his chair.

****

Petronovich was disoriented when he woke up; he heard movement in the kitchen. He dressed, then followed the scent of strong coffee. A hot cup was waiting for him on the table. Jason looked up from the news he was reading on his iPhone.

"Have you heard from Marina?" Jason asked, wondering if picking her up from the airport would keep them from the mine.

"She texted me the flight number and time," Vladi said. "It looks like she gets in at 11:30 in the morning, flying Delta. I'm glad it's not United, with their endless cancellations or delays." He sat down and pulled the cup of coffee to him.

So much for going to the mine tomorrow, thought Jason. He heard the scratching at the door and got up to let Rosie in, along with a crisp chill. The morning temperature was 29 degrees. He would need a warm coat, at least initially.

As usual, Rosie was standing by the door at 5:30. Jason didn't bother looking at the time. "Let's hit the road," he said as he zipped his parka. Vladi did the same as he carried a thermos to the Jeep. It was a 1955 classic, in great running condition, perfect for the back country they traveled to the mine. The year before, after their adventure, if it could be called that, Jason had exposed one of the largest veins of gold found in Montana in the previous 150 years. The only people to know about it were his brother Mike, his girlfriend, Brenda and soon, Vladi. And Rosie, of course, but Jason knew she could keep a secret. Aside from his recent discovery, Jason was wealthy. In fact, he was somewhat of a legend when it came to mining. This success gave him the luxury of picking and choosing contracts to work. His mine had been very successful.

It was still dark when they dropped into a small gully and pulled up in front of the mine shaft. "Grab a pick and shovel in the back of the Jeep, Vladi," Jason said. "Let's get started." He followed Rosie to the mine's entrance.

Petronovich, his gear in hand, flicked on the hard-hat light and entered the mine. Surprisingly, it was much warmer than outside. He unzipped his coat and followed the beam of light in front of him. Jason turned a corner. When Vladi caught up, his jaw dropped as he looked at the wall of gold in front of them.

"Impressive, isn't it?" asked Jason, without turning. The

gold glistened in the beam of light.

"That's an understatement!" whispered Vladi, as he reached toward the wall and ran his hand along the vein. "Why don't you have guards here?" he asked, still in awe.

"The more people that know about this, the less safe it is, even with 24-hour security," Jason said. He brought out a small hand pick and used it to knock rock away from the gold.

Chapter 2

Bert Mooney Airport, located three miles south of Butte, is serviced by Delta. All connections for Butte must travel through Salt Lake City, one of Delta's hubs. Marina left Orange County at 6:30 in the morning. The layover in Salt Lake gave her time for breakfast at one of the airport restaurants. She strolled through Terminal 2 and spotted The Market Street Grill. She asked for a seat next to the window and ordered eggs Benedict from the waitress. The Rocky Mountains in the distance reminded her of her hometown in Almaty, Kazakhstan. Almaty sat at the base of Trans-Illi Alatau mountains. Marina had been born and raised in Almaty and missed her family and friends. She shook her head to jar herself from her reminiscence and refocused on the information she had inadvertently stumbled upon. Marina worked for AdvanChem, a small, privately-owned company in Irvine, California. AdvanChem does work for the Federal Government; most of it is extremely sensitive. The owners and scientists have nothing but top-secret security clearances.

Half an hour before boarding, Marina left the restaurant and merged into the stream of travelers heading to various gates. A man who looked to be Middle Eastern quickly came up from behind and knocked into her. He apologized and moved on. Marina was stunned by the brief, yet seemingly innocuous encounter. A moment later, she felt her arm begin to sting, almost as if she'd been stung by a bee. Suddenly, light-headed, she found an empty chair at the closest gate. She sat down and began to perspire. Her breathing grew labored and she felt a tightness in her chest. She was losing control of her muscles, including her bladder, when the seizures began. A crowd surrounded her; many dialed 911. Marina, given her background in biochemistry, thought *nerve agent,* she then convulsed, closed her eyes, and died as a single tear rolled down her cheek.

Petronovich and McClintock arrived at the airport in Butte fifteen minutes before Marina's flight was scheduled to arrive. Jason found a seat in front of one of the two baggage carrousels in the claim area. Vladi was drawn to the picture windows off to the side and stood mesmerized by the beauty of the mountains surrounding the valley. In the distance, he caught a glimpse of the sun reflecting off the plane as it began its final approach. Vladi walked back to McClintock, "I think the plane is arriving. It looks to be ten minutes early," he said.

"Once she gets her bags, we'll head to lunch," Jason said. "I think she'd enjoy The Montana Club. So will you." He rose from his chair and stretched his back.

Twenty minutes later, the passengers began their descent down the escalator to baggage claim. Jason stood well off to the side while Vladi remained closer to the crowd, searching the passengers as they descended. As the last passenger to deplane walked past Petronovich, he looked at Jason, who shrugged, palms up, as if to ask, "Where is she?" Petronovich dialed Marina's number. It was answered by a strange voice, "Hello?"

"Who is this?" asked Vladi.

"This is Salt Lake City International Airport security.

Who am I speaking with?"

"This is Vadimir Petronovich. I am a friend of Marina Mikhailov. Is she okay?" he asked.

"This is Rich Harrington. My team and I found Ms. Mikhailov unresponsive at one of the gates. Emergency personnel administered CPR until an ambulance arrived. We have her handbag as well as carry-on luggage. I do not know her status," explained Harrington.

"Which hospital has she been taken to?" asked Petronovich.

"LDS is the closest; I'm sure she's there," answered Harrington. "We'll keep her belongings for her or a relative to pick up. Unless law enforcement feels compelled to get involved."

McClintock saw the look of concern on Vladi's face. He walked over and listened as best he could to his friend's side of the conversation. Jason's mind began to race. *What happened*? he thought.

Petronovich thanked Harrington, then found a seat. He looked up the number for the LDS Hospital and dialed.

"LDS Hospital, how may I direct your call?" asked the receptionist.

"I'd like the emergency room, please," replied Petronovich.

"Emergency Room," said a voice on the other end.

"I'd like to check on the status of a patient who was brought in recently from Salt Lake International," Vladi said. "Her name is Marina Mikhailov."

"How are you related to Ms. Mikhailov?" asked the individual.

"I'm a close friend, my name is Vladimir Petronovich,"

said Vladi, feeling anxious.

"Mr. Petronovich, please hold for one moment. I'll get someone to help you." For the next five minutes, Vladi listened to elevator music that was mostly static.

"This is Dr. Jake Sterling," a voice finally said. "Mr. Petronovich, unless you are family, we cannot release details of Ms. Mikhailov's condition."

"Is she okay?" asked Petronovich, obviously upset, as Jason looked on.

"As I said, we can't release any information regarding her condition, end of story," Dr. Sterling said. "Does Ms. Mikhailov have any relatives we can contact?"

"Her family is in Kazakhstan. I'm the closest one to her in the U.S.," said Vladi.

"If you can contact them and have them call, that would be helpful," said Dr. Sterling.

Vladi hung up and slumped in the chair. With all that had happened in the last forty minutes, he was emotionally spent. "Come on, Vladi," Jason said. "Let's go home, we have a lot to talk about." He stood and helped Vladi up.

****

Jason worked his way up the dirt road to the cabin. "Looks like Brenda is here," he said as he pulled in next to her Range Rover. Brenda was an artist, concentrating on oils of western landscapes. She had a show in Chicago and had been gone for a week, but when the two men entered the cabin, they found Brenda in the kitchen cutting cheese and salami and singing to a Bee Gees song on Pandora.

Jason moved across the room and gave her a hug and a

kiss, "I'm glad you're home," he said.

Brenda kissed him on the cheek and went straight to Petronovich. "Hi, Vladi," she said. "Welcome to Montana." She threw her arms around him. Sensing that something wasn't right, she looked at Jason. "What's wrong?" she asked.

"Brenda, you are as beautiful as ever," said Vladi as he sat the kitchen table.

Jason pulled a chair out and sat down as well. He brought Brenda up to speed, beginning with the call Vladi had received from Marina the two days before. He ended with the events that had transpired today.

"My God! Vladi, I am so sorry, I hope she's okay," exclaimed Brenda as she stood near the kitchen sink. "What coud have happened to her! What are you going to do? Don't you have to call the authorities?" she asked both men.

"And tell them what?" Jason asked. "We have no idea what Marina's condition is, or what she was going to tell Vladi."

Vladi straightened up and with a look of resolve said, "I'm not waiting, Jason. I want to look through her purse and luggage. I'll start with security at Salt Lake City International. Harrington said he had all of Marina's things." Vladi rose from the table and marched to his room. "I must pack. When is the next flight to SLC?" he asked.

Brenda was on it. She had two options. The next flight out of Butte left at 5:30 that evening and the last flight was at 8:00. Jason stood, "Reserve two seats on the 5:30 flight," he said. "We can make it. I better pack my bag as well."

****

The landing in Salt Lake was hard, with the small jet buffeted about by strong cross-winds. At the gate, as they were deplaning, Jason stopped and asked the flight attendant where the main security office was located. It was 7:30 when they entered the office. Petronovich had spoken with Harrington at 12:30 that afternoon. "I'll bet Harrington has gone home for the day," said Vladi as he approached the counter.

A young blonde woman looked up from her computer. "May I help you?" she asked.

"I'm looking for Rich Harrington," said Vladi.

"Well, I think you're in luck. Rich is still here, I'll get him," said the woman as she went through a side door.

A moment later, Harrington walked through the door wearing his dark blue uniform. He looked to be in his mid-thirties with a short-cropped haircut. "What can I do for you?" he asked as he approached the counter.

"My name is Vladimir Petronovich," Vladi said. "I spoke with you earlier today about my friend, Marina Mikhailov." He offered his hand.

"Mr. Petronovich, I didn't expect to see you this soon," Harrington said. "I thought maybe tomorrow." He shook Vladi's offered hand. "And you are?" Harrington asked as he looked at McClintock.

"Jason McClintock. We came to retrieve Marina's personal items."

"I'm sorry. I can't release her personal property without authorization," Harrington said.

Petronovich had been afraid this would happen. In fact, he and Jason had discussed the possibility on the plane. "Fine. Can I look at her belongings here with you present?" asked Vladi.

Harrington hesitated then nodded, "I'll give you fifteen minutes. Let me get her bag and purse."

Petronovich and McClintock started with the purse and worked their way through it and the luggage. Nothing stood out to them; they were finished in ten minutes. Vladi said, "Thanks for your help, Officer."

"I'm sorry I couldn't do more." Harrington turned and left.

Jason looked at the woman behind the counter. "Miss," he asked. "Can you suggest a hotel in town?"

Without hesitation, the woman looked up and said, "My favorite is the Grand America Hotel, hands down." She smiled and turned back to her monitor.

"Thanks for the tip," said Jason as they left the office and called for an Uber.

****

McClintock and Petronovich sat in overstuffed chairs listening to the soft piano music in the background. The Grand America was everything a 5-star hotel should be. Each man seemed lost in thought. The mood was disrupted by the hum of Jason's phone. He looked at the screen and answered, "Hi, Mike, how are you?"

"Good. The question is, how are you? Brenda called and said you and Vladi may have a problem. You're in Salt Lake, right?" asked Mike, Jason's brother.

Jason brought Mike up to speed on what had transpired over the past last 72 hours. "Tomorrow, we'll go to the hospital," he said. "I want to meet the ER physician and see if we can find out her status."

"If there's anything I can do to help, just ask," said Mike. "I still have my contacts." He had retired a little over a year before from the FBI in the Chicago field office. At that time, he'd moved his wife, Julie, and two kids, Zach and Samantha (Sam) to the Santa Ynez Valley, just north of Santa Barbara. They'd bought a small vineyard, trading criminals for wine-making. He couldn't have been more content.

"There's not much to do," said Jason. "I'll let you know what we find tomorrow."

"Sounds good. Tell Vladi I'm sorry about his friend," Mike said and hung up.

****

The Uber ride from the hotel to LDS Hospital took less than ten minutes. The driver pulled up in front of the Emergency Room. "Here you go," he said.

Petronovich was three steps ahead, striding towards the E.R. doors.

The waiting room was full. Children were crying and people sat in hard, plastic chairs, coughing and sneezing. It wasn't an inviting scene. Without looking up, the receptionist slid a form towards Petronovich. "Sign in and note the time," she said. "I'll need to see identification and your insurance information."

"I'm not a patient, I'm here to see Dr. Jake Sterling," explained Petronovich, on edge.

Sensing his anger, the receptionist looked up. "Have you noticed how busy we are? I can guarantee that you won't be seeing Dr. Sterling any time soon."

"Who the hell do you think you are?" replied McClintock, raising his voice as he stepped forward. The loud room became eerily quiet.

A man wearing a white coat with a stethoscope draped around his neck emerged from one of the exam rooms. "What's the problem, Melissa?" he asked.

"These men," she said, pointing to Petronovich and McClintock, "are demanding to see you, Dr. Sterling."

While Jason and Vladi were not small by any stretch, Dr. Sterling was even bigger. "What's this about?" he asked. "Can't you see we're extremely busy?"

Without apologizing, McClintock said, "We flew in to see you. We have a few questions regarding Marina Mikhailov, the woman from the airport who was brought in yesterday."

"I see," said Sterling. "I've requested additional help. Once they arrive, I can talk. Not until then. You might consider waiting outside. I'll come out when I'm available." Sterling didn't wait for an answer. He turned and moved quickly to the next exam room.

McClintock and Petronovich went to stand outside in the crisp morning air, away from the waiting room of sick and injured people. The sun was shining but the temperature was still too cold for short sleeves. McClintock spotted a bench by the sliding door and pointed. After close to an hour, the doors opened, and Sterling stepped out. "Okay, I can give you five minutes. But if you're not a relative, I have very little I can say. If you are an emergency contact for Ms Mikhailov, we can talk," he said.

Petronovich jumped to his feet. "I'm her closest friend in the U.S. Our families are very close in Kazakhstan. All we wanted was to check on her status."

"Until I know that I am authorized to speak to you, I can't," Sterling said becoming annoyed.

"Give me one second," said Petronovich as he dialed

airport security at Salt Lake International.

The phone was picked up and Vladi asked to speak to Harrington. Once on the line Vladi said, "Officer Harrington, the is Vladimir Petronovich. I'm at the ER with the doctor that was with Marina Mikhailov yesterday. I need to have you check the contacts list in her cell phone and see if she has anyone listed as her Emergency Contact. Can you do that?"

There was a hesitation at the other end, then finally, "Give me a second to power up the phone. Her things are sitting right here," responded Harrington. He came back on, "Under Emergency Contacts, your name is listed."

"Thank God! I'm handing my phone to Dr. Sterling. Please tell him what you told me," said Petronovich as he handed the phone to the doctor.

Sterling listened, then handed Petronovich his phone, "She died in the ambulance, there was nothing we could do. The results of the post will give us more information. I can say though, that there were no outward signs of struggle or foul play. Had there been, it would have been noticed in a crowded terminal."

"What do you mean by post?" asked Petronovich, clearly upset.

"Sorry, autopsy," explained Sterling. "That should be happening right now. I've told the guys upstairs to let me know what they find. As soon as I hear, I'll call. I have your number, Mr. Petronovich. I've got to be going. For some reason, we're really busy today."

****

Petronovich and McClintock sat in the lobby of the Grand America, listening to the soft background music being played on the Steinway piano. Jason was checking his emails while Vladi played a word game. His phone rang. He didn't recognize the number, but he answered, "This is Petronovich."

"Mr. Petronovich, this is Dr. Sterling. I just got off the phone with the doctor who performed the post on Ms. Mikhailov. From a toxicological standpoint, there was nothing out of the ordinary; no alcohol or drugs in her system. Ms. Mikhailov did, however, appear to have had a myocardial infarction; a heart attack. It is unusual for someone her age, especially someone who appeared to be in good physical condition. But it does happen. If she has a family history of cardiovascular disease, that could be the cause. Genetics should not be ignored. We see it all the time. They are going to rule the death a natural cause, myocardial infarction; total blockage of the left anterior descending artery. I hope this will provide some closure for you and her family. If I can help in any other way, please call."

"Thank you, Doctor," Petronovich said, and hung up. He sat in silence, absorbing the information.

"What do we do now?" asked McClintock.

"The results of the autopsy only strengthen my belief that there was foul play," Vladi said. "When I was with the GRU, we had access to chemicals that, if injected into a victim, would cause a heart attack. The compound would dissipate in the system within minutes, leaving no trace. I think we need to search her apartment and interview her colleagues."

"Why don't we ask the doctor who did the autopsy to search her body for an injection site?" suggested McClintock.

"If I'm right, the needle used is so small that it would be, pardon the pun, like looking for a needle in a haystack. They wouldn't find it, of that I'm certain," Vladi said.

Chapter 3

The Canadair jet made its final approach into the Santa Barbara metro airport from the north. One never tired of the beauty of this small coastal city. Mike McClintock and his family lived thirty miles north, over the Santa Ynez Mountains. Mike owned ten acres, six of which housed mature Syrah grape vines. It wasn't large, but those six acres produced 2,150 cases of wine each season. The other four acres were dedicated to their home, wine processing buildings, and equipment.

After the phone call with Dr. Sterling, Jason and Vladi had decided to meet with Mike to see how he might be able to help with the investigation. He had only been away from the Bureau for a year and a half, so he maintained many contacts. Early spring was busy for Mike, but not nearly as busy as it would be a month or so before harvest, in September. He could spare the time for his brother and his old friend.

Jason and Petronovich turned off Refugio Road and onto the dirt road that led to Mike's property. Mike was on a tractor, spraying the vines with an organic pesticide. He didn't notice the approaching car. Julie, his wife, heard the vehicle and stepped out on the porch. Zach and Sam were in their rooms doing homework. Zach is 10 and Sam 7. They dropped what they were doing and sprinted outside. With Uncle Jason and Vladi visiting, schoolwork went out the window.

Jason parked the car next to the house and the kids ran to greet him.

"There are my two favorite munchkins!" said Jason as he lifted Sam into the air.

Julie walked over to Petronovich and put her arms around him. "It's good to see you, Vladi."

"How'd you two sneak up on me?" Mike asked.

"Mike, you look like you have a real winery going on," said Vladi as he gave him a Russian bear hug.

The reunion was everything you'd expect when close family members got together after some time apart. "So, Vladi," Mike asked later at the dinner table, "what have you been up to since Uruguay? We heard you took a trip home."

"That adventure last year was a bit rough for me," Vladi said, "so I took some time off and went back home to Kazakhstan in June. It was nice to see family and friends. I hadn't been back for probably ten years. Last month I returned and thought a trip to the great state of Montana was in order."

"Well, we're glad you were able to make it, Vladi," Mike said. "It's a real shame about your friend though."

"Tell us what Kazakhstan is like, Vladi," Julie said as they dined on the grilled tri-tip.

"I am from a place called Almaty, the largest city in the country. That is where I met Marina. Our families were close friends, though she was fifteen years younger. The city is surrounded by the Trans-Illi Alatau mountains, which rise to a little over 4,900 meters."

"What's a meter?" Sam asked.

"Oh, that's a European measurement," Vladi said, smiling. "Converted to feet, it's about 16,000." Sam's eyes grew wide. "The mountains are huge and quite a sight to see."

The banter continued through dinner. After the kids had gone to bed, Mike spoke up, "Why don't we take a walk?"

Julie had finished the dishes and waved them off. "Go," she said.

Mike, Jason, and Vladi walked over to the small tasting room. Inside was a bar with high top chairs. Mike went behind the bar, placed three wine glasses on the polished oak surface, and poured each of them a glass of last year's Syrah. He raised his glass, "To us and those like us."

Jason followed, "Damn few left."

"To life!" Vladi chimed in.

Mike walked around the bar and sat down. "Now, what are your plans?" he asked.

Petronovich told Mike about Marina's autopsy results as well as his suspicions about what really happened.

Mike nodded, "We are aware of hits like this from the GRU and other bad actors. It's difficult to prove."

"Hence, the reason the technique is used so often," said Petronovich. "We are going to visit Marina's employer, AdvanChem and interview the employees, if that's possible."

"There's no way they'll allow that, especially if they're culpable," said Mike without hesitation. "You need some leverage. I think I may have the answer. Kevin Mitchell is in Los Angeles doing a field office audit. The timing couldn't be better."

Mitchell worked for the FBI out of Washington D.C. He and Mike had gone through the Academy together and were as close as brothers. Their families tried to vacation together at least once a year. "Maybe I can arrange for Kevin to join you when you visit AdvanChem," Mike suggested.

"That would be helpful, Kevin is a great guy," replied

Jason.

"Okay, it's done. I'll text him when we go inside," said Mike and sipped his wine.

****

Mike's normal routine was to be up by 5:30 and working in the vineyard by 7:00. When he entered the kitchen the next morning, he was surprised to see the coffee already brewed and ready to go. Jason was sitting at the table with his mug. He had forgotten that Jason's day normally started even earlier than his own.

"Morning, pal," greeted Jason as he looked up from the Santa Barbara NewsPress he had found on the front porch.

"Anything in the news?" asked Mike as he grabbed a mug from the cupboard.

"Usual stuff. Crazy ISIS jerks randomly killing. If it's not France or Belgium, it's London," said Jason as he looked back at the article he'd been reading.

"At least we've kept them from our shores these last twelve months, knock on wood," said Mike. "But you know it only takes one asshole getting through to cause a major problem."

"Have you heard back from Kevin?" asked Jason as he watched Mike doctor his coffee with cream and an excessive amount of sugar. "You know, I've been reading a book about the Primal diet," he said without waiting for an answer. "Mary, my neighbor, gave it to me and it says that sugar is about the worst thing you can ingest."

"I don't care," Mike said. "As old as I am, and after all I've been through, I'm not changing. Anyway, in answer to your question, yes. Kevin said he'd be glad to join you and would position FBI involvement as a preliminary investigation into Marina's death, given her Russian background. He did say that there was no way he had the right to ask for proprietary documents of any kind."

"Understood. We would have never expected that. Is his schedule flexible?" Jason asked.

"He has to be back in D.C. day after tomorrow, so you really only have two days. You have his cell number?"

"If it hasn't changed in the last year, then, yes. I'll call and coordinate with him. Thanks for making the call, Mike."

"I thought I heard some chatter," said Petronovich as he entered the room. "So, we are good to go with Mitchell?"

"We're on," said Jason. "I'll call him in a few minutes."

After coffee, Jason walked out onto the front porch and dialed Kevin Mitchell. He picked up immediately, "Jason, how are you?" he asked. "I hear you might need a little help. My audit of the L.A. Field Office is done, so I'm free whenever you are."

"Good to talk to you, Kevin," Jason said. "Can we shoot for 1:00 this afternoon? We're up at Mike's place in Santa Ynez. That's me and Petronovich. The drive to Irvine should take us about three hours, assuming reasonable traffic. The company we'll drop in on is AdvanChem." Jason gave him the company address as well as background on what had transpired with Marina Mikhailov.

"Sounds good," Kevin said. "We'll have a talk with those in charge and see if we can get a feel of where they're coming from. I'll call you when I'm close," said Kevin.

****

Kevin was located only forty minutes from AdvanChem, so he had time to do a little checking. The field office was full, but Kevin found an office that wasn't occupied for the moment. After inputting his ID, he accessed the system, and pulled up the AdvanChem website. *This will be interesting,* he thought as he began with the bios of the firm's twenty employees. The two principals, Abdullah Mohammed and Majid Al-Hamaidi had started the firm twelve years ago after obtaining their doctorates in Biochemistry at UC Berkeley, one year apart. The remaining employees had advanced degrees in Biology, Organic Chemistry, Biochemical Engineering, and one in Systems Engineering. All except one employee, Marina Mikhailov, appeared to be of Middle Eastern descent. This seemed odd to Kevin, if not a little unsettling. This was a highly-specialized group. He ran a background check on Mohammed and Al-Hamaidi. When the data came back, there were no immediate red flags. Kevin looked at his watch. He had one hour before he was to meet McClintock and Petronovich. It was lunch time so he thought he'd better hit the road in case traffic was a problem. He knew traffic could happen at any time, twenty-four hours a day in this jungle of humanity of Southern California.

****

McClintock and Petronovich had just merged from Highway 101 to the 405 South. Traffic was horrendous, coming to an almost complete stop. They had an hour before they were scheduled to meet Mitchell outside AdvanChem. The company was located in an industrial park at the north end of the Irvine city limits, so they didn't have far to go once the traffic finally began to move.

Mitchell pulled to the side of the road, two blocks from the nondescript, single-story building that housed AdvanChem. It was twelve forty-five when he dialed McClintock. "Jason, I'm here," Mitchell said.

"We're ten minutes out, see you in a few," responded McClintock.

Mitchell checked his messages while he waited for the other two. Before he knew it, a candy apple-colored Yukon pulled up behind him. Jason stepped out and walked to Kevin's window. "Pull up directly in front, we have nothing to hide," said Jason.

Mitchell led the way into the building. The reception area was sterile, with four folding metal chairs. There were no plants or decorations of any kind. There was a nondescript side door, but nothing more. The message was obvious: "Don't get comfortable." The girl behind the counter looked a little surprised to have visitors. Kevin held out his FBI credentials. "I'd like to speak with Dr. Mohammed and Dr. Al-Hamaidi," he said. "We don't have an appointment."

The girl stammered for a moment before speaking. "Dr. Mohammed is out of town on business," she said. "I'll see if Dr. Al-Hamaidi is available. Can I tell him what this is about?"

"We are investigating the death of one of your employees," said Mitchell in a crisp, business-like manner.

"Oh, my God, you mean Marina! She's the only one not here today!" said the girl as she covered her mouth. "She was so nice. Let me get Dr. Al-Hamaidi." She rose from her desk and almost ran to what appeared to be a heavy steel door. She input a ten-digit code on the keypad and the door opened. It shut immediately after she entered the next room.

Five minutes later, Al-Hamaidi came out, followed by the girl. He walked around the counter and introduced himself. "I am Majid Al-Hamaidi," he said as he walked past the men, towards the side door. "This is our conference room, please come in, take a seat." He gestured toward the executive leather chairs. The conference room was nothing like the reception area. The décor was simple but wreaked of wealth. "May I see your ID?" he asked.

Mitchell flipped open his FBI credentials, showing them to Al-Hamaidi without releasing them. "These men are with me," he said, gesturing to Vladi and Jason. "They are not with the Bureau."

"I need to see their identification," demanded Al-Hamaidi.

"Let's get this straight. You don't need to see anything. We can do this the easy way or the hard way. You can answer my questions here and now, or we can take a ride downtown and you can answer them at our main office in Los Angeles. I promise, we'll be there past midnight. Which is it?"

Al-Hamaidi's attitude changed immediately. "My receptionist said Marina Mikhailov is dead. What's this about?" he asked.

"She was in Salt Lake City when she apparently had a heart attack," said Mitchell. "Did you know she was traveling out of state?"

"No, she only said she had some personal business to attend to and that she needed a few days off. I thought nothing of it. This is quite a shock," said Al-Hamaidi.

He's saying the right thing, but his tone and body language don't match the words, thought Mitchell. "What was she working on?" he asked.

"I'm not at liberty to say," replied Al-Hamaidi. "Most of our work is with the Department of Defense and classified."

Mitchell knew he was not going to get anywhere with this line of questioning. He needed to prove that Marina had been in danger but he had nothing to go on other than her phone call to Petronovich. They had to check her apartment. Mitchell stood up. "We'll be back," he said. He turned and left the room; McClintock and Petronovich followed. Al-Hamaidi remained at the table.

Chapter 4

The Boeing 777 descended through the clouds and lined up for final approach to Kandahar Airfield, in Kandahar, Afghanistan. The flight time for the direct FedEx flight from Memphis, TN had been approximately 16 hours. The airfield was about ten miles outside of Kandahar City and serves as a U.S. military base as well as a public airport. Once on base, you'd never know there was a war going on. You could stroll along a boardwalk and sip coffee from a shop with outdoor seating, eat pizza from a pizzeria, or buy trinkets from local vendors. They even had a Popeye's Chicken, Burger King, and a TGI Friday's restaurant.

The pilot touched down with near perfect accuracy and taxied to the designated cargo area to off-load. After going through the post-flight procedures with his co-pilot, the pilot, Aaban Qasim, grabbed his carry-on and headed for the exit. The cabin door was open and the portable stairs ready. Qasim couldn't wait for a nice hot shower. He took the first shuttle available to Amtex Village, a small, but clean hotel next to the airport. The van dropped Qasim off in front of the lobby.

He walked up to the registration desk and was greeted by the clerk, "Welcome, good to see you again, Captain Qasim."

Qasim made this trip once a week, so he had become friendly with the people he encountered. "Good to see you, Pasha," he said.

"I have a note that was dropped off for you," said Pasha as he handed the envelope to Qasim.

"Thank you," replied Qasim as he slid the note into his pocket and signed the hotel registration paperwork. "See you tomorrow," he said as he walked down the hallway toward his room. He had twenty-four hours before his return flight.

Qasim dropped his carry-on on the floor and sat on the bed. He opened the note, which read simply: "Friday's, 7:00 pm." He lay back, closed his eyes, and was asleep in minutes.

A thirty-minute power nap did the trick. After a quick shower, he would be ready to go.

The restaurant was no different than any other TGI Friday's in the States. It was very busy with an elevated noise level that made it difficult to hear what someone said at the table next to you. This was why they always chose this location. Qasim stood in the entryway and looked around. He saw an arm waving and recognized the face.

As Qasim sat down, he told the waitress, "I'll have what he's having."

Ibraham Bashara looked at Qasim and shook his head, "I wish this was a Long Island iced tea, instead of just iced tea." Alcohol was strictly prohibited on any U.S. military base in a war zone. Bashara was Muslim, but once out of country, the strict Muslim tenets went out the window. He was a Saudi contractor working with both the U.S. and Afghan governments. His ties to the royal Family were extensive but concealed, even to Qasim.

Bashara slid an envelope across the table. "Confirmation of the deposit to your account at Credit Suisse is in there, along with instructions."

"What's our timetable?" asked Qasim as he took the

envelope.

"It's all in there. But we want to be operational within three weeks. It depends on the progress AdvanChem makes in producing the sarin crystals. They are two-thirds of the way there, but still need to produce several hundred pounds."

"That seems like a lot," said Qasim.

"The tank mounted on the converted DC-10 holds 12,000 gallons. The mixture is one part crystal to nine parts water. The crystals are placed in the tank first, then the water is added. At that point, the sarin crystals dissolve into a solution. That's the lethal combination. Picture a DC-10 air tanker over a wildfire. When the plane is over the target, the pilot releases the fire retardant. The drop itself takes eight seconds and covers a path 300 feet wide by one mile in length. But we're not dropping a fire retardant. When our mixture is released, the water evaporates in the atmosphere, leaving sarin gas," whispered Bashara.

Visualizing the air drop, Qasim began to sweat. "Allahu Akbar," he whispered.

****

"That guy is hiding something," said Mitchell as they walked to the car. "Where is Marina's home?" he asked, looking at Petronovich.

"She lives here in Irvine. I've never been to her place, but I have the address." Petronovich pulled out his phone to search his contacts.

"Okay, I'll follow you two," Mitchell said.

Marina's condo was close to Anaheim, on the fringe of a middle-class neighborhood. It was on the third floor of a modest, nondescript, three-story complex. Mitchell went directly to the manager's office for a key. When he returned, McClintock and Petronovich were waiting at the unit. Mitchell slowly opened the door. Cushions from the sofa were slashed and strewn about; stuffing was everywhere. The drawer to the end table was on its side, its contents spilled on the floor. The same was true for the kitchen and bedroom drawers. The place had been ransacked.

Mitchell dialed the Los Angeles field office and asked the agent to send Irvine P.D. and inform them of the break-in, possible foul play, and the FBI's interest in the case. Mitchell wanted the condo thoroughly inspected for anything, especially prints. "I might stay an extra day or so," he said after he hung up.

****

After the brief meeting with Mitchell, Jason, and Vladi, Al-Hamaidi phoned Mohammed. "Where are you?" he asked.

"We just landed," said Mohammed. "I'll be at the office within the hour."

"Good, we need to talk." Al-Hamaidi put the phone down and thought about the last three days.

Marina had her own lab, away from the rest of the group. She was working on a U.S. Government-sponsored project to find a quicker, more easily administered antidote to sarin gas. Atropine was the current drug of choice, but it requires patient dosage adjustments depending on the level of exposure to the gas. In a battlefield scenario, with multiple casualties, it wasn't practical. Marina's job was to come up with an antidote for sarin that could be injected once for any patient, regardless of the level of exposure. This was no easy feat. Marina seldom ventured from her lab. Three days ago, that had changed. Marina needed additional funds for her project. She had wanted to discuss this with Mohammed or Al-Hamaidi.

She walked out of her lab, down a long sterile corridor past other secure doors, each locked, requiring separate codes for entry. The hallway ended at a T-corridor which housed single offices for each of the other researchers to the left and right. Al-Hamaidi's office was first on the left. As Marina approached the door, she heard Mohammed raise his voice, "How can they expect us to have 400 pounds of crystal ready within a week? It's not possible!" Al-Hamaidi looked up and saw Marina standing at the door.

"I'm sorry, I can come back when it's more convenient," Marina said as she turned to go.

"No, wait, Marina, Dr. Mohammed and I were just finishing up," explained Al-Hamaidi, "What do you need?" Al-Hamaidi ignored the potential implication of what Marina may have heard.

Mohammed rose from his chair. "I have a conference call in five minutes," he said. "I must go." He passed Marina in the doorway.

Later that morning after Marina had returned to her lab, Mohammed entered Al-Hamaidi's office, closed and locked the door behind him. "How much do you think she heard?" he asked.

"Can't be that much."

"But I mentioned crystals. What would she think of that?" asked Mohammed. "This operation is too important to risk being compromised."

"What do you suggest?" asked Al-Hamaidi.

“I don’t know, let me think about it,” responded Mohammed.

Back in her lab, Marina sat at her desk and thought about the conversation she’d had with Al-Hamaidi. The additional funding for her research did not seem to be an issue. In fact, Al-Hamaidi acquiesced without a single question, which surprised her. What troubled Marina was what she had overheard. *What were they talking about? The company is under contract to work with nerve agents, but nothing in crystalline form. On the other hand, maybe they have a contract to work on something like that, that I don’t have access to.* Marina shook her head and let her thoughts drift. After fifteen minutes or so, she thought, *something doesn’t feel right. Mohammed was upset and couldn’t get out of the office quick enough. Al-Hamaidi, on the other hand, was nonchalant, especially about the funding. He was covering up something, but what and why?* Marina needed to speak to someone. The only person she could think of was Vladi. She had picked up her phone and dialed.

After speaking with Petronovich, she emailed Al-Hamaidi and told him that she had to take a few days off for personal reasons.

Al-Hamaidi read the email and grew nauseous. He forwarded it to Mohammed, then walked to the other man’s office, closed the door, and said, “Check the email I just sent you.”

“Crap,” Mohammed said. He looked at Al-Hamaidi. “Have her followed and monitor her emails and texts.”

Al-Hamaidi went back to his office and opened the wall safe. He took the slip of paper that had been given to him by a member of the Saudi royal family. He had been instructed to call the number listed only if it was extremely necessary. With the project in jeopardy, the situation qualified. He dialed the number.

After two hours, Al-Hamaidi's phone rang. He looked at the screen; the display read "Unknown Caller."

"Hello?" he answered.

"She is talking to a guy by the name of Vladimir Petronovich. She seems upset and is going to meet him in Butte, Montana tomorrow late morning. She has a Delta connection in Salt Lake City."

"Fly to SLC tonight? I want her neutralized. You have the necessary tools, correct?" asked Al-Hamaidi.

"You need not ask."

"What about this Petronovich?" asked Al-Hamaidi.

"He is in Montana now, but his phone records place his home address in Dana Point, California. He hasn't used any credit cards, so we can't see where he's been. He will return home at some point. We will wait for him."

"You're ahead of me. After you take care of the problem in Salt Lake, do the same in Dana Point, Montana, or wherever. We can't have any loose ends."

"It will be done. This is the last you will hear from me," the voice said. The line went dead.

****

Inside his room, Qasim sat on the bed and pulled the contents from the envelope. The first page was a confirmation of $1,000,000 USD deposited into his Credit Suisse account in Zurich. The second gave the contact information for Abdullah Mohammed, one of the owners of AdvanChem. He had been told that Mohammed would coordinate the transfer of an undisclosed substance from Irvine to the Southern California Logistics Airport (SCLA) in Victorville, approximately 80 miles inland. In addition, he had confirmation that a converted McDonnell Douglas DC-10 had been purchased from Cal Fire and that he, Qasim, was authorized to act on behalf of the plane's owner, Advanced Aerial Fire Response, AAFR, a shell corporation based in Europe, with respect to the plane's operation and control. He had also been told that immediately upon his return to Memphis, he should take a leave of absence. He would contact an American named John McCaffrey who had tasked with retrofitting the recently purchased aircraft. McCaffrey was located at the private El Mirage Adelanto Airport, 8.5 miles from SCLA.

The final item Qasim pulled from the envelope was a corporate credit card in his name, and a fake passport with the name Sadik Sarraf. He shook his head, placed the envelope in his carry-on, and prepared for the weekly flight back to Memphis which included eight hours of uninterrupted sleep.

Chapter 5

Outside the condo, Kevin looked at his watch. It was getting late and traffic to the office downtown would soon become a parking lot. "I've got to get back," he said. "When I hear from Irvine PD, I'll let you know. Where will you be staying?"

"My place is in Dana Point, about half an hour south," said Vladi as he looked at Jason. "We can stay there tonight, then decide what to do tomorrow after we see what the police come up with."

Petronovich's home was a newer double-wide in a high-end mobile home park. It was situated across the Pacific Coast Highway from Doheny State Beach, made famous by the Beach Boys. The views were nothing short of spectacular.

Before heading home, Petronovich made a stop at the Post Office to pick up mail that had accumulated while he'd been gone. "Hang on to this," he said as he handed the bundle of mail to McClintock.

When they reached Vladi's home, Jason opened the car door, stood, stretched, and said, "This is a million-dollar view."

"Actually, not quite. I think the place is worth somewhere between five and six hundred thousand. For a mobile home, mind you! Can you believe it?"

"I can," said Jason as they walked toward the house.

Vladi stood at the front door. "Come in, let me pour us a

drink," he said. He placed the mail on the counter, then reached for glasses and the bottle of Grey Goose. Glancing at the mail as he poured, he noticed a large envelope. He stopped, handed the glass to Jason, and picked it up.

"Look at the post-mark. This was mailed from Irvine," he said as he ripped it open.

Inside was a smaller envelope with a note on the outside: "Open only in case of my death." It was signed by Marina. Vladi slowly eased himself down on one of the barstools and stared at the envelope. "She knew she was in trouble."

Petronovich opened the envelope and read the brief note. Marina had indicated that she was working on an antidote to sarin gas. She believed the other researchers were working on projects for the U.S. Government related to nerve agents. She didn't know any more. She explained that she had overheard Mohammed mention "400 pounds of crystal" but she didn't know what type. She knew only that that much crystal was well beyond what was necessary for research. She believed the principals were hiding something. They were acting out of character and this concerned her.

****

Marina's note left McClintock and Petronovich with little appetite. They ate a small dinner of cheese, crackers, and Grey Goose. At about nine p.m., Vladi retired to his bedroom. Jason wasn't yet ready to make his way to the guest room. "I'm going to take a walk," he said as Petronovich closed his bedroom door.

"No need to lock the door, it is safe here," replied Vladi. "See you in the morning."

McClintock grabbed a bottle of water and walked out into the cool night. The smell of salt and the sound of soft rolling waves was therapeutic. He crossed the highway and walked north along the water's edge.

The emotions of the last few days, as well as the note from Marina, combined with a fair amount of vodka to put Petronovich over the edge. When his head hit the pillow, he was out immediately. A tsunami wouldn't have woken him. What did was the sting in his arm.

The two men, both masked, had searched the home and realized Petronovich was alone. They went into his room and one injected the poison into his arm. They were out of the house before Vladi realized what had happened. He woke with a start. He began to feel nauseous, started drooling, and began to lose control of his motor skills. His distant experience with the GRU and the skills he had acquired as a trained killer told him he had been injected with a nerve agent. He had no more than a minute, and one chance of surviving before total incapacitation. Petronovich stumbled out of bed, opened the closet door, and reached for the emergency kit. In it, he had one large dose of Atropine. He dropped to his knees and dumped the contents of the kit onto the floor. Grabbing the syringe, he rammed the needle into his abdomen, fell to his side convulsing, and defecated.

****

Jason walked for about an hour. When he returned, the front door of the house was ajar. He distinctly remembered closing it when he'd left so he was on high alert.

When he opened the door, he was met immediately with

the foul stench of excrement. He ran to Vladi's bedroom and found him out cold on the floor. He checked his friend and found a slight pulse and labored breathing. Jason dialed 911, requesting immediate medical assistance. When the EMTs arrived, they found every light in the house on and the front door wide open. Jason waited on the steps and waved the ambulance into the driveway. The emergency crew jumped out of the truck.

"Where is he?" one of the EMTs asked.

"In the back bedroom," replied Jason. "He's in bad shape. Where's the closest hospital?"

"Mission Hospital, about three miles," said the EMT, as he began checking Vladi's vitals and administering oxygen.

Soon, the house was full of firefighters and paramedics. They strapped Petronovich to the gurney and rolled him out of the bedroom. One of the paramedics noticed the syringe on the floor. "Grab that," he said to his partner. They were out the door in minutes, sirens blaring on the way to the ER.

After two hours, the ER doctor on call came out and met with McClintock who had been waiting. "I'm doctor Walker, are you related to Mr. Petronovich?" he asked.

"I'm a friend," said Jason. "How's he doing?"

"He's lucky. One of the parameds found a syringe in his room and brought it in. We had the contents analyzed and found it to be Atropine, an antidote to various nerve agents. We continued with that therapy and he's now stabilized. BP and heart rate are up. He's intubated and breathing with a machine for now, but we plan to remove it in the morning. The bottom line is that someone tried to kill him. If he hadn't self-administered the Atropine, he would have died. I'm going to have to call law enforcement."

“Before you do, can I make a call?” asked Jason. “I think the FBI will have an interest in this.”

“I’ll give you ten minutes, then I call the authorities,” said Walker.

Jason dialed Kevin Mitchell, while Walker waited. It was after one in the morning, but Kevin answered. Jason explained what had happened and what Walker had said. “He wants to talk with you,” said Jason as he handed the phone to the doctor.

Walker listened, nodded, and said, “I understand. No local law enforcement involvement. You will have people here within the hour.” He handed the phone back to McClintock and said, “We’ll take care of your friend,” as he walked back into the ER.

****

Al-Hamaidi looked up from his desk as Mohammed walked in, shutting the door behind him. “We have a problem,” said Al-Hamaidi as Mohammed took a chair. “The FBI came by asking questions about Marina.”

“What would cause that?” asked Mohammed.

“I don’t know. They asked what kind of work we were doing, and I declined to answer. They left after I refused to cooperate.”

“I wouldn’t worry about it. At least not yet. How are the crystals coming along?” Mohammed asked as he rose from the chair and paced the room.

“We are working 24/7. It will be difficult to meet the deadline requested. The best thing we did was to lease a different location for production. If the FBI should come back with a warrant to search our premises, they won’t find anything."

"True, I'm glad we made the decision," Mohammed said. "What time do you plan on going over there? I'll go with you."

Al-Hamaidi looked at the time on his phone, "I could go now if you want."

The walk to the production unit took only ten minutes. It was in the same complex as their primary office, but leased to a different corporation without any ties to Al-Hamaidi or Mohammed. Security at this site was comparable to a bank vault. No one passed the threshold without proper access codes. The unit had a secure loading dock in the back and a large room housing stainless steel vats for sarin production, a huge industrial rotary dryer supported by steel columns to delete the moisture, industrial vents, and tanks to house sarin crystals. The entire line was fully enclosed and anyone working in its proximity wore a self-contained chemical biohazard suit. Mohammed and Al-Hamaidi entered the exterior lockout room and watched the two men on the other side of the window as they monitored the machinery. Al-Hamaidi pressed a speaker on the wall, "Good afternoon gentlemen," he said.

The men stopped and turned slowly in their biohazard suits wearing goggles, gloves, and respirators. They waved and muffled, "Hello."

Mohammed pressed the button and asked, "How is production going?"

One of the suited men responded, "We're averaging around 50 pounds a day."

The men had no idea what they were working on. Al-Hamaidi had led them to believe they were producing crystals for a chemical company that planned other uses for the compound. The men were paid very well and in turn, asked few questions. At this rate, it would take about eight days to produce the remaining 400 pounds needed. They would be close to the target date, assuming no glitches.

****

Kevin Mitchell had positioned an agent at the hospital outside Petronovich's room within the hour. After the agent arrived, Jason returned to Vladi's home. He arrived to find Mitchell supervising a forensic team. Kevin looked up as Jason entered. "I doubt we'll find anything, but we've got to try."

Jason nodded, "Sure. How much longer?"

"Twenty minutes, max."

Jason sat on the sofa and watched as the agents worked through the home, concentrating on Vladi's bedroom. As the last of the agents left, Mitchell closed the front door and sat on a side chair across from Jason. "Looks like we hit someone's nerve," he said. "The guys that did this were professional. That is a huge concern."

"Could it be AdvanChem?" asked Jason.

"The only ID we gave them was mine. How would they know where Vladi lived?" Kevin asked as he sat with his head back and eyes closed. "The sooner we get Vladi out of the hospital, the safer he'll be. What do you think about taking him up to Santa Ynez until he's on his feet?"

"I'll phone Mike first thing in the morning," Jason said. "Right now, I think we both need to get some shut eye. Why don't you take the guest room?"

"No, I'm good on the sofa, if you can find a blanket, I'll be fine," Kevin said.

Jason rummaged through the bedroom closet and came up with a blanket and pillow. He tossed both at Mitchell and rubbed his eyes, “See you in the morning.”

The sun was up at 5:20. Kevin and Jason were dressed and ready to go after a fitful two hours of sleep. Mike was eager to have Vladi stay with them and said he’d have a room ready when they arrived. Petronovich’s carry-on was sitting next to the bed, still packed from the night before. Jason and Kevin threw everything into the Yukon and headed to Mission Hospital three miles away.

When they approached Vladi’s room, the agent looked up from his phone. He was sitting on a chair next to the door. “Any problems last night?” asked Mitchell.

“No sir, everything was quiet,” replied the agent.

“Good,” said Kevin. “You’re relieved, we’ll take it from here. Get some rest.”

“Yes sir, thank you.” The agent grabbed his coat and left.

Jason opened the door to Vladi’s room and stepped in with Kevin following. They weren’t surprised to see Petronovich up, dressed, and sitting on the side of the bed.

“I was wondering when you’d get here,” he said. “They took the tube out about half an hour ago and told me I had to rest. As soon as they left, I got dressed.”

“Do you remember what happened last night?” asked Jason.

“I felt a sting and my arm began to throb,” Vladi said. “I didn’t see anything or anyone. I knew I needed my medical kit for the Atropine. I kept thinking of Marina and didn’t want to go just yet.”

“If you hadn’t taken the action you did, we wouldn’t be talking this morning,” Kevin said. “Who has a syringe of

Atropine in their medical kit?" Kevin held up his hand. "Never mind. I know the answer: a trained assassin."

Vladi smiled and shrugged his shoulders, "I guess it pays to be prepared."

"Okay, I'm going to find someone to discharge you so we can get out of here," said Mitchell as he walked to the door. "They won't be happy, but there's nothing they can do."

Jason sat in the chair across from the bed. "We're going back to Mike's place," he said. "Your body has suffered major trauma and you really do need to rest for a couple of days. We need to take some time to determine what we do next anyway, and a vineyard is as good as it gets."

"No argument there," said Petronovich as he tried to stand, but quickly sat back down. Just then, the door opened to an orderly entering pushing a wheelchair.

"The doctor in charge was kind of ticked off, but he relented," explained Kevin as he followed the orderly into the room with a smile.

The orderly positioned Petronovich in the chair and pushed him out the door Jason held open. Kevin walked ahead and sprinted to the parking lot to pull the Yukon around. With Vladi secured in the car, they headed north to Santa Barbara wine country.

Chapter 6

After landing in Memphis and another short night's sleep, Qasim found himself at the airport taking a commercial flight west to Los Angeles. He had reserved a rental car and with any luck, would be on his way to Victorville by one p.m. With the lunch hour past, the drive, though busy, was not as bad as it could have been. Two hours after leaving LAX, he parked in front of the administrative building at the Logistics Airport. He would meet with the Airport Director, David Hull, to introduce himself and complete the necessary paperwork to take custody of the newly acquired DC-10.

Qasim walked into the lobby. The secretary looked up from her desk. "Hi there," she greeted him.

"I'd like to see Mr. Hull, my name is Aaban Qasim," he answered.

"One moment," she replied as she lifted the phone and dialed an extension. The buzz could be heard close by. "I have a Mr. Qasim here to see you," she said. "Yes sir, I'll tell him."

She put the phone in the cradle and looked up. "Mr. Hull asked that you take a seat. He'll be out shortly."

"Thank you," said Qasim as he reached for the latest copy of *Plane and Pilot* magazine and sat down.

Ten minutes later, Hull stepped out of his office and walked over to Qasim, "Hello, I'm David Hull," he said, offering his hand.

Qasim introduced himself and shook Hull's hand. "I'm here to take custody of the Cal Fire DC-10 my company recently purchased," he said.

"I see, well, come into my office, I've been expecting someone," Hull said. "I have the paperwork ready to go." Hull turned toward the office with Qasim following. "Have a seat," said Hull as he motioned to a chair in front of his desk.

The file for the DC-10 was in a folder on his desk. "I'll need to see your FAA identification." Hull opened the folder and spread out the paperwork. "Most of this is completed. We just need to fill in the data from your ID."

Hull took the card Qasim offered and examined it. "It looks like everything is in order." He called out the door, "Crystal, would you come in here please?" The secretary walked in and Hull handed her Qasim's ID and paperwork. "Please fill in the blanks and make copies of everything, including the FAA ID," he said.

Crystal took the ID and paperwork and left.

"What do you boys have planned for the DC-10 out there?" Hull asked as they waited.

Qasim had anticipated the question. "My firm, Advanced Aerial Fire Response, AAFR, will act as independent contractors and hire out when needed for fires. We are thinking of moving our base of operations to Idaho to be centrally located in the west," he said.

"Not a bad idea," said Hull. "Several firms have made that move."

Crystal came back in and placed the forms and ID in front of Qasim, indicating where he should sign. She kept the original and gave the copy to Qasim.

"Well, that does it," said Hull as he stood with his hand

out. “Best of luck to you. That’s a nice airplane you have. Cal Fire keeps up on all required maintenance and then some.”

“Thanks for your help, Mr. Hull,” said Qasim. “Where’s the aircraft?”

“It’s in hangar two down the way,” he said. “I believe it’s fueled and ready to go.”

“Good to hear,” said Qasim. “Thanks for your time.”

Qasim drove his car to the hangar, parked, and walked inside. The aircraft was massive, but seemed even larger because of the modifications made to the undercarriage. Qasim shuddered slightly when he thought of the cargo that would soon be loaded into the empty tank. But before that happened, he had to meet McCaffrey at El Mirage airport.

****

The smell of tri-tip barbecuing over an oak pit was enticing. Mike had the heat on the stainless steel grill raised high enough to slowly cook the meat without burning the savory cut. Chairs were positioned in a semi-circle away from the wood. With drinks in hand, everyone seemed content to watch the flames as they licked at the meat.

Kevin finally broke the silence, “This afternoon I secured a court order to surveil AdvanChem and its principals.”

“Smart move,” Mike said. “After all, who else could be responsible for Marina’s death and Vladi’s attempted murder?”

“It’s a place to start,” Kevin said. “We’ll monitor office and cell phones as well as texts.”

“Is there anything else we can do?” asked Jason as Julie listened and the kids rode their bikes around the yard.

"For now, I think that's it," Kevin said. "We need evidence that they're involved. The real question is, if they are, what could be so important that they would resort to murder?" Kevin sipped his Syrah. "I have a contact at the Pentagon, I'll try to find out what AdvanChem is up to."

Kevin set his glass on the table and walked across the yard towards the tasting room. He dialed an old high school buddy from the Army, now stationed at the Pentagon and a Major General. "Dan, this is Kevin Mitchell, how are you?" Kevin asked.

Dan Nelan was friendly enough, but when it came to the military, he was all business, "Kevin, good to hear from you. Are we still on for golf next week?"

"Probably not. I'm working on a case in the Los Angeles area and will probably still be here. I need a little help you might be able to provide."

"What's that?" asked Nelan.

Mitchell gave him the details. "Any way you can dig into what a company called AdvanChem might be doing for the government? That could be helpful."

"Let me see what I can do," Nelan said. "Give me 48 hours, I'll get back to you." With that, the General hung up and Kevin walked back to the group.

****

Qasim sat at the desk in his room at the Holiday Inn in Victorville. He dialed the number for Abdullah Mohammed.

Mohammed was in his office at AdvanChem when his cell rang. "This is Dr. Mohammed," he answered.

"I am calling to give you an update. The aircraft is secure.

I have some work to do on the plane. I do not know how long it will take but I will call when I am finished, and we can arrange our meeting."

"Can you be more specific with respect to the timetable?" asked Mohammed.

"I am in the dark. I do not know the extent of the modifications that are to be made to the plane. Our mission is in Allah's glorious hands. His will be done. Praise Allah," said Qasim.

"Praise Allah," said Mohammed as he heard the line drop.

****

Kevin, Jason, and Mike were sitting in the kitchen with their coffee when Kevin's phone rang. Petronovich was still asleep. "Mitchell," Kevin answered as he looked at the time. It was seven on the dot.

"Agent Mitchell, this is Larson. We've been monitoring the traffic at AdvanChem as well as their personal devices. There has been nothing out of the ordinary except for one call."

"Give me the details, Larson," said Kevin.

Larson relayed what they'd heard from the phone call between Mohammed and Qasim.

"You identified the caller, correct?" asked Mitchell.

"Yes sir. His name is Aaban Qasim. He lives in Memphis and is a pilot for FedEx. He's clean and as far as we know, he's not on anyone's radar. The call originated out of Victorville, about 200 miles south and east of your current location," replied Larson.

"Okay, thanks, Larson. Continue to monitor Qasim's

number along with the others and let me know if you get any more hits." Kevin hung up and told Jason and Mike about the call.

"There sure seems to be a multitude of Arabs involved in our investigation," said Mike, forgetting that he was no longer with the Bureau. "It's beginning to make the hair on the back of my neck stand up."

"I know what you mean, Mike," said Jason. "That has been in the back of my mind for some time, and the name of this caller just kicked my concern into high gear. I don't know about you two, but I think we need to take a little trip to Victorville. What airports are in the area?"

"I'll check," replied Mike as he looked at his phone. "Vladi can stay here and rest. This shouldn't take too long."

"Looks like there is the Victorville Airport, known as the Southern California Logistics Airport. I think this is where Cal Fire keeps their fire-fighting aviation assets. Then there's a small public facility, Apple Valley Airport, and last, a private site known as El Mirage Adelanto Airport. This place is leased to a company out of San Diego. It looks like they work for the military in testing unmanned aerial vehicles. I don't think this is our target."

"I agree," said Jason. "I think our best shot is with the Apple Valley airport. I can't imagine we'd find much at the Logistics Airport."

"Then it's set. Let's head to Victorville and see if we can find anything about this guy, Qasim," said Mike as he rose from the table.

****

Mohammed walked into Al-Hamaidi's office and sat in front of the desk. "I just received a call from the guy that has the aircraft. I asked for a timetable, but he couldn't give one," explained Mohammed.

"I must say that I'm a bit nervous. That agent with the FBI said he would be back. It's been two days and we've heard nothing. I think we can assume that our communication is being monitored. When we speak about our mission, going forward, nothing is to be said over the phone, by text, or email. We speak in person only and when we do, we need background noise in case someone is using a parabolic listening device," said Al-Hamaidi.

"Don't you think you're being a little paranoid, my friend?" asked Mohammed.

"If you had seen and heard this man, you would be acting more cautiously, I assure you, Abdullah," said Al-Hamaidi. "Are we in agreement?"

"Yes, of course. I agree. Somehow, we need to communicate this to our brother with the aircraft," said Mohammed, his voice tinged with concern.

****

Qasim left his hotel room and drove the short distance to El Mirage Adelanto, the private airstrip on the outskirts of town. As he approached the gate, he noted that as far as the eye could see, the property was fenced off and topped with barbed wire. The gate was manned by a uniformed armed guard, but he wasn't military. As Qasim approached, the guard stepped out of the small office.

"Can I help you?" he asked, after Qasim rolled down his

window.

"I'd like to meet with Jordan McCaffrey," said Qasim.

"Do you have an appointment?" asked the guard.

"No, but he is expecting me. My name is Aaban Qasim, with AAFR."

"One minute," said the guard as he went back to the office and picked up the phone. While he was talking, he looked back at Qasim, said something inaudible, then came back out. "Mr. McCaffrey will see you. Straight ahead there are several hangars on the left then a one-story building at the end. His office is there. Park in front and don't wander. There are cameras everywhere." He opened the gate and motioned Qasim through.

McCaffrey was outside the building watching as Qasim's car approached. "I've been waiting for you," he said. "Your firm must have some strong financial backing."

"Why do you say that?" asked Qasim.

"The price we quoted was intended to scare you off. We have more work for the military right now than we can handle. Your firm is paying us very well to drop everything and make the modifications to your aircraft immediately. I understand you have it at the Logistics Airport?"

"Yes. What do you plan on doing to the plane?" asked Qasim as they walked into the building.

McCaffrey stopped and looked at him. "As you know, we design and test unmanned aerial vehicles. We've been hired to convert your DC-10 into an aircraft that can be flown remotely. With our resources and expertise, we should have the project completed in about three weeks."

"We are on a tight schedule, with fire season approaching. Can it be done any sooner?" Qasim asked.

"Your home office people asked the same thing. All I can say is that we'll try," said McCaffrey. "Let me have you sign some paperwork and we'll get started tomorrow."

****

Mike drove the three men south towards Victorville. Kevin was frustrated. Since monitoring the communication with AdvanChem, there had been no further calls or texts out of the ordinary. Mitchell could not involve the FBI without evidence. So far, AdvanChem couldn't be implicated in any nefarious act. As he ran through the options in his mind, his phone rang.

"Kevin, this is Dan, do you have a minute?" asked Nelan.

"Sure, Dan, what did you find?" Kevin was anxious to hear.

"My sources tell me that AdvanChem is legit. They're working on an antidote to sarin gas poisoning for the military," explained Nelan.

"I thought we already had one?" asked Mitchell.

"We do, but we need a single dose that would be good for all. I'm sorry I don't have more to tell you. Let me know when you're back in town so we can schedule a round of golf."

"No problem, Dan, thanks for your help. I'll give you a call when I'm home," said Mitchell as he ended the call.

"That didn't sound good," said Mike as he drove along the two-lane road ten miles outside of Victorville.

"It wasn't. He said AdvanChem is working on an antidote to sarin. So that means they have access to sarin. That's what most likely was injected into Petronovich," explained Kevin. "We need to find Qasim and see what kind of mission he and AdvanChem are on that involves an airplane."

Mike drove through town then toward the airport, just south of the city limits. The trip from Santa Ynez had been just shy of four hours. Turning into the airport facility, they parked in front of the administrative office. After stretching, Kevin turned toward the door. "Why don't you let me do this on my own?" he said. "It's intimidating with all of us in there."

"Have at it," said Jason.

After twenty minutes, Kevin returned. "They've never heard of Aaban Qasim. Our next best option is the Victorville airport."

"Hop in, we're wasting time," said Mike as he climbed behind the wheel. They were about thirty minutes from the logistics airport, but with Mike's driving, they made it in almost half the time. Mike rolled to a stop and Kevin jumped out.

Kevin walked up to the secretary and flashed his ID. "I'd like to speak with the person in charge of the facility."

The secretary, Crystal, looked at the ID and went into Hull's office. He came out immediately. "I'm David Hull." he said.

"Kevin Mitchell, FBI. I'd like to know if you're aware of a man by the name of Aaban Qasim? Does he have an airplane located here?"

"Unless you have a warrant, I'm not at liberty to discuss whether or not the individual in question has or does not have any business with this airport," replied Hull firmly.

"Qasim may be involved in a murder and an attempted murder," said Mitchell.

"Bring me a warrant and I'll discuss this as much as you like, but not until then," said Hull. "At this point, you're wasting your time." Hull turned and walked back into his office. Crystal followed.

"What do you think?" she asked Hull.

"Qasim doesn't strike me as being the type to commit murder. That said, I really don't want any trouble here."

****

Mitchell walked out of the office shaking his head. "What happened?" asked Jason.

"The manager wouldn't answer any questions without a warrant. He basically said that he had to respect his client's right to privacy. As long as we're close, let's make a stop at the Los Angeles field office. Maybe I can make a case for securing the warrant."

It was three thirty when they started toward the city. Traffic would begin to slow significantly within a half hour and the drive would take them at least an hour.

****

Hull dropped everything and headed out the office door for hangar two, a couple hundred yards away. As luck would have it, Qasim was inside sitting on a stool by a tool bench. "I'm glad I found you," said Hull. "About twenty minutes ago, I had a visit from a guy with FBI credentials. He was asking about you and your aircraft."

"What did you say?" asked Qasim, trying not to fidget.

Hull noticed. "You're not hiding anything, are you?" he asked.

"Of course not," said Qasim firmly. "I've been busy coordinating the retrofit I'm making to the plane. That should begin tomorrow."

"I thought this aircraft was pretty tight. What more are you doing?" asked Hull.

"Just minor modifications," said Qasim, realizing he was giving too much.

"Okay," Hull said. "I did not give him any information. I told him to come back with a warrant if he wanted me to talk. I doubt he'll be back. Good luck with the modifications." Hull left the hangar and walked back to his office.

Qasim waited ten minutes then locked the hangar, jumped in his car and headed for Irvine. About half a mile from AdvanChem, Qasim noticed a small coffee shop. He stopped, went inside, and ordered an iced coffee. Finding a table in the corner, he scanned the store and noticed a guy with a backpack and tablet, obviously a student. He scribbled the AdvanChem address and the names Mohammed and Al-Hamaidi on a napkin. He approached the student with the note and a one-hundred-dollar bill.

He sat down next to him. "How would you like to earn a quick hundred?" asked Qasim as he placed the money on the table. "Just deliver this note a few blocks away and the money is yours."

"Nothing illegal, right?" asked the student.

"Absolutely not. The office address is here. Ask for either of these two researchers and suggest they join me," said Qasim as he handed the student the napkin.

"You got it," said the student.

"Leave your backpack and books. They'll be waiting for you when you return," said Qasim, making certain the kid would do what he asked.

The young man grabbed the money, went out the door,

and peddled his bike the two blocks to AdvanChem. Inside the office, he explained to the receptionist that a guy was waiting to meet either Mohammed or Al-Hamaidi at the coffee shop. With that, he left and rode back to finish his coffee and studies.

Qasim was in back at a corner table when the student returned twenty minutes later. The kid noticed Qasim and gave him a smile and a thumbs-up. Qasim nodded, finished his cold drink, and headed for the door.

****

Kevin turned into the underground parking structure. The elevator opened to a large glass reception area. The large open space in the background had cubicles in the center and enclosed offices on the perimeter. Kevin input a code in the door and entered. "Follow me," he motioned to the McClintock brothers. He passed the cubicles and noticed Agent Larson in one of the side offices. He tapped on the door and poked his head in, "Any more hits in the AdvanChem surveillance?" he asked.

"None. After the first call, there hasn't been anything out of the ordinary, sorry," said Larson.

Mitchell closed the door and continued to the corner office in the back. Jack Schumacher was the agent in charge of the Los Angeles field office. He noticed Mitchell and two men marching toward him. Kevin opened the office door. "Jack, do you have a minute?" he asked.

"Sure, Kevin, come in," replied Schumacher.

"This is Jason and Mike McClintock," said Mitchell as he introduced the brothers.

"I know Mike, how's retirement treating you?"

Schumacher asked.

"It certainly hasn't been dull, Jack, good to see you," said Mike.

"I've heard about you, Jason. I read the after-action report detailing the help you gave us in Uruguay last year," said Schumacher. "So, what are you guys up to now? I know we have surveillance happening with that firm in Irvine. I understand that nothing has come of it?"

"Jack, we did have one call that was suspect. It was between one of the AdvanChem owners and a guy by the name of Qasim. They mentioned an airplane and a mission," said Kevin. "We'd like to obtain a warrant to check this guy out further."

"Kevin, you know we can't do that. On what basis do we ask the court? You have nothing and I'm not going to put my reputation on the line or hang this office out to dry because of an unsubstantiated phone call. I can't do it. If you can get me something to hang my hat on, I'll consider it; end of story."

"Jack, you know that half of what we do is because of gut instinct," said Mike. "And, from my experience, my gut is telling me something isn't right with AdvanChem or this guy Qasim."

"That may be the way you worked in Chicago, but out here, we do things by the book," replied Schumacher. "I've got nothing more to say on the matter. Get me something solid and I'll have your back."

Mitchell rose from his seat, "Okay, Jack," he said. "We'll see what we can do." They left the office and headed to the garage.

****

Qasim waited outside the coffee shop in his car. When Mohammed pulled up, Qasim got out and opened the passenger door. "Are you Mohammed or Al-Hamaidi?" he asked.

"Get in. I'm Mohammed, you must be Qasim," replied the driver. "What's wrong?"

"The FBI have been to the Victorville Airport asking about me and the aircraft. Fortunately, the manager would not give any information without a warrant. We are going to have to neutralize this guy, whoever he is. He's getting too close."

Mohammed sat in silence. "It must be the same guy I met. He had two others with him at that time. His name is Kevin Mitchell. How would he know about the Victorville Airport?"

"The phones must have been monitored when I made the call to tell you about the aircraft," Qasim explained. "I mentioned the airport."

"Let me see what I can do. From now on, the only communication we have is face to face," said Mohammed as a bead of sweat trickled down his face.

Chapter 7

Inside the car, Kevin suggested they stay the night in the Los Angeles area so they could continue their investigation in the morning.

The McClintocks agreed. "Where do you suggest we stay?" asked Mike.

"I always stay at the Marriott across from Staples Center," said Kevin. "It's only a few blocks from here and it has easy access to the freeways."

Kevin directed Mike and within ten minutes, they were in the hotel parking garage. Mike and Jason roomed together with Kevin right next door. After checking in and freshening up, they made their way to the bar. A corner table away from the people in town on business allowed for a more relaxed conversation.

"Where do you two suggest we start tomorrow?" Jason asked.

"I would love to have access to the client files in the office at the Victorville airport," said Kevin. "But with the way Hull acted, that won't be possible without the warrant."

"Maybe not," said Mike.

"What do you mean?" asked Kevin.

"I have an idea. I'll explain in the morning once I get everything worked out in my mind."

"You're starting to scare me," Jason said as he sipped his

drink.

Mike smiled, shrugged his shoulders, and stood. “I know it’s not late, but I need to call Julie. I think I’ll order room service.”

“Sounds good, we won’t be long,” said Kevin. “I’m kind of tired as well.”

Mike walked out of the bar to the gift shop where he bought two Lakers ball caps before heading to his room.

****

After meeting with Qasim, Mohammed drove back to the office and went directly to Al-Hamaidi’s office. “You have to make a call to the number in your safe,” said Mohammed. He explained about his meeting with Qasim and the concern he had with an agent getting too close and possibly interfering with their plans.

“I’ll make the call as soon as you leave,” said Al-Hamaidi. Mohammed left the office, shutting the door behind him.

Al-Hamaidi drove to the corner store. After inserting the coins in the pay phone, he dialed the number and waited. “What now?” a voice answered. Al-Hamaidi explained the situation.

“You can stop right there. I know who you’re speaking about,” said Omar Antar on the other end of the line.

“How could you know?” asked Al-Hamaidi.

“After Petronovich survived, we went to the hospital and asked some questions. Naturally, we had the proper credentials. We learned that the agent in charge was Kevin Mitchell. He’s out of D.C., doing some work here. It shouldn’t be too hard to find him. We couldn’t identify the other two. I will have my people monitor any credit card transactions that Mitchell might make. That will tell us where he's located, or at least where he's been. We'll also monitor AdvanChem should he show up there again. I'll be in touch." The line went dead.

Al-Hamaidi slowly hung up. He realized that he was losing control of the situation, a position he was not comfortable with given the enormous stakes.

****

An hour later, Jason walked into the hotel room he was sharing with his brother. Mike was relaxing on the far bed with his shoes off. "Okay, now you can tell me what you have in mind regarding the files at the Victorville airport," Jason said as he sat in the armchair in the corner of the room.

Mike sat up and swung his feet onto the floor. "I didn't want to say anything in front of Kevin, because he can't know should something go wrong. But you and I are going to Victorville tonight. With any luck, we'll be able to go through the client files and find out what Qasim is doing."

"I really don't feel like spending the night in jail for breaking and entering," replied Jason.

"If it doesn't look safe, we'll turn around and head back here. I think it's worth the chance, especially since it's not that far."

"What about alarms?" Jason asked. "You'll have law enforcement there in minutes."

"This is Victorville, Jason, not downtown Los Angeles. Every building isn't equipped with an alarm system, especially if they have security on-site," said Mike.

"And that's supposed to make me feel better?" he asked. He sighed. "All right, I'm in, let's try to get a couple of hours' shut-eye before we leave." Jason flicked off the light, laid his head back in the chair, and nodded off.

It was midnight. Before leaving the room, Mike handed Jason a Laker's cap. "What's this for?" Jason asked.

"We'll wear them when we approach the building. If there are cameras, I don't want our faces seen. I also have a box of disposable gloves in the trunk. We'll wear those as well."

"Why would you have gloves in your car?" Jason asked.

"I know it's weird, but when I check the engine, I hate to have grease or oil on my hands, so I wear gloves. It's an issue, let it go," said Mike, looking at Jason with a smirk on his face.

They left the hotel parking garage and merged onto the freeway. The traffic wasn't much different than it had been mid-day. Once they were clear of downtown, traffic started to lighten up. The drive would take about ninety minutes, which gave Mike and Jason plenty of time to think about what they might encounter at the airport.

At an elevation of close to 3,000 feet, the temperature in Victorville during the middle of the night in the spring could drop to the mid-forties. There was a bite to the air when they arrived at the airport. Mike approached the entrance, rolled past it far enough to be out of sight of any cameras, then pulled over to the side of the road. Floodlights lit up the hangars and the exterior of the administration building. Mike handed Jason a pair of gloves. "Keep the hat low, over your eyes, and don't look up. Let's stay out of the lights and see if there might be any windows left unlocked in the back of the office," said Mike as he reached for the flashlight in the glove box.

"I'll follow you," Jason said as he quietly closed the car

door.

The two men went through the gate into the darkness behind the office building. Mike pointed to the first window, "Check that one and I'll get the next."

The window was locked. Mike checked the next one as Jason pulled on the frame on the following window. Both were locked. As they rounded the corner, a sliver of light from the parking lot touched the next window. Mike pulled on it, expecting the same result, but was surprised as it slid open. "Keep an eye out for any security, they probably make the rounds several times a night," he said.

"I didn't hear an alarm," said Jason, his back against the wall as Mike pushed in the screen.

"That's a break we needed." Mike hopped up on the windowsill and swung his legs over the barrier onto a desk, clipping a lamp and knocking it to the ground with a loud crash. The sound echoed through the building. Jason was quiet, but knew if security was near, they were toast. Both men waited, unmoving, for several minutes.

When it seemed they were alone, Jason followed Mike into the small office. Mike flicked on the flashlight and kept the beam low to the ground, away from any windows. They went out into the lobby area behind the secretary's desk. The file cabinets against the wall were the obvious place to start. As luck would have it, the files were in alphabetical order and Advanced Aerial Fire Response was the first one. Mike pulled out the file and flipped it open. The pages Qasim had signed to take possession of the aircraft were on top. "We couldn't have had better luck than this," he said as he shined the light on Qasim's name, showing his brother.

"Let's get out of here," Jason said. "I don't want to push

our luck, this has been one heck of a night." He closed the file and moved toward the office. Mike picked up the broken lamp and placed it back on the desk, out of the way. Leaving the screen inside, they jumped out the window and moved along the side of the building, out the gate to the car.

****

It was one in the morning when Antar, the man Al-Hamaidi had phoned entered the hotel lobby. He had used his extensive contacts to track Kevin Mitchell's credit card use. The transaction at the Marriott earlier in the evening gave his location. Dressed in a dark suit, he approached the registration desk in the hotel lobby. The young guy behind the counter smiled.

Antar opened his wallet and placed $100 on the counter. "Can you tell me what room Kevin Mitchell is in?" he asked. "I'm a friend and I want to surprise him."

"I'm sorry, sir, I can't do that," the desk clerk said.

Antar placed a second, then a third bill on the counter. "I'm sure you can."

The clerk looked at the cash, picked it up, then checked his computer, "Do you want his friend's room as well? I checked the three men in together."

"Yes, please."

The clerk wrote the room numbers on a piece of paper and slid it across the counter. Without another word, Antar picked up the paper and turned toward the bank of elevators. Once inside, he put on plastic gloves and checked his gun to see if a round was chambered. He screwed the suppressor tightly onto the weapon.

The elevator doors opened. He walked quietly down the hall to the first room on the slip. It was Mike McClintock's room. He knocked and received no answer. Then he went to Mitchell's room. Kevin woke with a start to the soft tapping at the door. He stumbled out of bed thinking it was Mike or Jason.

"What's going on?" he asked as he opened the door. Antar pushed Mitchell back into the room. He stumbled backward and fell to the floor. "Wait!" he hollered as he looked up at the weapon pointed at him.

With the gun raised, Antar fired three shots. Two hit Kevin in the center of his chest and the third hit him directly above his right eye. His last breath was a gurgle and sigh. The killer left the room quietly, shutting the door behind him as he walked casually out of the hotel to the parking lot.

****

The pushback tug had the plane outside the hangar and ready for Qasim at seven. He began his pre-flight inspection, preparing for the short flight to Adelanto Airport. McCaffrey wanted to begin modifications to the aircraft by eight and he expected Qasim to have the plane there by that time.

After the exterior check, Qasim boarded the plane and took his seat on the flight deck. He spooled up the engines. Once all gauges were in the green, Qasim radioed the tower for permission to taxi. He was second in line behind a Cessna Citation business jet. After the Citation had rolled, Qasim was given clearance to take off. He positioned the aircraft on the runway, pushed the engines to full power, and released the brake. The DC-10 normally requires a crew of three, but for this 8-mile trip, Qasim broke the rules and lifted off solo. With a light load and the power of the two turbofan engines, the thrust slammed Qasim back into his seat. At the proper speed, he rotated and lifted easily off the runway. His climb was short and within minutes, he was instructed to make a slight turn and line up for the landing at Adelanto.

After landing, Qasim was directed to a hangar at the far end of the small airport. Outside, McCaffrey waited as the ground crew directed the aircraft into position and gave instructions to cut the engines. Qasim was on the tarmac, meeting with McCaffrey within minutes. "Ready to start?" he asked.

"We're good to go. I have a full crew working this modification. I know you want it done soon, we'll do our best," McCaffrey said. "I have a driver ready to shuttle you back to So Cal Logistics."

"Great, keep me posted," said Qasim as he watched the car pull up next to the hangar. "I'll call in a few days for an update if I don't hear from you." He turned and walked to the waiting car.

****

After a short night, Mike and Jason were ready for strong coffee and a large breakfast. Before heading to the restaurant, Mike called Kevin's room next door. The phone rang, but there was no answer. Jason had the file on Qasim and he knocked on Kevin's door as they passed but got no response. "Maybe he's in the shower, let's get something to eat. He'll meet us downstairs," said Mike as they reached the elevators.

With his coffee in hand, Jason flipped open the folder and

began scanning the pages. “It appears Qasim works for Advanced Aerial Fire Response,” he said. “We’ll get Kevin to do a background check on them.”

“Where the heck is he?” asked Mike as he dialed Mitchell’s cell number. The phone rang several times and went to voicemail. “That’s odd. He’s never far from his phone.”

Jason was focused on the file. “Nothing in this file appears to be out of order or cause for concern,” Jason said. “But that begs the question, why is AdvanChem involved with Advanced Aerial Fire?”

“I don’t have a good feeling about Kevin not responding,” Mike said while picking at his food, his appetite gone.

“It’s out of character. If he doesn’t answer the door when we get back to the room, we’ll get someone to open it.” Jason finished eating and looked at Mike, “You ready?”

Mike knocked on Kevin’s door while Jason walked down the corridor toward a hotel maid’s cleaning cart. She had left the room door open, so Jason called, “Hello?”

“Yes sir?” she asked.

“We have a room a few doors away,” he said, pointing to where Mike stood down the hall. “Our friend is in the room next to us. We’ve tried contacting him but he’s not answering his phone or the door. Can you please open it? I’m concerned.”

The maid pulled the master key from her pocket and walked toward Mike. Mike looked up. “Still no answer,” he said.

The maid opened the door, stepped inside, and screamed. Kevin lay on his back, eyes wide open in a pool of blood. The maid passed out and Jason caught her just before she hit the floor. Jason laid her down gently in the corridor and dialed 911, while Mike, white as a ghost, staggered to his room and phoned hotel security.

****

The Marriott Hotel was swarming with FBI Agents and local law enforcement. Jack Schumacher, the agent in charge, coordinated the activity. Mike and Jason stood back as the gurney with the black body bag was rolled out of the room. Schumacher approached the McClintocks. "Can you think of any reason why this happened?"

Jason handed the file to Schumacher. "Somehow it's got to be related to AdvanChem and Advanced Aerial Response. We haven't had any problems until we started looking at these two companies. Kevin did some checking on AdvanChem with his military contacts and he was told they were legitimate, working on a universal antidote to sarin. We don't know much about Advanced Aerial. I would bet that whoever tried to kill Petronovich is behind both Kevin and Marina's murder. There is also this," said Jason, handing the note Marina had sent to Petronovich.

Schumacher flipped open the file. He handed it back to Jason. "I don't want to know how you got this, but I can't keep it," he said. "I noted the two companies you mentioned. We'll check both." He read the note Marina sent Petronovich. "400 pounds of what type of crystals?" he asked.

"Marina never said. I don't think she knew. The facilities AdvanChem occupies are not big enough for that type of production," said Jason.

"Okay, I suggest you maintain a low profile away from here. Go home. We'll let you know if we find anything," said Schumacher.

"What about Kevin's wife, Amy?" asked Mike.

"You know the drill, Mike, she and her daughter, Megan will have the backing and support of the Bureau. They'll be taken care of in every way possible."

"My wife and Amy are friends. Kevin and I went through the Academy together, so our families have a lot of history. Whoever did this is going to pay," said Mike.

"We'll find them, Mike, let us do our job."

"Jack, if you don't, I will. Let's get the hell out of here, Jason," said Mike.

****

After leaving the hotel, Antar made a few calls from his vehicle. He found that Mike McClintock owned two cars, a black Suburban and silver Cadillac STS. With both license plate numbers in hand, he searched the hotel parking garage but came up empty. That made sense, he thought, since they didn't appear to be in their room. He would come back early in the morning to check the garage again. In the meantime, he drove to Al-Hamaidi's home in Irvine, which was in an affluent part of town where most homes were valued in the millions. A thick coastal fog had rolled in, making it difficult to see. Antar parked and walked to the front door, knocking several times. He waited two minutes and knocked again more loudly. A few minutes later from the other side of the door, Al-Hamaidi asked, "Who's there?"

"You know who this is, open the door and let me in!" Antar said.

Recognizing the voice, Al-Hamaidi opened the door. Antar walked in, stopping in the entry way. "I'll make this brief. Mitchell, the FBI Agent, is dead. The two men with him are brothers. I've been ordered to eliminate them. We can't have any loose ends."

"Do you know where to find them?"

"That is my business, not yours. Your only concern is to make certain the crystals are ready as scheduled." Antar turned and left, leaving Al-Hamaidi staring at the closed door.

****

As the McClintocks walked down the hallway, Mike's cell phone rang. He looked at the screen. "It's Julie, I can't tell her about Kevin over the phone," he said to Jason. "Hello?"

"Hi, Mike, have you found anything?" Julie asked.

"Nothing yet. Right now, we're on our way home. We should be there in about two and a half hours."

"Good. Amy phoned, she's been trying to reach Kevin. Have him call her, she's worried."

Mike stopped next to the elevator doors. He looked at Jason and shook his head, not wanting to tell Julie like this, but realizing he had no choice. "Julie, where are you?" he asked.

"In the kitchen, what's wrong, Mike, I know that voice."

Vladi was sitting at the kitchen counter listening to the conversation. "Julie, it's not good," Mike said. "Kevin's been murdered. We found him in his room."

There was silence on the other end of the line. Julie pulled out a chair and sat down at the table.

"Oh God, Mike. What do we do?" Julie began to cry.

"Nothing, right now," said Mike. "We'll talk when we get home."

"What should I say to Amy?" she asked.

"Nothing. She can't be told over the phone. The Bureau is sending people to meet with her right now. She'll be taken care of," explained Mike. "We'll call later and talk with her."

"Mike, I'm afraid. First Vladi, now Kevin," Julie said. "What have you guys gotten us into? You and Jason are in danger as well, you know that!" she almost screamed.

"We'll be okay. Tell Vladi. We'll be home soon. I need to go. I love you," said Mike.

"I love you too, be careful," said Julie. She looked at Vladi. His face was contorted with rage.

"I heard everything. We've got to stop these animals now," he whispered through clenched teeth.

Mike and Jason took the elevator down to level two of the parking garage. Antar watched as the two men headed towards the Suburban. When the McClintocks merged onto the 101 Freeway north, the assassin was three cars behind.

Chapter 8

With the modifications to the DC-10 underway, Qasim turned his attention to one of the most important aspects of the mission. He needed to purchase and set up a remotely piloted aircraft (RPA) systems console. But before doing that, he had to have a base from which to operate and a hotel room would not do. The furnished one-bedroom apartment on the outskirts of Victorville was perfect. The system he wanted required less than 20 square feet of space and was portable. Designed by a company called Zedasoft, the portable simulator desktop (PSD) could be set up in 45 minutes, perfect for this operation. He placed the order online, paying for expedited shipping, assuring delivery within three days.

****

Julie and Petrononvich sat on the front porch, waiting for Jason and Mike to arrive. The kids played on the swing set while the sun dropped below the mountains and the two-hour estimated driving time turned to three hours of waiting. Julie had phoned Mike, concerned that something had happened. He assured her the delay was due to traffic, nothing more. She was about to phone again when the Suburban turned onto the long drive. Petronovich watched as the SUV moved slowly down the dirt road towards the house. What caught Vladi's immediate attention was the white sedan that appeared to have followed the McClintocks. It slowed to a crawl, passing the vineyard entrance as Mike made the turn into his property.

"I have a really bad feeling about this," Petronovich said as he watched the vehicle move further down the road.

"I'm just happy they're home," said Julie as she ran to meet the car, ignoring the sedan.

****

Julie walked into the family room after putting the kids to bed for the night. Jason and Mike sat on either end of the sofa while Petronovich sat in a recliner nursing his Grey Goose. Nobody spoke. Julie sat between the McClintock brothers, slumped over with elbows on her knees and her hands over her face. She looked up and asked, "What are we going to do?" The silence was deafening.

Vladi set his drink on the side table. "We are too exposed here," he said. "Whoever followed us in Los Angeles will certainly know where this place is. We need to have Julie take the kids somewhere safe while we find out who's responsible."

"I think we should send them to Montana. They can stay with Brenda," said Jason. Brenda lived in Butte, about half an hour from Jason's cabin. They've been in a relationship for years. As often as Jason traveled, living apart was not an inconvenience, especially since Brenda spent most of her time in the studio attached to her home. She has been gaining a name for herself since having had two successful shows, displaying her paintings in New York City and Chicago in the last year. "Once we get the flight schedules, I'll phone her," he said.

Vladi looked at Mike. "When you drove in this afternoon, did you notice the white sedan behind you?"

"I saw him. He followed us from the 101 Freeway."

"I think we need to keep all exterior lights on and maintain a watch during the night," Vladi said. "Someone is following us, and we know what they're capable of."

"I'll get the flight reservations and do the first three hours," said Mike as he went to the kitchen cupboard and pulled down his Glock. "You guys get some sleep."

Mike walked around the house, checking all the doors and windows. The exterior floodlights illuminated the property. After getting the reservations, he turned off the interior lights and sat, looking out the kitchen window towards the driveway and the road beyond. It was close to one in the morning when the white sedan passed slowly by the property. Mike went to Jason's room and woke him. "The white car just passed the house."

Petronovich was standing behind Mike. "I couldn't sleep. I heard what you said."

****

Antar drove slowly by the McClintock vineyard. The place was lit up like a sports stadium, with bright lights turning night into day around the entire house. There would be no element of surprise, especially with several men keeping watch. He drove on, deciding to head back to Los Angeles, realizing that the McClintocks were not going to make this easy for him.

****

Jason spoke with Brenda who was excited to have Julie and the kids stay with her. The circumstances put a damper on the visit and Brenda was scared, given the danger Jason, Mike, and Vladi were in, but she agreed to help however she could.

Brenda cleaned the house, which didn't take long given the way she kept her home. The flight left Santa Barbara at two p.m. and arrived in Butte at 11:29 p.m. with stops in San Francisco and Salt Lake City. *This was going to be a long day for the McClintock family*, she thought. It was ten a.m. when Jason called. Brenda had an entire day in front of her, so she fell into her regular routine and headed to her studio to paint.

Mike had Julie and the kids at the Santa Barbara Municipal Airport an hour and a half before the scheduled departure. After checking in, he led the family up the escalator to the security checkpoint. The line was short, as it was most of the time in the small airport, so the process was quick. After hugs and kisses all around, Mike let them go. Julie, Zack, and Sam waved goodbye to Mike. He smiled, waved back, and headed for the exit. He tried to push away the thought that this might be the last time he saw his family, but it lingered in the back of his mind as he drove home.

****

It was a half hour drive from the airport to the vineyard. On the way back, Mike dialed Jack Schumacher, the agent in charge of the investigation into Kevin's death. "Schumacher," he answered.

"Jack, it's Mike, have you found anything?"

"We checked into AdvanChem and they're legitimate. We're still looking for a reason to get a warrant. We also checked Advanced Aerial Fire Response. They're a corporation based in London. The company purchased a DC-10 from Cal Fire. According to the Airport Director at the Logistics Airport in Victorville, their plan is to base the aircraft in Idaho and hire out as an independent resource to fight fires in the west. They also seem to be legitimate. Mike, we'll keep looking. If we come up with anything solid, I'll call you."

"What about prints in the hotel room?"

"There were none that we couldn't account for. It was a professional hit."

"Hotel surveillance should give you a picture of the guy or vehicle. Have you checked that?"

"That was the first thing we went after. About one a.m. a guy in a dark suit entered the lobby. We got a brief look, but nothing more. His head was down. We're running the partial face we have through the national database for recognition."

"Send me what you have. Maybe we've seen him," said Mike.

"That's not standard protocol, but I will," replied Schumacher.

"What about the vehicle?"

"The car had no plates," said Schumacher. "It was a white Toyota Camry."

"Oh shit! I bet that's the car that followed me to Santa Ynez. Someone followed me in a white sedan. It could have been a Camry. It drove by my house in the middle of the night, last night," explained Mike.

"I'll have a team posted at your home in the next three hours," Schumacher said. "I don't have to tell you to keep your eyes open."

"No need for that, Jack. Julie and the kids are on a plane,

headed for Montana. Jason, Vladi, and I will be coming your way. We're going to get this prick!"

"Mike, it's better that you keep a low profile somewhere other than Southern California," said Schumacher. "You don't want your kids growing up without a father. As I said, I'll keep you posted."

"Send the picture, Jack." Mike ignored the comment and hung up.

Chapter 9

The Delta Bombardier CRJ dropped through the clouds into the valley, lining up for final approach to the Bert Mooney airport south of Butte. The flight was five minutes early. Brenda waited at the escalator next to the baggage claim for the passengers to make their way down. Sam spotted Brenda and waved happily while Julie and Zach looked exhausted. It had been a long day, which had seemed even longer with the stress of the last few days. After collecting their bags, they stepped out of the terminal into the crisp evening air. The temperature was below freezing and there was a chance of snow showers. Julie inhaled deeply and felt a sense of relief, knowing that they were far from any immediate danger.

"Brenda, thank you for meeting us at such a late hour. We could have taken an Uber," said Julie as they walked to the car.

"Don't be silly! I could hardly wait to see you," Brenda said. "I know it's late, but are you guys hungry?" She started the car and pulled out of the parking lot.

"I think we're just beat. A good night's sleep is what we need right now," Julie said.

"The rooms are ready. I think you'll be comfortable. We can talk in the morning and you can bring me up to speed on all that's happening. Jason has been too preoccupied to keep me in the loop. I get the broad strokes and that's about it. I was really sorry to hear about Mike's friend," she said as she drove along the empty freeway back towards town.

"It's sad and scary at the same time," Julie whispered, not wanting the kids to hear. "Whoever killed Kevin is still out there and Vladi was close to being killed as well." Julie starred out the window and realized her sense of relief had been short-lived. She realized they could still be in danger and now they had exposed Brenda as well.

****

Qasim pulled into the parking lot next to the hangar. Inside, he could see the huge DC-10 being worked on. Men were working inside the cockpit as well as outside. The nose of the plane had been removed, exposing a nest of wires and cable.

McCaffrey was standing under one of the wings when he noticed Qasim at the entrance. He waved him over. "Impressive, isn't it?" he asked.

"It really is. How's the modification coming along?" The way things looked, Qasim was certain that the project wouldn't be completed for another two or three weeks.

"We're doing well. Our first test flight should be in about a week," answered McCaffrey.

"You're that far ahead?" asked Qasim.

"We do this all the time, Mr. Qasim. When I said one week, that's giving me a little room for unexpected issues. We'll most likely be ready for the first test even earlier than that."

Qasim was impressed and anxious to get back to Al-Hamaidi and Mohammed with the news. "That's fantastic, Mr. McCaffrey, I'm excited to see the end product."

"Please, call me Jordan."

"Certainly, and you must call me Aaban," said Qasim with a smile. "I'll let you get back to it. Thank you for the update. If you need anything, you know where to find me."

"As a matter of fact, I do have one very important question," said McCaffrey as they walked towards the hangar entrance. "Have you selected an RPA console?"

"Yes, we have. We went with a Zedasoft product and should have it in the next day or so," explained Qasim.

"Perfect. They make a good console. When we are ready, we'll call you so that we can interface your system with our modifications." With that, McCaffrey turned and walked back towards the swarm of technicians.

****

Qasim left Adelanto airport and merged onto I-15 west towards Los Angeles. He was anxious to relay the news about the plane's modifications to Al-Hamaidi and Mohammed. It was frustrating that he couldn't simply phone, but he would adhere to Al-Hamaidi's instructions that they communicate only in person. The possibility that they were being monitored by authorities was very high. The drive to Irvine would take a little over an hour, assuming reasonable traffic, which was never a given in Southern California.

The receptionist looked up as the office door opened and Qasim entered. "Can I help you?" she asked.

"I'd like to see either Dr. Al-Hamaidi or Dr. Mohammed. My name is Aaban Qasim."

"Do you have an appointment?"

"I do not, but I'm sure one of them will make time to see me," said Qasim as he took a seat on one of the few metal chairs in the stark room.

The receptionist phoned Mohammed's office. She looked up at Qasim, "Dr. Mohammed will be out to see you in a few moments."

"Thank you," said Qasim as he skimmed through the messages on his phone.

The door to the back offices opened and Mohammed poked his head out, "Come with me," he said to Qasim, holding the door open.

Qasim slipped his phone into his pocket and walked through the door. "First door on the left is my office. We'll meet in there," said Mohammed.

When they walked in, Al-Hamaidi was already seated. He nodded to Qasim but said nothing. Qasim sat down in the chair next to him as Mohammed asked, "What news do you have?"

"I just came from Adelanto airport. The modifications to the DC-10 are moving faster than expected. I'm told that the first test flight of the remotely piloted system will be within the next two weeks. How are the crystals coming along?"

"We will be ready when you are," said Al-Hamaidi. "Will you be able to pilot the plane?"

"The console I will use is configured to mimic the aircraft cockpit, so it should not be difficult. By the time we are ready to proceed, I will have had several hours of practice. Have you had any more issues with the FBI Agent that was checking on me?"

"Let's just say the problem is resolved," said Al-Hamaidi as he stood. "The next time we meet, it will be for you to give us the good news that the modifications are complete." He opened the office door and left the room.

From behind his desk, Mohammed said, "You know the

way out." Qasim rose and left the office.

****

Jason and Vladi were sitting on the porch when Mike returned. Mike pulled up a chair, "Okay, so what's the plan?" he asked.

"Vladi and I have been talking, and I think we need to split up. We've got to figure out the relationship between Qasim, the guy in Victorville, and AdvanChem. I'll go to Victorville. You and Vladi go down to Irvine," said Jason. "But, before we go, will you call Jack Schumacher at the L.A. Field Office and see if he can get the home addresses for Qasim, Al-Hamaidi, and Mohammed?"

"Will do, but he's going to be suspicious and may not release the information," explained Mike. "I'll do what I can to get him to tell me."

"Do your best," said Jason.

"We didn't get very far playing by the rules, so this time we need to be more aggressive," said Petronovich matter-of-factly. "After what has happened to Marina and Kevin, as well as what they did to me, I have no problem using my skills to get them to talk."

"I don't either, but what I don't want is law enforcement after us," said Mike.

"If Qasim and the researchers at AdvanChem are dirty, as we suspect, the last thing they will do is bring attention to themselves by calling the authorities," said Petronovich. "What they will do is unleash their hitmen and we will need to be aware and prepared for that eventuality. These assholes will stop at nothing to get us once they realize we're after them."

"It's settled then. Let's pack up and hit the road," said

Jason as he walked to the door.

****

Brenda was in the kitchen brewing her first cup of coffee when she heard footsteps coming down the hall. “Good morning, you’re up early. I have coffee almost ready,” she said. “Cream and sugar are on the counter.”

“Thanks, it smells great,” said Julie as she waited for the Keurig to finish. She took the cup from Brenda and settled onto a bar stool at the counter.

Brenda stood on the other side and sipped from her cup. “Tell me what happened,” she said.

Julie recounted the tragic events of the last couple of weeks. “So far, the FBI hasn’t come up with anything solid. Mike pointed them in what he believes is the right direction, but if they’ve made any progress, nobody is telling him. Because of that, and the fact that the guys believe our lives are in danger, they decided to act on their own. They believe they know who is responsible for the murders, but they can’t prove it yet. They’re trying to find evidence that the FBI can work with. You know, it’s been two years since Mike retired from the Bureau and our life has been more stressful than when he was working for them. I’m afraid for the guys and I’m afraid for us. The people responsible are ruthless.” Julie stared at her coffee and shook her head, “I’m sorry to have dragged you into this.”

“Julie, there’s no need to be sorry,” Brenda said, putting her hand over Julie’s on the counter. “We’re in this together, and we’ll get through it.”

Chapter 10

Petronovich drove the car south on the 101 Freeway. As they approached Interstate 5, the traffic came to a grinding halt. It was stop and go for the next twenty minutes. Mike heard his phone ping from the center console. The text was from Schumacher that read: "I hope this helps." The picture was from the hotel surveillance camera and showed a partial face of a man in a suit. His facial features looked Middle Eastern.

"Look at this," said Mike as he showed the photo to Petronovich. After the picture, three addresses were listed; one each for Qasim, Al-Hamaidi, and Mohammed.

"Looks Middle Eastern," said Petronovich as he took the phone and looked more closely at the picture. "I just had a thought. If we can place this guy in the same terminal as Marina up in Salt Lake City, we are a very large step closer to determining if he's the killer. We need to make a call to the guy in security at the airport up there."

"Rich Harrington," said Mike.

"Make the call, Mike. After that, you better call Jason with Qasim's address," Petronovich said.

Mike phoned the airport and asked to be directed to security. The traffic seemed to lessen as he waited for Harrington to get on the line.

"This is Harrington."

"Mr. Harrington, this is Mike McClintock. My brother

Jason and our partner were in to see you a couple of weeks ago regarding Marina Mikhailov."

"How can I help you, Mr. McClintock?" asked Harrington.

"I'll make this brief. When you reviewed security tapes in the area where Marina was found, did you notice anything out of the ordinary?"

"Nothing really. It was a busy time of day with several aircraft off-loading passengers. We were able to monitor her for about fifteen minutes before she sat down and slumped over. She had breakfast at a place close to where we found her. As she left the restaurant, there was something that caught my attention. I didn't think much of it. But a guy knocked into her pretty hard, held her arm, keeping her from falling, said something to her, and moved along. With so many people, this is not unusual," explained Harrington.

"Did you get a good look at this guy?" asked Mike.

"If I recall, he was nicely dressed, suit and tie. Seemed like he was traveling on business. Like I said, I didn't think much of it."

"Can you take a look at the tape and get a screenshot of him?" asked Mike.

"I could, but this is airport property. I can't release it to just anyone."

"Mr. Harrington, I'm working this case with the FBI," said McClintock.

"Send me a photo ID and I'll get you the screenshot," Harrington said.

"I can't," explained McClintock. "I just retired."

"My hands are tied, Mr. McClintock," Harrington said. "There's no way I can release it to you."

"Fine. Email it to the FBI Field Office in Los Angeles. Direct it to the attention of Special Agent Jack Schumacher. I'll phone him and tell him to expect it." Mike thanked Harrington and looked at Petronovich. "My gut tells me this might be our guy."

****

Jason had about ten miles to go before he reached the Victorville Logistics Airport. He was headed that way when his phone rang. Seeing that it was Mike, he clicked the hands-free button and answered. "What's up, Mike?"

Mike recapped his conversation with Harrington and then gave Jason Qasim's address. "How do you plan on handling this?" he asked his brother.

"I can't just knock on his door and ask him what he's up to. If I confront him, he might run. We need to know what he's doing at the airport and how he's associated with Mohammed and Al-Hamaidi. I'll stake out his place and follow him. It won't be easy given that it's just me. But I may get lucky. Where are you?" asked Jason.

"We're approaching LAX and should be in Orange County in less than an hour. I'm not sure how we'll approach AdvanChem. Vladi wants to confront them using some of the KGB methods he knows. Given what's happened to him, I can't say I blame him," said Mike.

"They say that discretion is the better part of valor. I wouldn't be so quick in using the hammer. You may find an easier, safer way to get proof they were involved in the murders once you get down there and assess the situation," said Jason as he entered the Victorville city limits. "I'll talk with you in a couple of hours. Stay safe."

Jason put Qasim's address in his Maps app. The apartment building was new and in a nice part of town. He turned into the parking lot, parked, and began to scout out Qasim's unit on foot. Within ten minutes, he had identified the place. It was a corner unit on the first floor. Jason walked past the apartment back to his car and began the vigil.

****

Antar's sources had been monitoring the McClintock's cell phones. When Jason called Brenda, Antar knew where Mike McClintock's wife and kids were: Butte, Montana. With McClintock's address as well as his girlfriend's, Antar scheduled a flight from LAX to BTM (Bert Mooney) for the next day. The flight from Los Angeles to Salt Lake was direct. When boarding was called for Butte, it was easy to spot Julie and the two kids with so few passengers. Antar blended with the group and took his seat for the short, one hour and twenty-minute flight. He had a rental car waiting for him at the terminal.

****

It was a cool morning in the mid-30's. After some discussion, Julie agreed with Brenda that they would be safer at Jason's cabin. There was only one dirt road to the home, and it could be watched for a half mile as it climbed the hill off the main highway. Julie and the kids loaded their luggage while Brenda packed her bag. The Jeep Cherokee was the perfect vehicle for Montana, as it had four-wheel drive. Jason's place was twenty minutes away in the hills overlooking Butte at the base of the Anaconda-Pintler Wilderness. Jason had several weapons at the cabin, but Brenda preferred her Colt Army Special 32-20. This was the last item she packed before grabbing Jason's dog, Rosie. The golden lab was smart and loving. Brenda held the gate to the Cherokee open and Rosie jumped in back next to the luggage. The Jeep was tightly packed for the short drive. The scenery was spectacular on the two-lane highway with towering mountains in the distance as they climbed.

"The cabin is about a mile from here," Brenda said. "After we make this turn up ahead, you'll see the driveway on the right and then the cabin on the hill."

"This is beautiful country," commented Julie as they turned onto Jason's dirt drive. "Jason's place has got to have spectacular views!"

"Wait until you see it. It's like a picture," Brenda said.

Brenda worked her way slowly up the hill avoiding potholes and larger rocks. "I've asked Jason to bring in gravel and smooth this out, but it's not one of his priorities," she said. "I really like that it's remote. After we get our things into the cabin, I'll show you around the property. We have a fire pit out back that we can use to roast marshmallows, maybe tonight. Would you guys like that?" She looked in the rearview mirror at Zach and Sam.

"That would be great," said Zach.

"Yes, please!" Sam piped up while Julie smiled.

****

Mike's phone rang as they passed LAX. It was Schumacher. "Did you get the email, Jack?"

“Where are you?” asked Schumacher.

“Heading to Orange County, just passed LAX,” replied Mike.

“You aren’t too far away, you need to see what came in. Can you meet me at the office as soon as possible?”

“Sure, see you soon,” said Mike. He hung up and looked at Petronovich, “Head downtown to the Field Office, Vladi.”

****

Jason watched as the freight truck pulled up next to the apartment building. The driver got out and approached Qasim’s door. When the door was opened, the driver spoke briefly with Qasim before returning to the truck. It took about twenty minutes for the driver to off-load the three large boxes and hand truck them into the apartment. Jason looked on, trying to determine what was being delivered. One of the boxes sat by the truck waiting to be moved. Jason got out of the car and walked by the box, noting the name stenciled on outside, Zedasoft. He returned to his car and searched for Zedasoft on his phone. “Zedasoft develops innovative man-in-the-loop and constructive simulation solutions for avionics.” *What the hell is in those boxes?* he wondered.

Qasim signed for the packages after instructing the freight driver to place them in the center of the small family room. The furniture had been moved to one side to make room for the RPA console. With a tool kit next to his chair, Qasim opened the first box and began the assembly. The website said the process would take no more than 45 minutes. Three hours later, Qasim wiped his brow, sat back, and smiled at the RPA console he’d put together. He picked up his phone and dialed the Adelanto airport. Jordan McCaffrey's secretary answered and transferred the call.

"This is McCaffrey."

"Jordan, this is Aaban Qasim. I wanted to let you know that the RPA Console is assembled and in working order. I am ready to move forward when you are," said Qasim.

"That's good news. We are still a few days away from being able to run the first test. I'll call as soon as we're ready," McCaffrey replied from the hangar floor.

Qasim walked to the bedroom, tossed his cell onto the bed, and lay down with the DC-10 Flight Training Manual in hand. Ten minutes later he was asleep.

****

McClintock and Petronovich were shown into Schumacher's office. Jack looked up from the desk and motioned for them to sit. He slid a file across the desk and opened it. "It seems we have a match," he said. "The picture from the hotel matches the guy in the screen shot we received from Salt Lake Airport Security." Schumacher held up a hand, "I know what you're going to ask, and the answer is no. We ran the picture through our database for facial recognition and came up empty. This guy is under the radar. We don't have a name."

"Well, we know that he probably killed both Marina and Kevin Mitchell," said Mike. "The question is, how do we find him before he kills again, and what is his relationship to AdvanChem and Advanced Aerial Fire Response?"

"Also, what did Marina want to tell you that was so important she had to speak with you in person, Mr. Petronovich?" asked Schumacher. "Whatever it was probably got her killed."

"Marina worked for AdvanChem and they are somehow involved with Advanced Aerial Fire Response. Has there been any more communication between the two companies since the one we know about?" asked Petronovich.

"None. We're watching them, but so far have nothing but crickets," said Schumacher. "Mike, given that this guy has been tailing you and we can assume he knows where you live, you need to assume that he has Jason's address as well. If I were you, I'd have my entire family, including Jason's girlfriend, tucked away in some remote location until we have this asshole apprehended. I would also be discreet with any communication in case he has listening capability. He's obviously a professional."

Mike looked at Petronovich and knew that Schumacher was right. *I made a rookie mistake sending Julie and the kids to Brenda's place in Montana.* "I think you're right, Jack," he said.

Chapter 11

The wood crackled and sparks rose slowly into the air as the fire caught and the flames grew. Brenda urged the fire on with an iron rod Jason had welded for that purpose. Julie, Zach, and Sam sat bundled in coats on chairs surrounding the firepit. With little breeze, the smoke rose straight up into the moonless night. Rosie parked herself between the kids as if to offer protection from the potential predators in the woods a hundred feet beyond. They were, after all at the base of the Anaconda mountain range and in brown bear country. Lights from the back porch lit up the area and the fire began to cut the cold evening air in a warm, cozy way. The worries that had consumed Julie had temporarily faded into the background. With a glass of wine in hand, she felt a sense of relief.

A wood crate turned upside down acted as a small table for the package of marshmallows and four bamboo skewers. Brenda sat next to the makeshift table with a shotgun propped up against a small tree behind her. Jason had loaded the shotgun with double-aught buckshot, followed by a slug, then buckshot once again, in that order. If an aggressive bear appeared, the idea was to fire at the snout first to ruin the bear's sense of smell and follow with the slug, which would be lethal. Firing accurately is never a given when faced with a charging bear.

****

It was late afternoon when Antar passed McClintock's house. He pulled over about a half mile further up the road. With a hill and dense woods between his car and the house, he began the climb. He wanted to be within sight of the house before sundown. Perched in the tree line above the home, he waited for the lights to come on and darkness to envelop the hills. It wasn't long before the porch light came on like a beacon and a woman whom he assumed to be Jason McClintock's girlfriend came out. She gathered wood for the firepit and set about lighting it. The rest of the family followed, with the kids throwing a ball and playing with a dog. With the fire going, the family settled into chairs and roasted marshmallows. Antar became concerned when the lab stood, turned in his direction, and lifted her head, sniffing. With the darkness and little breeze, he doubted he could be seen. But Brenda noticed the dog and asked, "Rosie, do you smell something?" She glanced in the direction the dog was looking. It was then that Antar saw her reach for her shotgun. *This isn't going to be as easy as I thought.* He sat back and watched.

****

Jason waited in the parking lot until the lights in the small unit went out. It was a little after ten p.m. and he was beat. He had passed a Motel 6 up the road and decided to crash there. The place would be clean and there were a couple of fast food restaurants nearby. That's all he'd need. A shower was the first order of business.

It was still dark when Jason headed back to Qasim's

apartment. The stakeout was tedious and boring, but it was all he could do. A little after nine a.m. the next morning, Qasim left the house and got into a small Toyota parked out front. Jason started his car and followed. Qasim turned into the Adelanto airport and stopped at the gate where he was motioned through. Jason watched from the road as Qasim parked in front of a large hangar. He could see what looked like a commercial aircraft inside with quite a few people actively at work, though what they were doing was unclear. It was important that Jason find out.

****

With the kids bathed and in bed, Julie sat on the sofa scrolling through her mailbox on her phone and deleting most of the messages. Her phone vibrated in her hand with an incoming call. "No Caller ID" flashed on the screen. Normally she wouldn't answer, but this time she felt compelled to. "Hello?"

"Hi, Jules," said Mike.

"Mike, where are you calling from?" she asked.

"I'm using a pay phone, Julie. Listen, I want you, the kids, and Brenda to quickly pack up the car and leave. Drive towards Idaho. Do not use any credit cards. I'll call in a few hours once I've got a destination in mind for you."

"It's after nine, Mike, can't we leave at first light?" asked Julie.

"Julie, you could be in danger. I'm not saying you are, but we can't take any chances. Please pack and leave. I'll call in a few hours. Tell Brenda if she gets a call from Jason, not to answer it. Our phones may be monitored," he explained. "You need to go. Now. I'll call in a few hours."

Brenda, sitting in the armchair across from Julie asked, "What was that about?"

Julie explained what Mike had said then began to gather their clothes. Brenda packed her things, glanced at the shotgun, and brought it as well. "We'll get the kids up once we're ready to go," said Julie. "They'll sleep as we drive. Let's keep the outdoor lights off as we pack the car."

Twenty minutes later, they were on the road with Rosie once again in back with the luggage. Brenda took I-90 west toward Coeur d'Alene, Idaho. It would take them about four and a half hours. They should be there by two thirty the following morning.

Antar sat on the hill overlooking the house, waiting for the lights to go out. He planned to make his move once it was dark. He heard car doors slam on the other side of the house and was surprised to see the Jeep Cherokee drive down the dirt road and wind toward the highway. Panicked, Antar jumped to his feet and ran as fast he could up the hill, through the trees. *I'm screwed!* he thought as he reached his car car twenty minutes later.

Chapter 12

After meeting with Schumacher, Petronovich and McClintock drove to Dana Point and Vladi's home for the night. Before they arrived, Mike stopped at a local convenience store and placed the call to Julie. Knowing the family was secure and on the road, he and Petronovich sat down to decide on their next move. Schumacher had attached a brief background of the three Arabs along with their home addresses. Al-Hamaidi was the only one who was married. He had a wife who stayed at home and cared for a two-year-old daughter. For this reason, McClintock and Petronovich decided they would visit Mohammed's home the next day while he was at work.

Mohammed lived in an upscale part of Irvine about two miles from his partner. Mike and Vladi parked the car a block away and walked to the door. Petronovich pulled his lock pick set from his coat pocket and had the door open within thirty seconds. The home was equipped with an alarm, but it was not activated. Mike and Vladi quickly determined they were alone and moved to Mohammed's office. His desktop was humming. Petronovich sat at the desk, inserted the USB flash drive, and began to download the files stored on the scientist's computer. "This shouldn't take long," said Petronovich as he watched the screen come to life.

McClintock paced the room wearing gloves. On the wall across from the desk were shelves of books stretching from the floor to the ceiling. One side of the shelves seemed dedicated to chemistry, molecular biology, and physics, while the other held books about religion and the doctrine of Islamic Jihad. "What the fuck is this all about, Vladi?" asked Mike as he held the book *Jihad and Death* by Olivier Roy. "He must have dozens of books about Jihad."

"I don't know, but chemistry and Islamic Jihad doesn't sound like a great combination to me," said Petronovich as the computer stopped downloading. He pulled the USB drive from the port, "Let's get out of here and see what's on this drive."

****

On the side of the road, Jason recalled what Kevin Mitchell had said about this small private airport. A company from San Diego leased the property and worked on unmanned aircraft, mostly military contracts. It was then that he connected the dots. The packages Qasim received yesterday were from a company called Zedasoft. *They developed simulation solutions for avionics! Those boxes must have something to do with unmanned aircraft and the work being done in that hangar! And Qasim is a pilot! I'll bet he's going to fly that DC-10 remotely! But why?* Jason needed to talk this over with Mike and Vladi. His next stop would be Vladi's place in Orange County.

****

Antar sat in the car, his hands clenched on the steering wheel. He was pissed. With a twenty-minute start, the McClintock family could be heading anywhere from Canada to Mexico.

His only option was to fly back to California and wait until his targets showed themselves again.

****

Brenda drove into Coeur d'Alene at about 2:45 in the morning. The kids were sound asleep. She looked at Julie and whispered, "Let's find a place to stop and try to get a couple of hours sleep before we move on."

"Sounds good to me," said Julie with a yawn.

They found a parking spot near the bathrooms of a city park. Brenda cut the engine, placed her handgun on the center console, and closed her eyes.

****

It was late when Jason walked into the house. Mike and Petronovich were at the kitchen table poring over files downloaded onto the drive. "What do you have there?" asked Jason.

Mike looked up. "We paid a visit to Mohammed's place and copied the files from his desktop. Did you have any luck?"

Jason told them about the boxes delivered to Qasim as well as the DC-10 at the Adelanto airport. "I think he plans to fly the plane remotely. But why would he do that?" Before waiting for an answer, he added, "By the way, I haven't talked to Brenda, have you been in touch with Julie?"

"Yes, they're headed to Coeur d'Alene. Schumacher thinks they should be somewhere remote. Any idea where we might send them until we get a handle on this?" Mike asked.

"If they're in Coeur d'Alene, I think we should consider

some place nearby. You know, there's Roosevelt Lake in Washington, about an hour or an hour and a half from them. Brenda's family have rented houseboats there for years. We joined them a couple of years ago. Brenda can handle a houseboat. The Marina we rented from was Seven Bays. I'll check that out," said Jason as he pulled up Google on his phone.

"Sounds like a good option, the kids would like that," said Mike.

Jason went to the Seven Bays website. It was off-season, so availability wouldn't be a problem. He could rent a 35-foot boat that slept four, with a full bathroom and kitchen. It was all they needed. He would contact the marina in the morning and confirm the reservation. That decided, he said, "Tell me what you've found in those files."

"A bunch of mumbo-jumbo scientific stuff," moaned Petronovich. "I'm falling asleep looking at this crap."

"Why don't you hit the sack, Vladi? Jason, you should too. We can talk this out in the morning. I'll give it another thirty minutes then shut it down as well," suggested Mike.

"That's not a bad idea," said Jason "Don't stay up too long."

McClintock and Petronovich called it a night while Mike continued looking through the files for anything that might be important. He was about to shut it down an hour later when the next file caught his eye. It was the purchase and delivery receipt for one industrial grade, 800-gallon stainless steel tank at $20,000, as well as a large rotary dryer and industrial vents like the kind used in the pharmaceutical industry. *Why would AdvanChem need equipment like this to test for a sarin antidote? They wouldn't, but they would if they were producing*

400 pounds of a crystal product. He logged off the computer and fell onto the sofa in the family room. With any luck, he'd get four hours of sleep.

****

McCaffrey was ready to establish the link between the DC-10 and Qasim's RPA console. He phoned Qasim. "Aaban, this is Jordan McCaffrey, we are ready to communicate with your console. I need to send a technician to work on the interface. Where is the system located?" he asked.

Qasim was reluctant to release the information, but he had no choice. "I'm operating out of an apartment." He gave McCaffrey the address and was told a tech would be there at eight a.m. the following morning. If everything worked well, they would be operational and ready for the test flight in about one week.

****

Jason was up and out the door early. He drove to the corner convenience store and used the pay phone to call Brenda.

Brenda's phone vibrated and woke her from a deep sleep. The sun was about to rise over the hill. She picked up the phone and quietly stepped out of the car, moving away so she wouldn't disturb everyone else who remained asleep. "Hello?"

"Hi, where are you?" asked Jason.

"We're in Coeur d'Alene. I stopped at a city park about three hours ago. How are you guys doing?"

"We're okay. I think Mike made the right call. I've got a place where you guys will be safe. Roosevelt Lake is about an hour from you. I reserved a small 35-foot houseboat in my name. Ask your dad to call Seven Bays Marina and pay for it with his credit card. We'll pay him back once this is over," said Jason. "How are you set for cash?"

"We've got enough for groceries and gas to last awhile," Brenda said. "We should be fine. How long do you think we'll be on the lake, Jason?"

"Not long, I hope. We're starting to piece things together and should have enough evidence for the FBI to get a warrant to search AdvanChem and the owner's homes soon."

"That's good. Just keep safe. I'll phone Dad and we'll head to the marina after we find a store. Houseboats are fun, but you need to pack right, or you pay through the nose at the marina store. You remember that I'm sure," said Brenda.

"I do. A six pack of beer for $15 was a bit steep. "I'll call you later today. Hopefully you'll be on the water." Jason hung up, went inside the store, and picked up doughnuts for breakfast.

Chapter 13

Mike was at the kitchen table with a cup of coffee going through the file he'd found the night before. He looked up as Jason walked in. "Take a look at this."

Jason sat down and scanned the document. "Why would they need a heavy-duty industrial tank, vent, and dryer?"

"I'm no chemist, but I don't think the type of work they're doing would require machinery like this. I can see a pharmaceutical company manufacturing drugs using this equipment," said Mike. "Or someone producing 400 pounds of an unknown crystal."

Petronovich entered the kitchen and poured a cup of coffee. He bent over and scanned the file. "I agree. I think you need to show it to Schumacher, Mike," said Vladi.

****

Brenda explained the plan to Julie when she woke up a few minutes later. The car was loaded with groceries as they continued west on I-90 into Washington, turning north onto highway 25 towards the lake. The marina was busy for mid-week in the fall.

They parked, and Brenda checked in at the office. The boat was ready for them and after several trips back and forth from the car, everyone, including Rosie, was eager to get going. Brenda had captained houseboats much larger than this, so her check-ride to make sure she could handle the boat was quick and smooth. They off-loaded the marina employee and slowly moved out of the protected bay. After leaving the no-wake zone, Brenda looked at Julie, "It's time to pop the cork," she said. "The champagne is in the cooler on ice. I know it's not a celebration, but I have never left a marina in a houseboat without a toast."

Julie smiled and popped the cork. "I'm good with that," she said. "Here's to a safe trip." They sipped their wine while Brenda increased the boat's speed and headed for her favorite cove.

****

The technician arrived at Qasim's place with nothing but a laptop computer. He introduced himself as Paul. He sat at the console, plugged a thumb drive into the RPA console USB port, and began to download data. The shared information would allow the console to access the flight deck of the DC-10. The instrumentation would show on the three large screens on the platform. In addition, with the cameras positioned inside the cockpit, the remote pilot would be able to see outside the aircraft even better than a pilot inside the plane. The entire process took about thirty minutes. Qasim sat off to the side and watched. Paul looked over at him when he was finished. "That should do it. Let me call Jordan and have him light up the instrumentation inside the cockpit."

Paul took out his phone and dialed, "Jordan, we're ready at this end. Power up the flight deck and let's see what we've got."

Jordan gave the command to the technicians working on board. "Okay, Paul. Your screens should be showing full instrumentation." At that moment, the three screens lit up the console, with all gauges in clear sight.

"That's amazing," said Qasim, as he walked over and examined the controls over Paul's shoulders.

"Looks like we're good, Jordan," Paul said. "We have a visual of the flight instrument panel."

Qasim pulled a chair next to the technician. Paul stood, "Take the seat at the console and tell me what you think, Mr. Qasim."

Qasim sat down and stared, "It's as though I'm in the left seat."

"You *are* in the left seat," said the technician. "When we're done with the plane's modifications, from here you'll be able to communicate with air traffic control and fly the DC-10 just as if you were in the cockpit. Keep the thumb drive in case you upgrade your RPA console."

****

Jason sat down with his coffee and doughnut. He told Mike and Petronovich about the boxes from Zedasoft that had been delivered to Qasim's place. He explained that Zedasoft sold consoles to fly aircraft remotely. He then reminded them what Kevin had said about the Adelanto airport and the company leasing the property. "They modify aircraft to fly remotely, mostly military contracts. The DC-10 is there being worked on. Combine that with the fact that Qasim is a pilot and he just received a Zedasoft product, probably an RPA console, and you can make a case for the DC-10 being modified to fly remotely."

"I don't see how a remotely controlled aircraft has anything to do with fighting fires," said Mike. "I would bet my favorite 2013 Syrah that Qasim's company is a front."

"Nobody in this room would take that bet," said Jason.

"Qasim is somehow tied to AdvanChem," said Vladi. "The question is, what is the connection between AdvanChem, their industrial equipment, 400 pounds of a crystal product, Qasim, and a remotely piloted DC-10?"

"And how are they all connected to Marina and Kevin's murder and your attempted murder?" added Jason. "And us being followed and watched in the Santa Ynez Valley?"

"I'll talk to Schumacher," said Mike.

****

Antar pulled up in front of the AdvanChem office. He walked in, past the receptionist, to the locked side door. Looking back at the young girl, he said, "Key in the code." This wasn't a request and she knew it. Without hesitation, she walked over and input the numbers. The door swung open and Antar walked directly into Mohammed's office. Mohammed looked up from the desk as Antar sat down. "We intercepted a call from the retired FBI Agent. He called the Los Angeles field office."

"We assumed he's been in contact with them," said Mohammed.

"Yes, but they know about your industrial equipment, the crystals you are cooking, and the modifications to the DC-10."

"How could they know about the equipment and crystals?"

“I don’t know, but they are too close. We need to shut them down.”

“What happened with McClintock’s family in Montana?” asked Mohammed.

Antar got up and paced the room, “They made a run for it as I was closing in. I don’t know where they are.”

“If you could find them, we’d have some leverage over these infidels. It could buy us the time we need to finish the crystals and get the plane modified.”

“Do you think I haven’t thought of that?” Antar snapped.

“What about any McClintock relatives?” asked Mohammed.

“The McClintocks have no other family. Their parents are dead, I checked. The Russian’s family is in Kazakhstan. I haven’t checked on McClintock’s girlfriend’s family. If she has any, they may know where she is.” Antar left the office abruptly, not waiting for Mohammed’s response. The next day he was back in Butte, on his way to Brenda’s home.

****

Brenda throttled back the power as she entered the cove. Steep cliffs towered above the small boat on each side. The cove narrowed at a bend then opened once again as they made the turn. About a half mile up, the fjord ended with the cliffs giving way to a small beach next to a trickle of a stream that in the rainy season was sure to bring down heavy waters from the mountainside.

“This is it! What do you guys think?” she asked as she moved the boat slowly to the end of the cove.

Julie was on the forward deck standing to the left as

Brenda guided the boat. "This is absolutely amazing, Brenda," she said.

"I never get tired of this place. The one drawback though is that it gets dark a little early. The canyon walls are narrow and high."

"I like it!" exclaimed Zach while Sam looked on in awe.

"Okay, this part is a little tricky. Julie, you need to help me. I'm going to steer the boat into position to land on the shore. You need to keep the boat pointed straight ahead with engines running as I jump off and secure the lines. I'm going to put it between those two trees," she said pointing, as she eased the boat forward.

As the boat slowly ground ashore, Julie took over the helm while Brenda jumped off the bow with the left stern line in hand. She scampered up the slight incline and secured the line to a tree. After the second line was in place, she climbed back on board and cut the engine. The silence was deafening.

"Why don't you two hop on shore and scout the area?" suggested Julie to the kids, thinking it would be good for them to burn off some energy. As the kids jumped off the boat, she admonished them, "Be sure to keep the boat in sight. I want to be able to see you!"

The two chairs on the bow deck were situated next to the gas grill. Julie sat in one as Brenda came out with two glasses of wine. Handing one to Julie, she sat down opposite and took in the scenery.

"Under different circumstances, this would be relaxing. I can't help thinking how the guys are doing," said Brenda. "Unfortunately, we won't know until we're in open water. There's no cell reception in this canyon."

Julie took a long sip of her wine, "I hadn't thought of

that."

****

It didn't take Antar long to find Brenda's father's home. They lived in a suburb, southeast of Helena, 68 miles from Butte, just off Highway 15. Antar merged onto the freeway for the one-hour drive just as the sun was setting. He needed to find the McClintock family before the brothers and the Russian got any closer to learning the truth about AdvanChem.

Brenda's father checked the lock on the front door and turned off the lamp in the living room before heading down the hall to bed. It was ten p.m. when he put his book down and turned the light off on the nightstand. He was alone. Brenda's mother had died two years earlier from pancreatic cancer.

Antar parked his car on a side street a block from the house. Before exiting, he attached a suppressor to his Glock 17. He slid the gun into the shoulder holster under his coat and made his way through the shadows to the house. The gate to the backyard was unlocked. Antar moved into the back, closing the gate behind him without a sound. As expected, the back door was locked, but opened with a credit card slid between the frame and the handle mechanism. Antar hadn't even needed to use the lock pick set in his pocket.

Brenda's father woke with a start when the light next to his bed snapped on. He adjusted his eyes and stared at the gun pointed at his head. "What do you want?" he asked. The man appeared to be of Middle Eastern descent. He didn't speak.

"I don't have any money in the house," Brenda's father said.

"I don't want your money," whispered Antar. "Tell me

where your daughter is."

Brenda's father's eyes opened wide and he began to perspire. "I don't know where she is."

"I don't have the luxury of time," said Antar as he lowered the weapon to the old man's calf and fired. The spit from the gun was followed by an eruption of bright red on the bed sheets and a muffled scream as Antar pushed a pillow down on the man's face.

"Don't scream and I'll lift the pillow," he whispered, pulling the pillow back. Brenda's dad was shaking as tears rolled down his cheeks. "I'll ask you one more time. Where is your daughter?"

The old man gritted his teeth and shook his head. "No," he said.

Antar raised the gun and fired again, hitting the old man's other calf. He muffled the second scream with the pillow. Brenda's father passed out. Antar waited a minute until he came to. Then he held gun to the old man's shoulder. "Where is your daughter?" whispered Antar. Brenda's father shook his head once again and waited for the searing pain that came instantly. His eyes rolled back in his head and he passed out again. The mattress was soaked in blood. Antar pointed the gun at the old man's left foot. He came to shaking, soaked in blood and sweat.

"Why are you doing this?" he asked between gasps.

"This isn't personal, just tell me where she is," explained Antar.

"I can't," answered Brenda's father as the gun spit once again, the most excruciating pain erupting from his left foot. This time, he was out cold for five minutes. When he woke, he saw the barrel of the gun pointed at his other foot. He didn't wait to be asked. Between gasps, he said, “She rented a houseboat at Seven Bays Marina on Roosevelt Lake in Washington.”

“Thank you,” said Antar placing the portable phone from the nightstand near him. “After I’m gone, you may call 911.”

Brenda’s father, sensing relief, closed his eyes, and took a deep breath. It was his last, as Antar pointed the Glock between the old man’s eyes and pulled the trigger.

Chapter 14

Schumacher sat at his desk and listened while Mike detailed point by point what he, Jason, and Petronovich had found over the last several days. After ten minutes, Mike finished and waited for a response from Schumacher. Schumacher looked up from his legal pad which was full of notes. "I'm not going to ask how you learned about the industrial equipment," he said. "But, Mike, there's nothing that you've said, whether it's the equipment purchases, the RPA console, aircraft modification, or crystal production that's illegal. Now, if we found that they had an elaborate meth lab going on, that would be a different story, but we haven't. The one thing we do know is that Kevin and Marina were most likely killed by the same guy. If we could tie him, whoever he is, to AdvanChem, we would have something. I have agents working on that angle. Why don't you guys take a break, lie low, and let us handle this? We are far more capable than you and your civilian partners now that you're retired."

"Why would AdvanChem need industrial equipment to develop an antidote to sarin gas? It just doesn't make sense. That equipment wouldn't even fit in their current facility," said Mike, thinking out loud. "They must have another place where the equipment is being used." Mike stood and walked over to the window. The busy streets of downtown Los Angeles were starting to pick up as the five o'clock rush hour approached.

“We’ll see if AdvanChem has any other property they’re leasing,” Schumacher said. “If they’re doing something illegal, I can assure you it’ll be a shell of some type and difficult to discover. If we come up with anything, I’ll call.” Schumacher stood and walked to the door. “Watch your back, Mike,” he said.

Mike drove out of the parking garage and merged into the late afternoon traffic, heading toward the 101 Freeway a mile down the road. Spotting a gas station at the corner, he pulled in next to the pay phone to the side of the building. He dialed Julie’s number but the call went immediately to voicemail. He checked the contacts list in his cell and phoned Brenda but got the same result. Frustrated, he slammed the phone into the cradle and walked back to the car.

****

Qasim was in the living room when the phone rang. It was Jordan McCaffrey. *I hope this is good,* thought Qasim as he answered, “Hello, Jordan?”

“Mr. Qasim, I hope I’m not disturbing you,” said McCaffrey.

“Not at all, how are you progressing?”

“We are ahead of schedule, about ready for the first test flight and we would like to begin tomorrow at eight a.m. We have an engineer licensed to fly this plane. He will be on the aircraft, acting as co-pilot and able to take control if something should go wrong. His name is Tony Cusseta. Since you are not on-site with the RPA console, there will be a short delay between your commands and the plane but it is minimal and will not be an issue. The airplane will be on the taxiway and powered up before you take control. Can you be available at your console in the morning? If so, I'll have a technician there to assist, should you need help."

"That's great news, Jordan! Absolutely, I will be ready," said Qasim. "Talk to you tomorrow." He hung up and stared at the RPA console he was about to use for the first time. As darkness settled, Qasim knew he wouldn't be getting much sleep; he was too excited.

****

It was mid-morning when Brenda started the engines and untied the stern lines. There was a crispness to the air, necessitating a light jacket . The kids and Rosie sat on the bow while Julie watched the back for shallow rocks and logs. Brenda backed the houseboat away from shore, turning it toward the mouth of the fjord and the open waters of the lake's main channel.

At 150 miles long with 630 miles of shoreline, Lake Roosevelt provided plenty of coves to explore. Brenda felt the need to put more than a few miles between their current location and Seven Bays Marina, should someone come looking for them. She headed north toward the Canadian border where the lake began. A manmade lake, Lake Roosevelt filled from Canadian snowmelt as well as the Columbia River. The lake's deepest point approached 400 feet; the most shallow being 14 feet close to Canada. Brenda's plan was to motor towards the northern half of the lake for safety.

A map of the lake encased in plexiglass hung on the wall next to the captain's chair. Brenda pointed to a cove. "This looks promising, Julie, it's about 7 miles north. That's where we're going."

Julie had a pot of coffee brewing on the stove. She walked over to Brenda and placed a steaming mug next to her as she scanned the map. "This is one big lake," she said, as she sat at the small kitchen table across from the helm.

"The size provides a certain amount of safety," said Brenda as she increased the boat's speed. "Anybody looking for us would have a lot of shoreline to check."

****

In the distance, the sun settled into the fog as it moved in from the ocean, across the Pacific Coast Highway towards Petronovich's home. Mike parked in front of the house, listening to the rhythm of the waves crashing against the shore. A moment later, he entered the living room as Jason leaned forward in the easy chair and Vladi explained what he was going to do. "Whoa, back up," Mike said, "let me hear this from the beginning."

"Grab a drink and have a seat," said Petronovich.

There was a half bottle of Syrah sitting on the kitchen counter, partially corked. Mike reached for the stemware on the sideboard. "Okay, what are you two thinking?"

"We know Mohammed is single," said Vladi, "and we know he's not prone to engaging his security system. I'm going to pay him a visit tonight and see if I can't use some of my expertise to get him to tell us what they are up to at AdvanChem. I can't be as aggressive as I'd prefer, which means he may not talk. But at least he will know that we know they're up to something and that we're watching."

"What if he calls the police?" asked Jason.

"I will ask him to do just that," Vladi said. "He won't because it could expose what's really happening at AdvanChem. I will press the issue by bringing up the industrial equipment, which should shake him up a bit. You two will be watching the home from a distance in the car. Should he leave the house after I'm gone, you will follow him. We leave in one hour."

"Let's do it," said Jason as Mike nodded in agreement.

The McClintock brothers parked a quarter mile down the block, with unobstructed views of Mohammed's driveway and garage. Lights illuminated the ground floor, indicating he was home. Petronovich drove further down and turned onto a side street closer to the house, parking near the same spot he had a couple of days before when he and Mike had broken into the home and downloaded the computer files. He couldn't see the house, but he could see the McClintock's car. When Jason and Mike thought the time was right, they would flash their headlights twice, giving Vladi the go sign. At 11:50, Petronovich was given the signal to move.

****

The technician was at the apartment at seven forty-five a.m. Qasim let him in and sat down at the console. It was turned on and ready to go. At precisely eight, the technician's cell buzzed. He answered, "Jordan, we are ready here."

Lights flickered as the screens came to life. Qasim sat at the RPA console and watched as the instrument panel came into view below the cockpit windows. His co-pilot sat to his right and could be seen checking and adjusting certain gauges. Qasim put on his headset and spoke into the mouthpiece,

"Good morning, you must be Tony Cusseta."

"That I am, Mr. Qasim, good morning. Do you have an unobstructed view of the instrument panel?"

"I can see everything perfectly."

"Good, then let's get started. As Mr. McCaffrey told you, I am here to intercede should something go wrong from the RPA standpoint. I doubt it will. Go ahead and call the tower for clearance to taxi."

Qasim did as he was told and before he knew it, he was taxiing the plane, immersed in the instrumentation, and feeling as though he was in the cockpit. After receiving permission to roll, he powered up and let the light DC-10 roar down the runway and catapult into the sky. The plane felt no different than it had when he'd flown it from the Victorville Airport to Adelanto. After leveling off at 5,000 feet, he heard McCaffrey in the headset. "So far, so good. How does it feel, Mr. Qasim?"

"It feels great. The airplane is responding perfectly."

"Okay, we're going to head east for ten minutes, then bring her home," said McCaffrey, giving Qasim the coordinates.

Twenty minutes later, with the tower's descent instructions, Qasim had the DC-10 lined up with the runway, floating down evenly. He touched down lightly, braked, and slowly began to taxi towards the hangar. "That was a soft landing, Mr. Qasim, good job," said Cusetta. "If you like, I can take it the rest of the way to the hangar."

"The airplane is yours, Tony, take her home. Thanks for your help," said Qasim.

"That went well, Mr Qasim," said the technician, "The interface couldn't have worked better. We will tweak a few things back at the hangar, but barring anything unforeseen, we are close to being done. Jordan will be contacting you shortly, I'm sure."

"Thanks for everything," said Qasim as the tech walked out the door.

****

The weather was overcast and damp when Antar pulled into the Seven Bays Marina parking area. The marina was quiet, with no customers in sight; only employees taking care of regular maintenance. Antar entered the marina office and approached the person he assumed was the manager sitting behind the desk. Pushing paperwork aside, the man looked up. "Hi there," he greeted Antar.

"I'd like to rent a ski boat," said Antar.

"That might be more boat than you need for fishing, young fella," said the old man. "Ski season is long gone with the water and outside temps dropping."

"I want to check out the lake for possible houseboat plans next summer," Antar said. "I'll be covering a lot of area in a short amount of time, so I'd like a fast boat. I have a neighbor on the lake right now. The name is McClintock. You wouldn't have any idea where they might have headed, would you? They were the ones who suggested I give Roosevelt Lake some thought for next year. I'd like to drop in and surprise them."

"No idea. This is a large lake; they could be anywhere. How long do you need the boat?" asked the manager.

"Probably no more than two days," said Antar.

The manager picked up the hand piece and spoke into it, "Jimmy, prepare a ski boat." His voice could be heard over speakers located throughout the marina. After twenty minutes, with paperwork complete, Antar was on the water, motoring slowly out past the docked houseboat fleet.

The marina manager sat at his desk and thought about the strange exchange that had just taken place. Something didn't feel right and his stomach seemed to be doing back flips. He reached for the marine radio on his desk. Set at Channel 16 he called, "Mrs. McClintock, this is Seven Bays Marina, come in, over."

The kids, dog, and Julie were in the cabin of the small houseboat with the sliding door to the bow closed to keep the biting fall air at bay. Brenda was steering the boat north up the main channel when the marine radio came to life. Brenda looked at the family, then back to the radio. She ignored the fact that the manager assumed she was Jason's wife, since he had made the reservation. She picked up the receiver, "This is the McClintocks, Seven Bays, over."

"Go to Channel 68, please acknowledge," said the manager.

"McClintocks switching to Channel 68, over," replied Brenda, as she reached for the dial and moved from 16 to 68. "Seven Bays Marina, go ahead, over."

"McClintock, this is Seven Bays. I just had a strange conversation. A guy looking like he's from the Middle East, I can't pronounce his name, came in and rented a ski boat. He mentioned that he knew you and asked if I might know where you'd be. He said he was a friend and wanted to surprise you. He rented the boat for a couple days, but the thing is, he didn't have any gear; no tent, nothing. Something didn't seem right, I thought you should know."

"Thanks for the heads-up, Seven Bays. We'll be on the

look-out. Keep us posted if you learn any more about him. McClintock out, changing back to Channel 16."

Brenda placed the handpiece in the cradle and turned to look at three faces staring at her from the kitchen table.

****

Petronovich placed the zip ties in his coat pocket as he got out of the car. He had his lock picks ready and the back door opened in a matter of seconds just as he had done a couple of days before. As before, the alarm was not engaged. With his handgun drawn, Petronovich made his way up the stairs. He remembered the office had a chair that was more like a dining room chair with a high back and arms, not the typical heavily padded office chair. He moved the chair to the bathroom and placed it next to the oversized tub. The lights were off in the master bedroom and he could barely see the curves of a human body underneath the heavy comforter. Petronovich walked softly to the bedside and whispered, "Dr. Mohammed."

Mohammed woke with a start, sitting straight up only to be met with a sickening crack as the Russian broke his nose, knocking him out cold. Using the fireman's carry, Vladi swung Mohammed over his shoulders, took him into the bathroom, and sat him on the chair. Using zip ties, Vladi secured Mohammed's arms and legs tightly to the chair. Petronovich then eased the chair backwards so that it rested on the side of the tub with Mohammed's head hanging over the back. Petronovich was careful to be sure the unconscious man's body was elevated higher than his flopping head. He grabbed a hand towel next to the bathroom sink and soaked it with water. After wringing it out, he placed it over Mohammed's mouth and nose as his eyes began to flutter.

Mohammed mumbled something incoherent as he tried to focus. Recognizing the Russian, his eyes grew wide and what would have been a high-pitched scream, had it not been for the soaked towel, emanated from the depths of his lungs as a gurgle. Petronovich smiled, turned on the tub's large faucet, and eased the chair backwards. Mohammed flung his head back and forth, trying without success to free his limbs from the zip ties. With the water running, Petronovich asked, "Why did you kill Marina and Kevin Mitchell?"

Mohammed shook his head and mumbled, "I don't know what you're talking about."

Petronovich eased the chair further back, running cold water over Mohammed's face. Whipping his head back and forth, Mohammed tried to avoid the flow of water. This only made the situation worse. The water poured into his upturned mouth and nose, filling his mouth, throat, and sinuses. Mohammed's lungs were clear, so his body still received oxygen though his mind told him he was drowning. Vladi had learned this waterboarding technique years before while working for the KGB. He slowly lifted the chair and let it rest on the side of the tub once again. He looked at Mohammed and asked, "What are you hiding at AdvanChem?"

Mohammed turned his head sideways and threw up toward the tub. The soaked washcloth caught most of it, causing it to drip down the side of his face and throat. Gasping, he said, "We are working for the Government to produce an antidote to sarin."

"Why would you need an industrial tank, vent, and dryer for that?" asked Vladi.

The surprise in Mohammed's eyes was evident as he

shook his head, "I don't know what you are talking about!"

Petronovich eased the chair back once more, flooding Mohammed's face with water. Mohammed's body began to shake as his eyes rolled back into his head. Vladi realized he had reached the point where he had to stop, or Mohammed would die. He lifted the chair up once again and removed the wet cloth. After throwing up again, Mohammed gasped and stared at Petronovich.

Vladi cut the zip tie to Mohammed's left arm, releasing it. "We are watching you, Mohammed," he said. "We will find out what you are doing, and we will nail your ass for the murders of Marina and Agent Mitchell. Please, call the police and report me. I'd really like to bring AdvanChem to the attention of the authorities." Petronovich left the bathroom, leaving Mohammed the task of undoing the other ties.

Chapter 15

After the tech left the apartment, Qasim powered down the console and headed for his car. He had to tell the researchers at AdvanChem about the progress being made.

Al-Hamaidi poked his head out of the door and spoke to Qasim who was sitting on the metal chair in the reception area. "Come this way," he said.

Qasim followed Al-Hamaidi to his office. Mohammed was sitting, his back to the door when Al-Hamaidi and Qasim entered. When he looked up, Qasim stopped in his tracks. Mohammed looked as though he had been hit by a truck.

"What in the name of Allah happened to you?" asked Qasim.

Al-Hamaidi pointed to a chair, "Sit down, Qasim and we'll tell you everything."

"I'm listening," said Qasim as Al-Hamaidi took his seat behind the desk.

"The people that were asking about you at the airport have not gone away. We eliminated one of them, but the others are still pursuing us. One broke into Dr. Mohammed's home and tortured him, as you can see," explained Al-Hamaidi.

"He waterboarded me," said Mohammed. "He is Russian and he knew what he was doing. If I had to guess, I'd say he was GRU or what was the KGB. He could have easily killed me, but he didn't. What concerns me most is that he knew about the industrial equipment."

"That is troubling. I piloted the DC-10 remotely this morning. The technician present said they were almost ready to release the aircraft to me," Qasim said. "I'd say the plane will be fully operational in the next few days. How close are you to being ready to move the crystals?"

"We are almost there. We will continue to produce until you receive notification that the plane's modifications are complete. At that point, we will proceed," said Al-Hamaidi. "These dogs are getting too close."

"Can you eliminate the threat?" asked Qasim.

"The contact we have is going after the family of the pigs who are causing us problems," explained Mohammed. "If he can get them, they can be used as leverage to bring these animals in, so we can kill them all."

"This is getting too complicated. The sooner the operation moves forward, the better," said Qasim as he stood and moved toward the door. "I'll let you know when the airplane is ready."

****

After the call from Seven Bays Marina, Brenda immediately steered the houseboat to the western shoreline and a cove that went back a half mile. Looking at Julie, she said, "I don't want to be in the middle of the lake at any time other than very early in the morning. We'll have some cover from the morning fog then."

"Zach, you and Sam take Rosie and go out on deck. Let us know if you see any logs in the water out front," said Julie. Zach and Sam grabbed their coats and went out onto the bow, closing the sliding door behind them.

“Do you think the guy that’s following us is the same one who killed Kevin and Vladi’s friend, Marina?” asked Julie.

“I’d say that’s a pretty good bet,” Brenda said. “Take the wheel, I’m going to load the shotgun, just in case. Keep the boat in the middle of the channel away from the shore.”

The shotgun was in the back of a closet and the shells were in Brenda’s suitcase. She loaded the weapon the same way she did for bear, triple aught buckshot followed by a slug. The triple aught shot would devastate anything within 35 yards. Brenda placed the shotgun next to the steering console, readily accessible if needed.

****

Antar was moving swiftly up the middle of the lake, about five miles south of Brenda’s location. The distance could be covered quickly if not for the coves on either shore that had to be checked. His cell phone rang as he crossed from one side of the lake to the other. “Hello?”

“We have a problem. The people tracking us are getting close. Mohammed was threatened and almost killed last night by the Russian you were supposed to have eliminated. Of utmost concern, however, is that they know about the industrial equipment. Where are you?” asked Al-Hamaidi.

“The McClintock family rented a houseboat on Roosevelt Lake, north of Spokane. I’m going after them, but the lake is large, 150 miles long. They have a lead time of one day, but the houseboat is slow, and I have a ski boat moving fast. That said, the process is time consuming.”

“Find them. Find them quickly. Our mission may be compromised and that can’t happen. Let me know when you have them," demanded Al-Hamaidi.

****

Mike walked in the front door of Petronovich's home. He'd tried to reach Julie once again from the phone at the local convenience store. Looking up from the kitchen table, Jason asked, "Did you talk to them?"

"It went right to voicemail. I'm really concerned," said Mike, just as Jason's phone buzzed.

"It's Brenda," said Jason, answering. "Brenda, we were worried, are you okay? You shouldn't be using your cell. Make this quick."

Brenda kept the boat at the mouth of the fjord as she told Jason about the call she received from the marina manager.

"Don't go into that cove, Brenda. Continue north and put as much distance between you and Seven Bays as you can. Mike and Vladi will catch the next plane out. They will meet you this evening or tomorrow morning. Keep your cell on and they'll be in touch. At this point, it doesn't matter if the call is intercepted. If you're out of cell range, try to find a hotspot and call Mike late today so you can coordinate a place to meet. I'm sorry you guys are going through this, Brenda, but they will be there soon."

"We'll be okay, Jason. I have my 12 gauge with us. If that shithead threatens us, I'll send his ass to meet Allah and his seventy-two virgins."

"That's my girl. Be safe." Jason hung up. Looking at Mike and Vladi, he said, "You two need to head to Spokane right away. The guy who killed Kevin is on the lake, looking for them. I'd go, but I think I'd be better off going to Victorville to confront Qasim. I need to see if I can put an end to this."

****

Mike was on the phone, making reservations out of LAX for a direct flight to Spokane before Jason finished his sentence.

His next call was to Schumacher. "Jack, this is McClintock. We're heading to Roosevelt Lake in Washington. We believe the guy who killed Mitchell is on the lake looking for my family and Jason's fiancée. They rented a houseboat."

"Where is this place, Mike?"

"About two hours north of Spokane. Can you send agents with a picture of the suspect to the Seven Bays Marina? The manager will be able to confirm if this is the same guy or not. If it is, my family is in danger."

"You got it, Mike. I'll have a team out of Spokane there within the hour," said Schumacher. "We'll keep you posted."

"Thanks, Jack," replied Mike as he grabbed his bag and headed for the car. Petronovich was in the driver's seat with the car running. Their flight left L.A. in two hours and they had an hour's drive to the airport. If they made the two p.m. non-stop flight, they'd be in Spokane by four forty-five and at the lake at about six thirty. It would be too dark to meet the girls. The rendezvous would need to wait until morning.

****

As the agent in charge of the Spokane field office, Rudy Hanselka took notes and waited for the email with the photograph of the suspect Schumacher had been talking about for the last five minutes. The email came in and Hanselka opened the attachment. "Got it. I'll copy this and take it to Seven Bays Marina. With any luck, we'll have the McClintocks in protective custody later this afternoon."

"Thanks, Rudy. This family has gone through enough. We need to make sure they're safe," said Schumacher. "Let me know if you need any more manpower or help in any way."

"We should be fine, Jack. I have a helicopter waiting to take us up to the lake. I'll let you know when we've got the family."

****

Schumacher was poring through the stack of paperwork he'd accumulated over the past three days when Agent Larson knocked at the door. "Enter," said Schumacher.

The agent stepped forward, "Sir, Al-Hamaidi just phoned someone regarding the McClintock family. He said something about a mission being possibly compromised and that they had to act quickly."

"Did he say what that mission might be?" asked Schumacher.

"No, sir, only that someone was getting too close."

"Did you check the number?"

"Yes, it was a burner phone, untraceable," replied Larson.

Schumacher picked up his phone and dialed the Spokane field office. The call was forwarded to Hanselka's cell. "This is Hanselka."

"Rudy, we just received positive confirmation that the McClintock family has a killer searching for them on Roosevelt Lake," said Schumacher.

"That changes things, Jack. I'm going to need help from

Seattle, ASAP. This lake is too big for the few people in my office, especially since we are under pressure to find the family quickly."

"I'll get you support, Rudy. In the meantime, get up there as soon as you can." Schumacher hung up and looked at Agent Larson.

"Was anything else said?" he asked.

"The Russian came close to killing Mohammed. I'd bet that's the guy with the McClintock brothers."

"I think you're right. Whatever this mission is, it must be important to them, especially if they're willing to kill for it. It's time to bring these guys in for questioning," said Schumacher. "That's all, Larson."

****

The closest airport to Seven Bays Marina was in Wilbur, 29 miles away. That wouldn't do, given the urgency of the situation. "Fly directly to Seven Bays," instructed Hanselka to the pilot. "Find an open field and land."

After circling the marina and surrounding area, the pilot selected a remote corner of a dirt parking lot. He came down slowly, dirt kicking up everywhere, covering the few cars in the lot with a coating of dust. The manager came out of the office and walked toward the aircraft just as Hanselka ducked out of the cockpit, jogging low below the slowly spinning chopper blades.

"This better be important. Our parking lot is not a landing strip," the manager said as he approached Hanselka.

Hanselka held out his FBI identification for the manager. "Let's go to the office, we need to talk," ordered Hanselka.

The manager turned. "Follow me."

Inside, the manager pointed to a chair, "Have a seat. What's this about?"

Hanselka placed a picture of the suspected killer in front of the manager. "Do you recognize this guy?"

The manager didn't hesitate. "Yes. He rented a ski boat yesterday. He was an odd character, seemed to be looking for a family that rented a houseboat the day before."

"Would that be the McClintocks?"

"Yes, two adult women, two kids, and a dog. I was concerned, so I radioed them to tell them this guy had a ski boat and was looking for them. I told them that if I had any more information, I would call. Do you want me to get them on the radio?"

"Yes, but first, can you have someone gas and ready two ski boats for me?" asked Hanselka.

The manager nodded.

While the ski boats were being prepped, he raised the McClintock houseboat on the radio. "Mrs. McClintock, I have an FBI Agent who would like to speak with you, over."

Hanselka took the hand piece. "Mrs. McClintock, this is Agent Hanselka from the FBI field office in Spokane. What is your current location, over?"

Brenda didn't correct the agent about her name. "We are in the northern half of the lake, in the middle of the channel. I'm trying to put as much distance between us and Seven Bays as possible. I think the next major marina is Kettle Falls, over."

"That's good, keep moving. We are going to try and intercept the man following you. I have agents in two ski boats on the way. I'll be in the air and once I've spotted you, I'll direct them to pick you up. In the meantime, stay the course, we will be in touch." Hanselka handed the handpiece back to the manager.

"This is Seven Bays, out."

"McClintocks, out," said Brenda.

Julie and the kids sat at the galley table and stared ahead as the boat moved north through the water.

****

It was three in the afternoon when Schumacher and Larson arrived at AdvanChem. They entered the office and flashed their ID at the receptionist, requesting to see Mohammed and Al-Hamaidi immediately. The receptionist picked up the phone and dialed Mohammed. Two minutes later, he came out.

"What do you want?" asked Mohammed.

"We would like to speak with you and your associate, Dr. Al-Hamaidi," said Schumacher.

Mohammed instructed the receptionist, "Call Dr. Al-Hamaidi and ask him to meet us in my office. Come with me." Mohammed gestured to the agents.

Schumacher and Larson were seated in front of Mohammed's desk when Al-Hamaidi entered. "We are very busy, why are you here?" he asked.

"We have some questions you need to answer," said Schumacher.

"What reason would you have for making such a demand?" asked Mohammed.

"We believe you are involved in the murder of an FBI agent and one of your own employees," replied Schumacher, gauging their response.

Mohammed didn't hesitate. "You have no evidence that

would stand up in court, otherwise you'd have arrested us already." Mohammed stood, "Don't bother coming back unless you have a warrant. You know the way out."

Larson and Schumacher stood and turned toward the door. "We're not finished with you two," said Schumacher.

"I'm sure you're not. You will be hearing from our attorney shortly," said Al-Hamaidi.

Schumacher and Larson left AdvanChem for the long ride back to the office.

****

The sun would be setting within the hour. Brenda turned to Julie. "Try giving Mike a call," she said.

It was closing in on five p.m. as Julie dialed. "If Mike's plane was on time, he should answer." The phone rang and Mike picked up almost immediately.

"I'm glad you called, Julie, we'll be leaving the airport as soon as we have our rental," said Mike. "Can you tell me where you are on the lake?"

Anticipating the question, Brenda was doing her best to estimate their location on the map next to the steering console. "I think we're just south of Daisy," said Brenda, "About 40 minutes south of the Kettle Falls Marina. It's going to be dark soon, so we may need to go into a cove and tie up. We can meet there tomorrow."

Mike put the marina in his GPS. "Okay, it looks like the marina is three hours away. We will be there tonight, so at first light, start moving. The sooner we get you off the lake, the better."

"We'll be there forty minutes after sunrise. Do you have

any idea what we're going to do next? Where will we go?" asked Julie.

"Not yet, but we'll figure it out. Be safe tonight," said Mike.

****

Antar, thinking the McClintocks would try to put some distance between themselves and the Seven Bays Marina, decided to go as far north as possible then work back south and try to locate them. He knew this was a long shot. He also knew that at 30 mph, he would cover the distance in short order. Racing up the middle of the lake, Antar spotted a small houseboat in the distance, close to three miles away. He pushed the throttle forward, giving the boat full power, hoping his search would be over soon.

****

After the call to Mike, Brenda turned the houseboat toward a cove. Before doing so, she glanced south and saw a ski boat moving toward them with a certain intensity. "Julie, look at that boat in the distance," she said.

"I see it. Looks like he's coming right at us," said Julie.

Brenda stood with her hand on the helm. "You've got the wheel," she said to Julie as she let go and grabbed the shotgun. "I'm going to the back deck. Zach and Sam, climb into the bunk and stay down. Take Rosie with you. Julie, once we turn the corner and enter the cove, put the boat in neutral and wait. If this is the guy who's looking for us, I'm going to have a 12-gauge surprise for him."

The kids moved down the short hallway with the dog and jumped on the bed. Zach closed the privacy curtain behind them.

Brenda pulled a box of shells from her suitcase before going out the back door. She knelt, the shotgun resting against the rail above the outboard engine, the shells on the deck at her side. The houseboat idled, hidden past the rock outcropping and the entrance to the cove.

****

Hanselka instructed the four agents to take the two ski boats and head north as quickly as possible. He would use the helicopter to locate the houseboat and direct the agents to it once they were spotted. With any luck, they'd locate the boat before it became too dark to navigate the lake. Given the time of year and size of the boat, it shouldn't be difficult to find. If it were summer, it would be a very different story.

Hanselka was strapped into and the aircraft was ready to go when he noticed the houseboats were numbered. Speaking to the pilot, he said, "Hang tight, I'll be right back." He jumped from the helicopter and ran to the office as the pilot dialed back the rotor's speed.

"What's the houseboat number we're looking for," asked Hanselka as he swung open the office door.

The manager picked up the log book and quickly spotted the McClintock rental, "57."

"Got it," said Hanselka as he sprinted back to the aircraft. It was only a minute after he was onboard that the pilot, with rotors spinning, lifted the craft into the air and headed north. The lake was virtually empty except for the occasional fishing boat. Houseboat season was over, though they were still available to rent. Once in a while, a group of guys would rent one for a long weekend of fishing and drinking.

About a half hour away from Seven Bays, Hanselka noticed the ski boat. “Look down there!”

“Yea, but look further north, a houseboat,” replied the pilot.

Hanselka raised the binoculars and tried to make out the boat’s number. “We’re a little too far out to confirm the identity.”

The pilot slowed and dropped the elevation, diving toward the ski boat, buzzing over him at about 500 feet. The ski boat slowed as the single male on board looked up.

“Swing around one more time for a closer look and pace him. I want to see his face,” said Hanselka. “I’m going to try and get a picture.”

The pilot did as he was told, this time about 200 feet closer and much slower. The spinning rotors whipped at the vessel causing the driver to slow and look up.

As the pilot came around, Hanselka snapped a Macro 15x lens to his iPhone. With the aircraft above the boat, he had a perfect image of the guy. The picture he took matched the photo from Schumacher. “This is our guy!” he said. “I would bet the houseboat ahead is number 57. Give the boat teams our location and tell them to get here, STAT!”

****

Brenda heard the thumping of the helicopter’s blades. She looked above the hills and spotted the aircraft. Just as suddenly as it appeared, it dropped out of sight. She could hear the rotors, muffled by the cliff in front of her. *Maybe help has arrived*, she thought. Julie poked her head out the back door. "Do you hear that?" she asked.

"They are south of us. I'm guessing close to the ski boat we saw," replied Brenda. "I don't know what they can do to help from a helicopter."

"Maybe just being here will scare the guy away?" suggested Julie.

"Better get back inside, Julie. The guy could turn into the cove at any time."

Julie closed the door and went back to the steering console, waiting for instructions to move. Brenda could hear the distinct whine of the ski boat's engine. The sound grew louder the closer it came to the cove. When it turned in, the deafening roar of the engines echoed off the rock walls. The boat slid to the right, with only feet to spare between the houseboat and the rock wall. The driver sent a plume of water high into the air as it entered, narrowly flipping the speeding boat.

Brenda raised the shotgun to her shoulder and fired the triple aught buckshot toward the bow as the boat sped by, missing the houseboat by inches. Julie, seeing the ski boat pass her, put the houseboat in gear, turned left, and gave it all the power she could. With the bow facing the entrance to the cove, Brenda, at the stern aimed at the ski boat as it idled. The driver seemed to be considering his options as he looked at the houseboat through the shattered wind screen over the bow pock-marked by the triple aught shot.

Hanselka hovered above the scene, watching and expecting a disastrous collision. The blast and flash from the muzzle of the shotgun surprised him as the boats avoided impact. The pilot contacted the four agents, told them about the ski boat and determined that they were 10 to 20 minutes out.

"Swing the chopper around. I'm going to try and get a shot at this guy," said Hanselka as he drew his service revolver and slid open the cockpit door of the helicopter.

The pilot did as he was told, but lifted and turned quickly away as Antar raised a rifle and fired at the rotors. They heard a loud thump and whine above their heads.

"We have a problem, sir. We're losing oil pressure and the rotors are slowing. I need to find a place to set this thing down before the engine seizes up," the pilot said calmly as he maneuvered out of the canyon and over the hill.

"Issue a mayday," said Hanselka.

"The radios are out, let's hope we can put this thing down safely," replied the pilot.

Brenda watched the helicopter as it turned away from the lake, dark smoke billowing from the turbine. It seemed to move slowly toward the other side of the hill, losing altitude as it dropped out of sight. Knowing that the man in the other boat had a rifle changed the equation. A shotgun is good at short distances, but a rifle, properly sighted and with an experienced operator could be accurate at 200 to 300 yards. They were sitting ducks. *What do we do now?* she thought as the sun set leaving behind a twilight that, at any other time, would have been impressive.

****

For the moment, Antar kept his distance from the houseboat. He knew that this impasse couldn't last, that he had to act.

There was no moon, only a slight silhouette could be seen toward the mouth of the cove. The soft purr of the idling engine was the only noise in the cove. Antar engaged the drive and moved the ski boat forward as slowly as possible, ready to throw it in reverse if shots rang out from the houseboat. The sun had set, and darkness came much sooner within the confines of the rock walls and hills surrounding the cove. He heard the sounds of engines before he saw the two ski boats enter the mouth of the cove a short distance beyond the houseboat. Their flood lights illuminated the houseboat. It sat silent and dark as though empty. The two boats approached with extreme caution, not seeming to notice Antar's boat. He knew his options were limited, especially when he heard the men in the boats identify themselves as FBI. Moving as quietly as possible, he slipped over the side of the boat and swam to shore, leaving the rifle and the shattered ski boat behind.

****

Brenda and Julie sat on the floor next to the back door and the bed where the kids and Rosie lay. They heard the engines before they saw the lights. Brenda peered through the sliding door leading to the bow deck as two boats approached them.

"This is the FBI, we're looking for the McClintock family, is anyone here?" asked one of the agents as he flashed light over the boat, not seeing the ski boat in the back.

Brenda hollered back, "How do we know you're FBI?"

"I'll throw my ID on deck. You can check it out." The agent idled the boat forward, tossing the badge. It landed open for Brenda to see.

"Are you okay now?" he called. Not waiting for a reply,

he continued, “Turn on all of your lights and come out, one at a time with your hands raised.”

“Julie, you get the back cabin and stern lights and I’ll get them here. I’ll go out first, then the kids will follow with you last,” Brenda instructed.

The entire boat was illuminated as the sliding door slowly opened. Brenda came out, her hands raised. “Stand by the rail with your back to me,” commanded the agent.

One of the agents from the other boat maneuvered to the stern and climbed aboard, gun drawn. He entered the main cabin as the kids were about to walk out, arms in the air. He noticed the pig-tailed little blonde girl with tears streaming down her face. Calling out to the other boat, he said, “The vessel is clear, passengers are safe.” The agent holstered his weapon. He picked up the girl, “You’re safe, honey, we’re here to help.”

Rosie yelped, wagging her tail.

“Thank God, you’re here,” said Julie taking Sam from the agent’s arms. “We were in trouble with that guy at the end of the cove.”

The agent looked up, surprised, “What guy? I didn’t see another boat.” He hollered out the sliding door, “Turn the flood lights toward the back of the cove, now!” The lights hit the damaged ski boat. “Everyone down, kill the lights. We have to secure that boat!” he yelled.

****

Jason turned into the main gate at the Adelanto airport, stopping in front of the security booth as the guard stepped out. “Do you have business here?” the guard asked.

"I'd like to speak to someone about work being done on an aircraft," replied Jason.

"You don't have an appointment, correct?" asked the guard as he scanned the interior of Jason's car. "Are you law enforcement?"

"I don't have an appointment, but I am working with law enforcement," said Jason stretching the truth. "I only need a few minutes."

"What's your name, and what is this regarding?"

"My name is Jason McClintock and I have a few questions regarding a client of yours by the name of Qasim." The guard picked up the phone and dialed the main office.

McCaffrey's secretary picked up, and after a few minutes, asked the guard to let McClintock through.

The guard directed McClintock to the main hangar. "The person to ask for regarding Qasim is Jordan McCaffrey. He's in the main hanger where you'll see all the activity."

"Thanks," said Jason as the barrier gate was raised. He drove to the hangar and parked.

McCaffrey was waiting outside the hangar. He approached Jason's car. "I'm McCaffrey," he said, as Jason stepped out.

"You're working on a DC-10 aircraft modification for a guy by the name of Qasim?" asked Jason. "We believe he is associated with a group of people who may have been involved in two murders and at least one attempted murder."

"Who is the 'we' you are referring to?" asked McCaffrey. "Let me see your ID."

Jason removed his driver's license from his wallet and handed it to McCaffrey, "My brother is, or was, FBI. A friend, another agent, was gunned down a few nights ago in Los

Angeles."

"I heard about that on the news. At the Marriott, right? Why isn't the FBI here asking questions?"

"They'll be talking to you, I'm sure," Jason said. "I've been watching Qasim for some time, and something isn't right. Look, Mr. McCaffrey, you don't have to tell me anything, but something you might say may save another life. Can we talk for a few minutes?"

McCaffrey handed Jason his ID. "I'll give you ten minutes, only because an agent was killed, and I've had a gut feeling that Qasim's story of fighting fires with the airplane, wasn't the entire truth. Come with me," said McCaffrey as he turned and walked toward the office door next to the hangar.

****

Schumacher was at his desk when the intercom buzzed. "Yes, Ruth?" he asked.

"Sir, Deputy Director Taddy is on the line."

"Put him through," said Schumacher.

"Jack, this is Taddy. What the hell have you been doing with AdvanChem? DOD is throwing a fit, complaining that we're interfering with their contractor's work. I know from your reports that you believe they're up to some nefarious activity. But hear me loud and clear, Jack, unless you have hard evidence that they're involved, back off! Do I make myself clear?"

Schumacher was stunned by the outburst from a man who was normally subdued. "Loud and clear, sir," replied Schumacher as the line went dead.

****

Antar watched, lying prone on the ground at the top of the hill. The FBI spotted his boat and approached from both sides. The intense lights lit the boat and cove like day. Bull horns blared, the FBI demanding the boat's occupant show himself. Inching closer, they realized the boat was empty. The search lights began to pan the shoreline, back and forth. They started at the bottom and worked their way towards the hilltop. Antar hugged the dirt, as the beam passed over and away from him. The two ski boats finally turned away from the shore. One attached a line to the bow of the damaged boat while the other dropped an agent off with the McClintocks to captain the houseboat. The three boats, with one in tow slowly headed out of the cove, turning north in the dark towards the Kettle Falls Marina.

****

Julie, Brenda, and the kids sat in the galley at the table, with Rosie underneath as the agent followed one of the two ski boats up the middle of the lake. The second boat with the tow, brought up the rear. "I'm going to call Mike," said Julie, as she rose from the table and headed to the back bedroom.

"When we get to Kettle Falls, they should only be about an hour away," said Brenda. "I hope they have an idea about what we're going to do."

The agent at the steering console jumped in, "Agent Hanselka will have some suggestions for you, including a safe house we have access to in Spokane. The place is very secure and watched by us 24/7."

"That would be great," said Brenda as Julie shut the bedroom door.

"I'm sure that's the direction Hanselka's leaning. This is a conversation that we need to have in person, not over a phone. You better tell Julie not to mention anything about what I just said."

Brenda went to the door, poked her head in, and relayed the agent's message.

Mike answered the phone as Vladi drove. "I didn't expect to hear from you so soon, Julie."

"We had a run-in with the killer, but we're all right. Brenda gave his boat a load of buckshot. The FBI, using two ski boats, found us and scared him off. We'll be at Kettle Falls Marina in about half an hour. Where are you?"

"We'll be there in an hour according to my GPS. I'll let you know when we're pulling in," said Mike. "See you soon."

"I can't wait, Mike. This has got to stop. It's one thing for you and me to be in danger, but it's unacceptable to have our children in harm's way."

"We're on the same page, Julie. We'll figure it out when we get there."

****

Antar watched the ski boats as they approached the houseboat. He knew he had to move quickly if he had any chance of following them when they left the cove. He walked down the other side of the hill, through the trees, parallel to the lake. In the distance, he spotted a campfire and two small tents at the lake's edge. Looking towards the water, about 200 yards away from the campers, he noticed a skiff with what looked to be a good size outboard engine. The silhouettes of two men could be seen in the darkness. *They must be hunters,* thought Antar as he studied the camp. The men were loud, sitting on folding chairs next to a card table. They were listening to country music from a boom box situated between two bottles of hard liquor. They had obviously been there drinking for some time. Antar skirted around the camp, moving quietly toward the boat. The bow line was tied to a log that had washed ashore. Antar untied the line, shoved the boat back into the water, and climbed in. He used an oar to push the boat away from shore before priming the engine and pulling the starter cord. He knew he had only a matter of minutes before the men would hear the commotion. Liquor and guns were never a good combination, especially when you were stealing a boat. He had one chance to start the outboard before the bullets would fly.

Antar pumped the fuel bulb, then pulled the choke all the way out. "Allah be with me," he whispered as he closed his eyes and pulled the cord, once, then twice, before the engine coughed and began to roar. He quickly pushed the choke halfway in while giving the engine gas. The boat lurched forward, the bow rising with the acceleration, then leveling out as it cut through the water toward the middle of the lake. After twenty seconds, he heard the discharge of a large-caliber rifle. The blast echoed from shore to shore. He was moving too fast for anything but an extremely lucky shot to hit him. Nevertheless, he ducked down and gave the boat as much power as he could, his silhouette fading as he careened north in the middle of the lake.

Chapter 16

Mohammed watched the men in the biohazard suits through the thick glass in the outer containment room. He pressed the intercom, "Good afternoon, gentlemen."

The two men turned and waved. Mohammed continued, "How close are we to the target production weight?"

One of the men spoke, "I'd say we are very close, no more than two days from our goal."

"Excellent," replied Mohammed. "There will be a nice bonus for you when the work is complete. Good job, I'll let you get back to it."

Both men waved and turned back to the task at hand. Mohammed smiled and left the facility. He knew it was time to start the final stage of the mission.

****

Jason sat in front of McCaffrey's desk. "Tell me what you know about Qasim."

"He is a representative for Advanced Aerial Fire Response, a European company. He is also a pilot. As I understand it, they plan to establish their business out of Idaho and fight fires under independent contracts."

"And they plan to do this remotely?" asked McClintock.

"It's entirely possible. Hell, look what the Air Force does

with aircraft in the Middle East piloted by men right here in the United States. It's bizarre! They bomb the shit out of a target in Afghanistan in the morning, then coach soccer in the afternoon, before having dinner at home. The technology is amazing."

"Has he hinted at using the aircraft for anything other than fighting fires? In other words, is there any doubt in your mind that he's telling the truth?" asked Jason, as he leaned forward.

"The only thing that raised a red flag for me was the fact that when AAFR approached me about the aircraft modification, they insisted it be done immediately. I told them we were extremely busy with military contracts and couldn't get to the job for at least a month. Then they threw an insane amount of money at me. So, I dropped everything to work with them," explained McCaffrey. "We'll have the modification done by the end of the week; maybe three days. We'll give it one last test flight, then hand the aircraft over to Qasim."

"That means, if they're up to no good, whatever they're working on is about to go down soon," said Jason. "Can you give me a call when you're ready for the last test? I'd like to be here to see how she operates. I might even be able to have a word or two with Qasim."

"He won't be here. His RPA console is at his apartment," replied McCaffrey. "The aircraft flies no different than any other plane except for the fact that the pilot is remote. That said, I will call you when we're scheduled to go. Leave your contact information with my secretary." McCaffrey stood and headed for the side door leading to the hangar.

****

The FBI agent cut power to the ski boat, passing the no wake buoy, as he turned towards the Kettle Falls Marina. The houseboat followed with the second ski boat bringing up the rear, the damaged boat in tow. The marina flood lights lit up the place. With most boats out of the water for the winter, there were plenty of docking options. Hanselka stood outside the marina store, watching the three boats enter the cove.

Marine personnel were on the dock waiting to assist in tying up the boats. The houseboat operator seemed to be coming in too fast and at an angle. One of the dock hands jumped on the bow and pushed the boat back before it hit the wood planking. He ran to the steering console. "Let me help you, sir," he said as he took control, putting the boat in hard reverse and then slowly easing it forward into position along the dock.

"Thanks for the assist," said the agent. "It's been awhile since I've handled one of these."

The dock hand laughed. "No problem. You get the hang of this after you've done it a couple times."

Hanselka waited for the bow and stern lines to be secured. Spotting the McClintock family as he jumped on board, he said, "You folks had us concerned. The suspect that followed you hasn't been apprehended. We need to get you out of here."

"My husband should be here soon," Julie said. "He flew into Spokane a few hours ago. We won't leave without him."

"Understood. Let's get your belongings, we'll wait for him in the office," replied Hanselka.

Hanselka and the agents helped pack the McClintocks and moved from the boat to the three Suburbans in the parking lot. After loading the vehicles, they waited in the office.

"Mrs. McClintock, will you please phone your husband

and see how far out they are?" asked Hanselka. "We need to leave as soon as possible."

As the phone rang, Julie looked out the office window just as Mike and Vladi pulled into the parking lot. Mike picked up, "We're here."

"I see you. Park the car and come into the office. There are some people I want you to meet."

****

McCaffrey sat at his desk reviewing the stack of work orders that had been piling up. *The modification of this DC-10 is going to back us up at least two months,* he thought. The door to the hangar opened and his foreman walked in. McCaffrey looked up, "Where do we stand, Hank?"

"We've tested all systems and back-up systems. That aircraft out there is as good as any we've done in the past."

"Good news. I'll call Qasim. Have the plane ready for one final test flight tomorrow morning at 8:00. Make sure Tony is available to fly in the right seat," said McCaffrey. "I can't wait to get that plane out of my hangar and back to our normal operations."

"Got it. We'll be fueled and ready," replied the foreman as he left the office.

Before McCaffrey called Qasim, he buzzed his secretary, "Linda, phone Jason McClintock. Tell him the final test flight is tomorrow. He should be here no later than 7:45 if he wants to see it fly."

****

Qasim had the RPA console powered up and linked to the DC-10 when the technician knocked at the apartment door. "The door's unlocked, come in," hollered Qasim as he stared at the console and the aircraft instrumentation. The plane was outside the hangar and ready to taxi to the runway.

The technician stepped in and took a seat next to Qasim. He dialed McCaffrey's cell, "We're ready here, Jordan. Mr. Qasim is already interfacing with the DC-10. We can see Tony in the right seat."

Qasim spoke into the headset, "Good morning, Tony, are you ready to fly?"

"Good morning! Yes sir! The airplane is yours, Mr. Qasim. I've contacted the tower and we are cleared to taxi. You have the airplane." Cusseta lifted his hands from the controls.

"I've got the airplane," replied Qasim as he gave the engines enough power to slowly move the plane toward the runway.

"Tower has cleared us for take-off," said Cusseta as he ran through the checklist.

Qasim gave the DC-10 max power. The thrust pushed Cusseta back in his seat. It was an odd sensation for Qasim, not feeling the same rush of power. He could see the runway roll by as he picked up speed and heard Cusseta through the headset, "Rotate." The plane lifted easily and rose swiftly into the air.

"We have instructions to follow Highway 15 toward Barstow, then circle back to Adelanto," said Cusseta. "Should take no more than twenty minutes."

"Roger that," said Qasim.

****

McClintock stood next to McCaffrey in front of the hangar and watched as the DC-10 rumbled down the runway, shooting into the sky. "You know, it's one thing to see a small drone piloted remotely, but it's another thing entirely to see a huge DC-10. That's incredible," said Jason.

"No, that's technology, Mr. McClintock. You have no idea what the government is working on and how things will change in the next few years," said McCaffrey as he watched. "We'll sign that plane over to Qasim after this flight. At that point, if you think he's up to something, he and that plane will be the FBI's and your problem."

"I don't know, McCaffrey," Jason said. "I've got a bad feeling about this guy and the group he seems to be working with. Thanks for letting me see the plane fly." He turned toward his car.

****

Antar saw the lights of the marina in the distance. Thinking this was the obvious choice for the FBI to bring the McClintock's houseboat, he increased the power and motored past the entrance, toward a small cove. After beaching the boat, he positioned himself on a small hill overlooking the marina. Two ski boats, one, with his boat in tow, as well as the houseboat turned toward the no wake zone.

An hour later, Antar watched as the family came out of the marina office and waited for two occupants of a car that had just pulled into the parking lot. He wasn't surprised to see one of the McClintock brothers and the Russian get out. He knew he had only minutes before they would leave.

****

Julie and Brenda waited on the porch as Mike and Petronovich crossed the parking lot. Sam and Zach bolted down the stairs with their arms open, ready to smother Mike in hugs. Mike clung to the kids, one in each arm, as he met Julie at the top of the stairs with a kiss. "We got here as fast as we could," said Mike.

"I know. I want you to meet the men who saved us tonight," said Julie as Brenda opened the door and ushered everyone inside.

Stepping forward, Hanselka offered an outstretched hand. "Mike," he said, "I'm Rudy Hanselka from the Spokane field office. Jack Schumacher sent us up here to find your family. I think we reached them just in time."

"For that, I will be forever grateful. This is Vladimir Petronovich," said Mike as Vladi stepped forward.

"I remember the name from an after-action report I read last year about an incident involving National Security that took place in Montevideo, Uruguay if I recall correctly. Nice to meet you, Mr. Petronovich. It seems as though you and the McClintock brothers are magnets for danger."

"My pleasure, Agent Hanselka. And you're right, it seems like we do attract a bit of trouble. Not that we're looking for it! May I ask what happened to the man who attacked the McClintock family?" said Petronovich as he sized up the other men in the room.

"I was in a helicopter lighting up the cove where the McClintock's houseboat was located. We came in low, trying to get a shot at the guy. He was quicker and managed to hit the rotor gears with a high caliber rifle. We were lucky to set the bird down without a disaster. When my men reached the cove, they approached the killer's ski boat but it was empty. The bottom line is that we don't know where he is. I happened to get a photo, have a look." Hanselka pulled his phone out and shared the picture with McClintock and Petronovich. "I've emailed this to Schumacher, but as far as I'm concerned, from the picture he sent me, it's a match."

"No question, that's the guy," said Mike as he handed the phone back. "What's the plan?"

"I'd like to take you, the family, and Mr. Petronovich to a safe house we have outside of Spokane. You can stay there until we get this guy. You know the drill, Mike, 24-hour protection. It's already been authorized."

"It sounds good for the family, but Vladi and I may need to get back down to California. My brother Jason is following up a few loose ends."

"I think it's better that you leave this to us," Hanselka said. "You know that's what Schumacher would say. If you have any leads that you haven't shared with Schumacher, let me know." Hanselka stared at both Mike and Vladi, looking for any hint that they might be hiding something. He saw nothing.

Mike sighed. "Everything we know we've given to Schumacher. I think his hands are tied. Someone, whether it's us or his men, needs to come up with concrete proof that the people we suspect are responsible for two murders. Beyond that, we think they're up to something more heinous. I wish I knew what."

"Okay. I can't keep you. God knows I would if I could. We'll care for your family until this is resolved," said Hanselka reluctantly. "That settles it, let's pack up and move out. My men will stop at Seven Bays Marina and pick up Julie's car. We'll keep it at our office in Spokane until you need it. Mike, you know I can't tell you where your family will be located. And while they're in our care, cell phones will be prohibited. Ladies, you might as well hand them over now. Mike, if you need to communicate with them, it will be through me, understood?"

"As you said earlier, Rudy, I know the drill, thanks," replied Mike.

Julie stepped forward, "Mike, I don't like this. I don't want you and Vladi to go. Stay with us."

"Jason needs our help. We can't just leave him, you know that, Julie." Mike turned to Brenda. "We'll get back to Jason and end this as soon as possible. Thanks for watching out for my family, Brenda."

Mike and Vladi stood on the porch as three of the Suburbans pulled in front of the office and the family was ushered into the vehicles. Mike held open the back door of one of the SUVs. "We'll put this behind us as quickly as we can. I love you all." Looking at the agents, he said, "Take care of them."

"Yes sir, we will," one agent replied as the door closed and the heavy Suburban pulled away.

****

Antar watched the scene from a distance at the far end of the parking lot. While everyone was inside, he had hotwired a Honda, determined to follow the FBI vehicles once they left.

****

Qasim landed the DC-10 at Adelanto and handed the aircraft

to Cusseta to taxi back to the hangar. Once the plane was in Cusseta's hands, the technician's cell rang. "One second, Jordan, here's Mr. Qasim," he said, handing the phone off.

"Hello, Jordan, your work is magnificent," exclaimed Qasim.

"I think we've accomplished everything you've asked, Mr. Qasim," said McCaffrey. "I need you to sign for the aircraft and fly it over to the Victorville airport, preferably today. We have work to get to and need the hangar space."

"Sure, Jordan, I'll shut down the console and get a ride over with the technician. See you in about half an hour."

****

Mike watched as the vehicles moved out of the parking lot. The last Suburban was followed by a silver Honda Civic. He couldn't see the driver, but felt uneasy, nevertheless. He jumped into the passenger seat of the rental, "Follow that Civic, Vladi."

"I was going to," said Petronovich as he gunned the engine and spun the tires in the gravel before gaining traction.

Antar noticed the headlights behind him immediately. As they passed through the town of Gifford, the city lights illuminated the vehicle enough for Antar to recognize the car as the same one that had pulled up at the marina office with the two men. They had backed off considerably, but he was certain it was McClintock and the Russian. The town was small, but still had side streets offering an opportunity to lose his tail. Given the distance between him and McClintock, he knew this was his one chance. Antar made a quick right, cut his lights, then a sharp left into an alley. He traveled a block, crossed a street and moved into a second alley. He pulled into an empty carport behind a store, killed the engine, and waited.

Petronovich saw the quick turn and hit the gas. He was two blocks back. “Crap, we’ve been spotted,” said Vladi.

“We can’t lose him, give it all you’ve got!” said Mike, holding onto the door as Petronovich turned the corner, tires screeching, almost losing control.

“No lights, no sign,” said Petronovich as he slowed and looked down each alley and street they passed. “We’re screwed.”

“Keep going, I’ll call Hanselka and let him know what happened,” said Mike as he made the call.

Hanselka responded, “We had the car in sight. We were letting him follow us and were going to take him as we got closer to Spokane. That plan has gone out the window. McClintock, I suggest you and your Russian counterpart leave this to us. Head back to California as you intended. We’ll call you with updates as warranted,” Hanselka hung up, furious.

“Did you hear that?” asked Mike, looking at Petronovich.

“I did. Fuck him! Who does he think he’s talking to? We’ll find that safe house and keep watch. The killer will find it as well. When he does, we’ll be there to end his pursuit for good. But first thing in the morning we need to find a sporting goods store and get weapons.”

“We’ll need to drive across the state line to Coeur d’Alene. Gun laws in Washington are too strict. Idaho is gun-friendly. But I’m retired law enforcement so I can purchase the weapons and have possession the same day,” explained Mike.

“Sounds good, let’s get out of here.”

****

After the short flight from Adelanto to the Victorville airport, Qasim secured the DC-10 in the hangar and took an Uber back to his apartment. He was on the road to Irvine within ten minutes of his arrival home. Mohammed and Al-Hamaidi had to be told as soon as possible that the airplane was ready to go.

Jason watched as Qasim pulled out of the parking space in front of his apartment. He followed at a discreet distance, hoping not to be noticed. When Qasim entered the Irvine city limits, Jason knew where he was going. McClintock drove a circuitous route to AdvanChem. As he pulled over a block from the office, he wasn't surprised to see Qasim's car parked on the street out front. What did surprise him was that Qasim was walking out of the office toward his car. *He couldn't have been in there more than ten minutes. What's going on?* McClintock thought.

****

While Antar slumped low in Civic, he dialed his contact and explained that the McClintock family was being protected by the FBI in the state of Washington. "This is an urgent situation. I need to know where they are now," he explained.

"I will call you back as soon as I have the location," responded the other person. "We have high level contacts in the Bureau, so it shouldn't take long."

The line went dead. Antar backed slowly out of the car port. An hour had passed since the near confrontation with McClintock and the Russian. *They must be gone,* he thought, as he drove down the dark alley and turned onto the road. He was half an hour into the drive toward Seven Bays Marina when his cell buzzed. “Do you have what I need?” he asked.

“Yes and no. Where they are now is not where they are going to be. The family will be taken care of. You are to come immediately back to Victorville. We are about ready to move ahead with the plan and we want you to keep close watch on the pilot, to make certain he hits the designated target without any outside interference.”

“What do you mean by that?” Antar asked.

“Listen to me,” the voice said in an even tone. “We have an asset in the FBI’s Spokane field office. He will eliminate the family.”

Antar listened, realizing he had a long drive ahead of him. He couldn’t fly, certain his picture was on every watch list. He was a quarter mile from Seven Bays when he pulled off the road. In the darkness, he moved the stolen Civic as far into the trees and brush as possible. Determined to stay in the shadows, he moved from tree to tree until he spotted his car from a distance in the gravel lot. The weapons cache in the trunk would probably be necessary in the next few days. Antar crouched low as he approached the vehicle. Jumping into the driver’s seat, he started the car and pulled out of the lot, turning on to the highway, moving west toward Seattle and I-5 south.

****

Mohammed sat behind his desk while Al-Hamaidi paced in front of the office window. He finally stopped pacing and looked at Mohammed. “It’s time. Use a pay phone, call and arrange for the chemical tanker to be here tomorrow morning. As we discussed, we need a water tanker as well. We’ll load the crystals first, then add the water from the truck. Once the sarin is in solution, it can be transferred easily from the tanker to the DC-10. We told Qasim we'd be at the airport the day after tomorrow. He'll be waiting."

"I wouldn't say that working with sarin is easy," replied Mohammed.

"You're right. All I'm saying is that it's easier to place the crystals into solution here rather than at an airport with prying eyes everywhere."

"I know you know this, but there is absolutely no margin for error. This mission must be completed," continued Mohammed. "Pay the technicians tonight. We will not need their services any longer."

Al-Hamaidi nodded, leaving the office and closing the door behind him. Mohammed left AdvanChem to phone the trucking company that had been contracted for them by their Saudi contacts.

****

Hanselka and his men turned off Highway 395 ten miles north of Spokane onto a nondescript road without any signs. After a mile, the house could be seen in the distance at the top of the next rise. It was modest in size, with exterior lights illuminating the perimeter. "This is it," whispered Hanselka not wanting to wake the kids as the driver approached the home.

"You were right when you said the place was secluded," said Brenda.

The kids had been sleeping, but they stirred when the motion of the car slowed and the adult chatter increased. Agents unloaded the McClintock's personal belongings, placing the kids in one bedroom and the two women in each of their own.

After tucking the kids into bed, Julie walked into the living room. Hanselka came in from outside. "The home is secure," he said. "We'll have an agent parked outside 24/7. There is no need to be afraid."

Brenda looked around. "Where did you put my shotgun and ammunition?" she asked.

"You won't need the weapon here. We've got you covered; the weapon is safe."

"If I don't have the shotgun, you won't be keeping us here," Brenda said.

Hanselka looked at her for a long moment, then nodded to the agent standing at the door. "Get the shotgun and ammunition." Five minutes later, Brenda had the weapon and ammunition in hand.

"Keep that in a safe place out of reach of the kids," admonished Hanselka.

"Agent Hanselka, we appreciate all that you're doing for us, but do not lecture a girl born and raised in Montana about gun safety."

"Enough said," he replied. "Let's talk about communications. The land line in the kitchen is a direct line to our field office. If you need anything or have any concerns, pick up the phone and someone will answer. There's no need to dial. You are safe here, get a good night's sleep." Hanselka turned and walked out the door. He posted one agent in a car in the driveway, and then Hanselka and the rest of his team headed back to Spokane.

****

As Petronovich drove across the Washington state/Idaho border into Coeur d'Alene, Mike phoned Schumacher in the Los Angeles field office. Recognizing the number, Schumacher answered, "Mike, I understand your family is in our care."

"Jack, that's the reason for my call. The killer is still out there. He followed Hanselka towards Spokane and spotted us about a quarter mile behind him. He's a professional; we lost him. The bottom line is he's still after my family, and I can't stand by and do nothing. I need to know the location of the safe house. We will be added protection only, leaving the investigation to Hanselka and his team."

There was a pause, then Schumacher responded, "Hanselka will be pissed, just as I would. Out of professional courtesy, I'll give you the location. But with the understanding that you stay out of Hanselka's way."

"Understood, Jack, you have my word," promised Mike as he wrote down the address.

He hung up and turned to Petronovich. "That was easier than I thought," he said. "Let's find a sporting goods store and get to the safe house."

Big 5 was in the Coeur d'Alene mall. The store was large and at first glance, Mike was certain they would have everything they needed. After forty-five minutes, with the help of an employee who knew his weapons, their cart was full. They had two Armasight Night Vision Goggles, two Glock 21, 45 caliber handguns, two Remington 870 short barrel shotguns, and plenty of ammunition. After presenting his law-enforcement ID and placing $7,000 on a credit card, Mike and Vladi headed for the car.

“The last time we purchased weapons, it was the middle of the night and we broke into that hardware store up in Truckee,” said Petronovich. “We left cash on the counter and got away before the police showed up.”

“Can you believe that was only last year?” asked Mike, shaking his head. “Seems like so long ago, another time, another story. How do we get involved in situations like this?”

“I don’t know but I had retired from this type of work long ago. Meeting you and Jason has been the best and the most challenging time in my life, including my days in the KGB.”

“I know what you mean,” Mike said. “Let’s get this gear in the car and get out of here.”

****

The tanker truck arrived and when the driver saw Mohammed and Al-Hamaidi in full hazmat suits, he became immediately uneasy. “What kind of chemicals are you loading?” he asked.

Mohammed answered through his mask, “No need to be concerned. Just stand back out of the way and we will handle the transfer. In fact, there is a coffee shop several blocks away. Take advantage of a little free time. We should be done in no more than two hours.”

The man shrugged his shoulders; he really didn’t want to be there. “Are you sure you’re good with the equipment?”

“No problem, we’ve loaded trucks like this many times,” explained Mohammed. After the driver left for the coffee shop, Mohammed and Al-Hamaidi got to work. The process was straightforward. The system was enclosed, prohibiting any exposure to air in moving the crystals from the industrial tanks in the lab to the tanker truck. The men rolled a gangway next to the truck, allowing them to access a walkway at the top. They securely connected the pipe from the lab to the top and through the pressurized system to begin the transfer of crystals. When the industrial tanks were empty and the crystals were in the tanker, Mohammed motioned for the water truck that had been waiting off to the side to move into position. Filling the tanker with water would take very little time. Within twenty minutes, the process was complete. The timing was perfect as the truck driver arrived as the water truck rolled away from the loading docks at the rear of the lab.

****

Once inside the Spokane city limits, the agents parted ways. Hanselka, driving the government vehicle by himself, noted the time when his cell rang. He listened to the instructions, then circled back out of town toward the safe house. He'd been told that two million USD had been wired to an offshore account he had established in Grand Cayman. Another two million would be wired as soon as there was confirmation the family had been eliminated. *About two hours before first light,* he thought as he circled back. Steering with his knees, a technique he learned at the Academy, he withdrew the Glock from his shoulder holster and attached the suppressor. He placed the handgun on the seat next to him and drove.

The agent, sitting in the car outside the house, noticed the light flicker down the road, alerting him to a vehicle coming his way. With his weapon ready, he tensed as the oncoming car climbed slowly up the driveway. Recognizing Hanselka, the agent relaxed and holstered the Glock. Hanselka pulled alongside the parked car and rolled down his window; the agent did the same. Instantly, Hanselka raised his handgun and pointed at the agent's head. Hanselka fired twice, blowing skull fragments, brain tissue, and blood across the passenger side of the car. Hanselka moved forward, past the dead agent's car, and parked in front of the garage. Fingering the keys to the house, Hanselka let himself in the front door. He entered and closed the door quietly behind him. As he did, he heard the distinct sound of a shotgun shell being chambered. The family room light flicked on.

"What's going on, Hanselka?" asked Brenda, looking at the weapon he was holding. *Why does he have a silencer on the gun?* she thought. *Something isn't right.*

"Our location has been compromised," he said. "You need to get everyone up, quickly. We've got to move to another safe house."

"What about the agent outside?"

"He's dead, Brenda. The killer is out there, we've got to go."

Brenda turned and walked down the hall while Hanselka waited by the front door. She shook Julie awake and whispered, "Get the kids up quietly and take them and Rosie into the master bathroom. Close and lock the door. Don't come out until I get you, now move!"

Julie roused the kids and shuffled them and Rosie through the master bedroom, into the bathroom. Brenda stood inside the door to the kid's room, the shotgun ready. She took a deep breath, trying to slow her breathing and calm her nerves. The old hunting trick wasn't working too well. She was almost hyperventilating. She heard Hanselka say, "Brenda, we've got to go!"

His footsteps clipped on the hardwood floors as he walked

towards the bedrooms. Brenda swung into the hallway in a crouched position, the shotgun aimed at the agent's chest. Hanselka, surprised by the move, leveled his handgun and fired twice. The suppressed "pffft" of first round was high and smacked the wall above Brenda's head. The second grazed her right arm as she pulled the trigger. The triple aught buckshot hit center mass, lifting Hanselka off his feet and blowing a huge plume of red into the hallway, onto the ceiling, and the walls. He hit the floor, eyes wide open in shock, but the blast had killed him instantly. Brenda waited to see if the loud discharge would bring anyone else into the home. After three minutes, and no additional movement, she retreated into the bedroom to check on Julie and the kids.

Julie opened the bathroom door after Brenda called to her. "What happened?" she asked.

Brenda grabbed two blankets from the bed, ignoring the question. "We're going to carry the kids out front to the car. Keep the blankets over their heads, it's a mess out there and they don't need to see it." Brenda picked up Zach while Julie carried Sam. The dog followed, everyone stepping over the remains of Hanselka. With the kids, Rosie, and Julie in the car, Brenda went back into the house, collecting the few items they possessed. On the way out, she patted the sticky front pockets of Hanselka's shirt, looking for his car keys. When she pulled her hand out with the key, it was covered with blood. Sickened, she wiped her hand as best she could on his lower pant leg.

Brenda glanced at the other vehicle in the driveway before climbing behind the wheel. The agent, obviously dead, appeared to have been thrown toward the passenger side of the car. *Hanselka didn't lie about that guy*. "Keep the kids down below the windows, Julie," said Brenda as she backed the

Suburban out, passing the grizzly scene.

****

Qasim was at the airport early the next morning. He hadn't flown the DC-10 with a full load and he wanted to do so before the sarin mixture was transferred to the plane the next day. After requesting a pushback tug and moving the aircraft out of the hangar, he filled the tanks with water. Leaving the DC-10 outside the hangar in taxi position, Qasim left the airport and headed back to his apartment.

Jason watched Qasim from a distance, outside the fenced airport property. He was certain that the plane was being prepared to fly remotely. Instead of following Qasim, he waited and watched the plane. One hour had passed, when suddenly McClintock heard the sound of the jet engines spooling up on the DC-10. After a short time, the aircraft lurched slowly forward, toward the taxiway and the takeoff hold position at the end of the runway. McClintock watched, mesmerized, knowing there was nobody in the plane's cockpit. The DC-10 sat at the end of the runway, then suddenly the engines roared with full power and the brakes released. The aircraft moved quickly, almost effortlessly down the runway, the engines screaming as the pilot rotated and lifted the DC-10 into the air.

Qasim sat at the console, following the control tower's instruction as the town of Victorville dropped away and out of sight. He planned to fly 60 miles over the high desert and then drop his load of water. Reaching his target area, Qasim dropped from 10,000 feet to 800, screaming across the desert floor. He switched the bay doors to the open position, maintaining elevation as the water dropped. When the tanks emptied, there was a noticeable lurch skyward as the aircraft's weight lightened significantly. Qasim closed the bay doors. While gaining altitude, he requested tower instructions for the return flight to Victorville Airport.

McClintock watched the silhouette of the large plane come into view, lining up on the runway while descending. The landing was soft as the tires met the concrete and the engines reversed thrust to slow down. Given the aircraft's light weight, it didn't take Qasim long to slow the plane down and taxi back toward the hangar. McClintock shook his head, amazed that he had witnessed an unmanned DC-10 take-off and land. *What is this guy up to?* he thought as he walked back to the car.

****

Mike turned off the highway as directed by the GPS. Vladi racked his Glock 19, forcing a cartridge into the chamber, and watched as they moved slowly down the road. In the distance, they spotted the house and a car in the driveway.

"That must be their FBI security," said Petronovich.

"No doubt. Keep your hands where he can see them as we approach," replied Mike, knowing how law enforcement officers operate.

As they approached the car, it became readily apparent that something was very wrong. Mike parked, his gun in hand, and got out to inspect the carnage. The mid-day sun and heat had attracted a swarm of flies and the stench of blood caused him to gag. "He's gone," Mike said, nearly panicking. "I pray to God Julie and the kids aren't inside!"

Instead of approaching the front door, they opted to move

around the perimeter and use a back entrance. Vladi turned the knob on the back door to see if it was locked. It was. The violence and speed that followed surprised Mike as Petronovich kicked the door open, tearing the door jamb from the wall and the door itself off its hinges. Mike was first through the hole, gun at the ready. The kitchen was clear as they moved through it into the family room. Glancing around the room, they stopped at the hallway. "Holy shit," whispered Petronovich as they approached the surreal scene. "It's the agent in charge who we met yesterday, what was his name?"

"Hanselka," answered Mike. "Let's clear the rest of the house."

The men moved with precision from room to room, quietly and methodically. Having confirmed that there were no other bodies, dead or alive, they inspected Hanselka and moved back into the family room. "Where are the girls?" asked Mike. "I sure as hell hope it was Brenda who used that weapon on Hanselka and not someone else. If it was her, they could still be alive and on the move. But why would she need to use it? I've got to call Schumacher. You drive while I call. I want to be far away from this place before any other agents arrive."

They left and turned onto the highway as Mike phoned Schumacher. "Jack, we just left the safe house. It's bad. Hanselka and another agent are dead."

"You've got to be shitting me! What about your family?" Schumacher asked.

"They weren't there. The agent on-site, was killed in his car, by what looked to be a handgun. Hanselka was hit by a shotgun. Nobody else was in the house. Call in the forensic team. We entered by the back door, they won't need a key. Are you aware of any other safe houses in the area?"

"I'm not. And I would bet there aren't any, Mike. We're

talking podunk Spokane, not Seattle. Have you phoned Julie?"

"She doesn't have a phone, neither does Brenda. Hanselka took them. We need to wait for them to call. As of right now, we have nowhere to turn."

"So what do you think?"

Mike thought for a minute, then answered, "I think we'll retrace their steps and head back toward Coeur d'Alene. If forensics finds anything at all, call me. Still nothing on AdvanChem? I know those assholes are involved in all of this."

"My gut tells me the same. We're monitoring their calls and have nothing to report. I'll call you if the forensic team finds anything. I've got to go. I have some calls to make, as you can imagine." Schumacher hung up.

Mike phoned Jason next.

****

The Bennett Bay Inn was a simple motel on the shore of Lake Coeur d'Alene. It was modest and unassuming, exactly what they needed. Brenda parked in front of the office and checked in. She paid cash for one night but was assured by the high school student at the front desk that it would be no problem to extend another night or two if she liked. She thanked the kid, taking the room key.

The room was standard for a two-star place. It had two double beds and small bath. Safely inside, Julie was concerned with its cleanliness. It passed the test as they unpacked. "I've got to get rid of this Suburban soon. Every law enforcement officer in the Northwest will be looking for it," said Brenda as she watched the kids walk Rosie in the dog park next to the motel.

“Where will you take it?” asked Julie.

“I’ll drop it at the other end of town, then catch a ride back. Don’t venture too far, I should be back in about an hour. When I return, we’ll find a pay phone. Mike and Jason need to know what’s happened.”

“Be careful, Brenda,” said Julie as she followed her out the door.

Brenda started the Suburban and headed toward the south end of town. Wherever she dumped the car, it had to be within walking distance of the city transit system. As she drove, a billboard advertising the Coeur d’Alene Casino popped into view. *That’s it,* thought Brenda. Open 24/7 with a full parking lot much of the time, there couldn’t be a better choice. In addition, the CityLink transit system provided service to and from the property for patrons from the surrounding area. She found a spot in the center of the large parking lot, as far away from security lighting as possible. She backed into the space so that the rear government license plates would be out of easy view, protected by the front grill of the car parked behind her. *Perfect*, she thought as she walked to the shuttle loading area to wait for a ride back into town.

****

Antar estimated the drive to Victorville would take about 20 hours, non-stop. It would be a long straight drive down Interstate 5. He was given Qasim’s address and told to shadow him everywhere. The mission depended upon Qasim’s ability to fly the plane and the Saudis wanted to be certain he wasn’t compromised.

****

Mike was talking with Jason when his phone rang. "Jason, someone's calling, unknown name. Let me get this, it might be Julie. I'll phone you as soon as I get off."

"Hello?" he answered.

"Mike, where are you?" asked Julie, relieved.

Mike ignored the question. "Are you safe? We went to the house and found Hanselka and another agent dead."

"We're okay. Hanselka killed the agent outside and was coming for us. He shot at Brenda and she killed him."

"Where are you?"

"In Coeur d'Alene at the Bennet Bay Inn. It's a small motel on the lake. We took Hanselka's Suburban. Brenda just got rid of it."

"You're not using credit cards, right?" asked Mike, concerned that their location could be traced.

"No. Cash only. I know the drill," answered Julie. "So, where are you?"

"We're about half an hour away," Mike said. "We'll pick you up and head back to California. I don't want us to be apart any more."

"I'm all for that, see you in a little bit," said Julie, relieved they would be together, but concerned that the assassin was still out there. "We'll be watching for you."

Julie and Brenda were standing outside the room when Mike turned the Yukon into the motel parking lot. Zach and Sam were playing with Rosie when they noticed the vehicle pull in. The kids and dog bounded over to the car, elated to see their father and Vladi.

Julie had the bags packed and ready. Ten minutes later, the family was on the road, driving south, out of town.

Chapter 17

Before leaving the lab's loading dock, Al-Hamaidi changed the Toxic placard on the tanker truck to one indicating the contents belonged to Cal Fire. This, along with a trucking manifest stating the load was fire retardant would ensure that any questions asked regarding the cargo could be easily answered. The truck began the two-hour trip to Victorville, followed by Al-Hamaidi and Mohammed in a separate car. With any luck, they'd be at the airport by three. Qasim would be waiting at the hangar for their arrival. The plan was to transfer the tanker's load immediately to the aircraft, then fly on the following day, anticipating the aircraft's arrival on target at rush hour. Pennsylvania Avenue runs between the Capitol building and the White House. Given the distance of 1.2 miles between them, Qasim's air drop, if precise, and with a slight breeze, should reach both targets. The thought was to execute the mission mid-week to ensure that most of Congress would be in town. The President's schedule had been checked and no trips had been noted. The mission and subsequent decapitation of the U.S. power structure was one day away.

****

After driving through the afternoon and night, with Mike at the wheel, the family crested the Santa Ynez Mountains. It was mid-morning when he drove over the San Marcos Pass into the Santa Ynez Valley, reaching his small vineyard on Refugio Road. After speaking with Jason along the way, a decision was made that Vladi would join him in Victorville. His interrogation skills could be used to persuade Qasim to reveal what he was doing with AdvanChem should the opportunity arise. Mike would stay at the vineyard with his family and Brenda.

"Everything's out of the car. Call Schumacher and let him know you're back at the vineyard with the family," Petronovich said. "You might also tell him what Jason and I are doing just to keep him in the loop. Take one of the shotguns, but leave both Glocks so Jason has a weapon. I've got to get going." Vladi gave hugs all around, then left abruptly, not one for goodbyes.

Mike walked out on the porch and watched as Petronovich drove away. He phoned Schumacher who picked up after the first ring. "Mike, did you find your family? I've been waiting to hear."

"Jack, we're in Santa Ynez. Did forensics find anything?"

"They confirmed that Hanselka killed the agent. And he was killed by someone with a shotgun. Does Brenda or Julie know anything about that?"

"Brenda killed Hanselka after he fired at her. One round missed, but she has a slight laceration on her arm where the second round grazed her. She's not coming in to answer questions, Jack. She's also not leaving my sight. I could use a couple of sheriff deputies to help make certain the property is secure, especially given that the assassin is still out there."

"We don't have him yet," Schumacher said. "Every law enforcement agency in the country has his picture. We're going through Hanselka's phone and email contacts to see if we can find a connection between him and the assassin. I'll phone the Santa Barbara Sheriff and have two deputies up there before nightfall. Where are Jason and the Russian?"

"Petronovich is meeting Jason in Victorville. Jason has been following Qasim. AdvanChem, the assassin, and Qasim are connected in some way. Are you still monitoring Mohammed and Al-Hamaidi?" he asked.

"24/7, and we've come up empty so far," Schumacher said. "Tell Jason to contact me immediately if he has, or thinks he may have anything substantial. I should tell you to tell him to back off and head home, but I know that would fall on deaf ears."

"Keep me posted. And thanks for the security detail," Mike said and hung up.

****

It was late when Antar arrived at Qasim's door. He peered into the living room through a gap in the flimsy curtains. The room was dark. Not wanting to draw attention to himself from neighbors, he knocked lightly on the door. After a minute, he knocked again. This time, from the other side of the door he heard, "Who's there?"

Antar responded, "A friend. Open the door."

"I don't know anyone here."

"Praise Allah, I have been sent to help you, open the door."

Qasim slid off the security latch and let Antar in. He stepped inside and walked immediately over to the RPA console. "So, this is how you fly the aircraft?"

"Yes, I can fly it from anywhere in the world with this machine," replied Qasim.

"I was told the mission is to commence soon, correct?" Antar asked.

"The cargo will be loaded onto a tanker truck tomorrow, then transported to the Victorville airport in the afternoon. That is when we will transfer it to the aircraft and fly the mission the next morning."

"Very good," said Antar as he moved to the sofa and sat. "I'm staying here tonight. Plan on me being with you until we have completed the assignment."

"I don't need a babysitter," responded Qasim as he stared at the man in front of him.

"Be assured, Qasim. I am anything but a babysitter. Do as you've been instructed, and you will have no problem with me. However, if you hesitate or falter in any way, you will learn the true extent of my capabilities."

The two men stared at each other for what seemed like several minutes. Finally, Qasim said, "I will complete my job. You have nothing to be concerned about."

"Good," said Antar as he swung his legs up and settled back on the sofa. "You'd better get some sleep, Qasim. Tomorrow will be a busy day." Antar crossed his arms and closed his eyes.

****

Jason and Petronovich sat in the car parked at the back of the parking lot. They had an unobstructed view of Qasim's front door. About mid-morning, the door opened. Jason nudged Vladi, rousing him from a nap. "He's coming out, but he's not alone," said Jason.

Petronovich looked up in shock. "Fuck me! Jason, that's the guy who killed Kevin and Marina! Schumacher showed me and Mike the pictures from the hotel and the airport. I guarantee you, that's the same son-of-a-bitch!" Petronovich chambered a round in his Glock and reached for the door handle.

"Wait, Vladi!" said Jason as he grabbed his friend's arm. "Let's follow them and see where they go. They haven't seen us, so we have the advantage. We won't let this guy out of our sight, I promise you. We should call Schumacher."

"Not yet, Jason," said Petronovich, shaking his head. I don't want a swarm of FBI agents descending on this place and scaring these guys off, or sending them to Allah before we determine what they're doing. We can handle it for now."

Qasim turned onto the highway, headed for the outskirts of town. "They're going to the airport," said Jason as he turned onto a road that ran parallel to the airport property. "I've found a place where we can watch, about a half mile from his hangar. It's not too close, and we shouldn't be seen. We'll keep an eye on him from there."

The car arrived at the hangar five minutes after McClintock was in position. After parking, Qasim opened the hangar and began prepping the DC-10 to move outside. Antar walked the perimeter, looking for potential problems. It was a busy airport, which made him uncomfortable. Thankfully, because the size of hanger needed for the DC-10 was large, the hangar stood on its own. That made it a little easier for Antar to patrol and provide security as he'd been instructed.

****

Mohammed parked his car on the side of the road about a quarter mile from the main airport gate. They watched as the tanker truck came to a stop at the guard shack and the driver presented the truck's manifest. The guard took his time, then nodded his approval while handing the document back to the driver. The gate opened and the truck passed through. Both Mohammed and Al-Hamaidi breathed sighs of relief as they realized their part of the plan was complete. AdvanChem had served its purpose, and for all intents and purposes, the company was finished. If they had any chance at survival, Mohammed and Al-Hamaidi had to leave the country immediately, before the attack. It wouldn't take the authorities long to tie the weapon of mass destruction to AdvanChem, and in turn, to them. They turned their car around and began the trip back to Irvine.

****

The tanker came to a stop next to the DC-10, which had been pulled out of the hanger in preparation for the cargo transfer. The driver appeared to be nervous as he began attaching the six-inch piping from the truck to the plane's tanks. "Why are you shaking?" asked Qasim as he watched the man closely.

The driver stuttered, "When your cargo was transferred from the lab to the tanker, the men were wearing Hazmat suits and wouldn't let me make the transfer. They did it themselves. I don't have that protection."

"Don't worry, my friend, this is a contained transfer. You are in no danger and, as you can see, I'm not wearing a Hazmat suit either. This is only fire-retardant material anyway."

The driver, realizing that Qasim was just as exposed as he was, began to relax. "This shouldn't take long," he said.

As the process continued, Antar walked around the hangar looking for anything out of the ordinary. As he turned the corner at the far side, he noticed a car in the distance, with what looked to be two men inside. They seemed to be intent on watching the DC-10. Antar moved away from Qasim's hangar to the next one over, near the airport fence. Between the fence and the hangar door were several 50-gallon drums. Crouching low, he hopped onto the barrel closest to the fence, then jumped over it. He ran across the road and down into a ditch that paralleled the road. Keeping as low as possible, he inched closer to the car. As he moved, Antar studied the profile of the man in the passenger seat. It hit him like a bolt of lightning. He was staring at the Russian!

Without hesitating, Antar sprinted across the street to the rear of McClintock's vehicle, his gun raised. Petronovich noticed movement in his peripheral vision and with cat-like reflexes, threw open the door and dropped to the ground while hollering at Jason to get down. As the words left his lips, two rounds shattered the car's rear window and tore through the windshield. The blast echoed across the runway. Antar had missed by inches. On the ground, Petronovich fired his Glock from underneath the car, hitting the ground next to Antar. Antar dropped and rolled, screaming in anger. He fired another two rounds in Vladi's direction. Both rounds landed in front of Petronovich, kicking rocks and pebbles into his face. Unable to see clearly, but knowing the assassin wouldn't have moved far, Petronovich fired three quick rounds in the same direction he had before. Clearing his eyes, he saw the killer lying in the dirt, blood pooling near his head. He thought one 9mm hollow point had hit him in the temple. After all, the kills Petronovich had under his belt, he was certain the man was dead.

"Jason, are you okay?" asked Petronovich.

There was a moment's hesitation before Jason answered, "Yes. We need to get out of here."

Petronovich moved the body off to the side, then jumped into the passenger seat. Jason started the car, accelerating quickly on the frontage road, back towards town.

Qasim had heard the gunfire and looked toward the sound. He saw the car that was near the fence leave the area, but nothing more. Checking the hangar but not finding Antar, Qasim instinctively knew he'd been involved. *Crap!* He thought.

With the cargo transfer complete, Qasim gave instructions to the ground crew to move the aircraft back into the hanger and secure the doors. Satisfied and with sirens screaming in the background, he climbed into his car and returned to his apartment. He had to leave. Someone was watching and the flight would be compromised if he were apprehended. The mission would need to be delayed.

Back at the apartment, he threw his personal belongings into his go bag, grabbed the thumb drive from the console, and headed out the door. The nearest airport was Burbank, but authorities would be watching. He had to get out of the country, but not by air. He would drive, and Mexico was the obvious choice. He could fly the DC-10 from anywhere in the world, but it wouldn't be from Victorville.

****

While Jason drove the back roads of Victorville, Petronovich

Googled the nearest car rental agency and reserved a sedan for immediate pick-up. They couldn't drive their current vehicle with the shattered front and rear windows without attracting attention. Jason dropped Petronovich off a block from the location and waited until he drove off the lot in a new, mid-size sedan. Petronovich followed McClintock out of town into the desert, turning off the two-lane highway onto a dirt road. They followed the road to the dead end, close to three miles, and ditched the car. They were surrounded by nothing but high desert Joshua trees. With any luck, their car would remain undetected for some time.

After transferring their belongings to the rental, Jason phoned Schumacher and explained what had happened at the airport and that Petronovich had killed the assassin. "We're going to Qasim's place next," Jason followed.

"Wait for my Swat team, Jason," said Schumacher.

"We can't. It'll take too long. I'll let you know what we find."

They headed back to town. Petronovich intended to provide Qasim with his first water-boarding experience. Outside the apartment, in the car, they waited until the sun set and darkness approached.

"I don't have a good feeling about this, Jason. There are no lights on inside," said Petronovich.

McClintock got out of the car and half jogged across the lot to the apartment's front door. He listened, then knocked. There was no response.

Petronovich took the lock pick set from the bag under his seat and walked to the door. He used the pick to open the door and stepped inside. Jason followed. The RPA console filled the small family room.

“Qasim is gone. Check the bedroom and see if any of his personal stuff is still here,” Jason said.

Petronovich checked the bedroom and came back into the living room shaking his head. “Nothing.”

Jason dialed Schumacher, “His place is empty, Jack. Everything’s gone except for the console he uses to fly the plane. It’s still here.”

“If the console is there, he’ll probably be coming back. How long has he been out of your sight?” asked Schumacher.

“Probably three hours or so.”

“That’s enough time to be anywhere if he’s running. I’ll notify Homeland Security and ask that he be placed on a watch list, especially at all airports. If I get a hit, I’ll notify you.”

“Can you get a search warrant for the hangar and plane?”

“If we can locate the assassin’s body, we can tie him to Qasim and I can get the warrant. Are you sure he’s dead?” Schumacher asked.

“Petronovich believes he killed him. But regardless, Qasim is tied to AdvanChem and somehow to the assassin. Something bad is going to happen. I honestly hope it’s not too late.” McClintock didn’t wait for a reply. He hung up and turned to Petronovich. “Let’s go back to Qasim’s hangar,” he said. “Whatever they’re doing involves the plane. We’ve got to try and figure out what that is.”

Chapter 18

Antar came to and realized he was knocked unconscious by a bullet that had grazed his head. He tore his shirt and pressed the cloth against the cut on the right side of his head. The bullet was a quarter inch away from killing him. The pain was unbearable, feeling as though he'd been kicked in the head by a mule. This was not the first time Antar had been shot. He fought through the pain, gained his footing, kicked dirt over the spilled blood on the ground, and ducked into the woods.

****

As he drove south toward the border, Qasim thought about where he might go. He'd been to Cabo San Lucas years ago and had promised to return. Cabo's airport was in San Jose del Cabo, which was a large, neighboring town. He decided that's where he was headed. He could cross the border into Mexico without anyone knowing, then drive down the entire length of the Baja peninsula. It would be long, but he had no choice, he couldn't stay in the U.S.

****

McClintock and Petronovich approached the side door of Qasim's hangar. The door was deadbolted and padlocked.

McClintock held the flashlight while Petronovich used heavy duty bolt cutters to snap the padlock. Setting the bolt cutter down, Vladi retrieved the lock picks from his pocket and quickly unlocked the dead bolt. Once inside, they turned on the hangar lights, revealing the massive DC-10.

"Where do we start?" asked Petronovich.

McClintock thought for a second, walking toward the aircraft's main cabin door. "We need the logbooks," he said. "That will give us a history of the plane. It's probably on board."

Stairs on rollers were locked against the body of the plane. The men bounded up the steps, two at a time. McClintock reached the door, pushed the cover, and grabbed the handle, lifting it all the way up. He pushed the door open into the locked position.

Once inside, they immediately went left to the cockpit. McClintock stepped inside and glanced around. There was a compartment in the side of the cabin next to the captain's seat. It was the obvious location. Jason sat down, opened the latch, and pulled the three-ring binder out. "This is it, Vladi! Lady Luck is with us tonight! Let's get out of here."

Retracing their steps without locking the hangar door, McClintock and Petronovich were in the car and on the road within ten minutes.

"Jason, we need a place to stay tonight. Qasim is gone, let's go back to his apartment," suggested Petronovich. "We can grab some food and get a couple hours of shut eye before continuing. With any luck he'll come back, and we can grab him."

"Sounds good to me. I'm anxious to see what this plane is all about," Jason said.

****

Antar knew there was no way he could return to Qasim's apartment to protect him. The pilot wasn't stupid; he would leave the area as well. But where should Antar go and what should he do now? He needed to stop all communication with his handlers if he was to survive. People were watching, and they were too close. His only goal at this point was to kill the Russian, his friends, and their family. They would all pay for the pain they had caused him.

****

After driving all night and most of the next day, Qasim entered the city limits of San Jose del Cabo. He remembered friends who had visited Cabo not long ago having nothing but great things to say about the Hyatt Ziva. He stopped at a gas station and asked for directions to the hotel. The property was gated, but the attendant let him pass without question. After giving the car keys to the valet, he grabbed his bag and entered the open-air lobby.

"I don't have reservations, but I'd like a room," Qasim said as he approached the reservations desk.

"That may be a problem, since we have two conventions this week. But let me see what I can do. All single rooms are taken, but we do have a two-bedroom suite with pool and ocean views available. Since we are an all-inclusive resort, the fee is $950 per night. How many nights will you be staying, Mr.?"

"Sarraf. Sadik Sarraf. I will be here one week," said

Qasim, intending to use the fake passport he'd been given.

"Very good, sir. Let me escort you to the private lobby and we will take care of the paperwork."

After paying in cash, Qasim was escorted by the bellhop to his room. He stepped into a living room adjacent to the dining area. Beyond the room were floor to ceiling, folding glass doors that led to an expansive deck.

"I think you will be happy with this suite, Mr. Sarraf," the bellhop said.

Qasim handed the young man $10. "I'm sure I will," he said. "Thank you for your help."

"Thank you," said the bellhop as he took the money. "If you need anything, please call. By the way, your bar is stocked. If there is a beverage you prefer and it is not there, let us know and we will provide it."

After closing the door, Qasim turned and took in the suite. It was larger than the apartment in Victorville, certainly more than he needed. He was anxious to complete the mission. But he couldn't do anything without the RPA console. His eyes were heavy and the only thing he needed was sleep. Ordering a new console would need to wait a few hours.

****

McClintock sat on the sofa in Qasim's apartment, reviewing the logbook. On the coffee table in front of him was a half-eaten burger and fries. Petronovich had finished his meal. "What have you learned, Jason?" he asked.

McClintock looked up. "The plane was initially owned by Continental Airlines. They flew it for years and eventually sold it to Cal Fire. At that point, it was retrofitted to fight fires, adding massive tanks for fire retardant. Cal Fire recently sold the aircraft to Advanced Aerial Fire Response. That's it. The log is straightforward, with nothing nefarious."

"Does it mention any modifications enabling it to be flown remotely?" Vladi asked.

"Let me see," said McClintock as he turned the pages to the most recent entry. "Yes, and it was signed off on by a Jordan McCaffrey at the Adelanto Airport. That's it, nothing more."

McClintock's cell buzzed. He looked at the incoming call and answered, "What do you have, Jack?"

"Jason, Homeland Security has nothing. My concern is that Qasim didn't fly, but drove. If I were in his position and knew I was being followed, I'd drive too. And I'd be driving into Mexico."

"The nearest point of entry is San Diego, Jack. But I can't imagine him going to Tijuana," replied Jason.

"I can't either. The largest city on the Baja peninsula is San Jose del Cabo, next to Cabo San Lucas. My guess is he'd go down there. Until he screws up and uses a credit card or his passport, he's going to be difficult to find. And if he rents a room, he'll need to show his passport."

"Unless he has a fake one," suggested McClintock.

"That's true. And that wouldn't surprise me since we don't believe we're dealing with an amateur. One more thing, Jason. I had a team go to AdvanChem this afternoon. They presented themselves as gas company employees needing to check the premises. They asked to speak with the owners and were told they weren't there. The secretary said she didn't know when they'd be back. They haven't been in the office for a couple of days and nobody has heard from them. Hearing that, I placed them on a watch list as well."

"Keep me posted about them. I think it might be time for a trip south of the border," said Jason.

"I can't stop you, Jason. What I will do is contact the PFM, or Ministerial Federal Police. They're Mexico's equivalent of the FBI. I have a contact I've worked with in the past that may be able to help us locate Qasim. Let me see what I can do."

Jason ended the call and looked at Petronovich. "I'm calling Mike. Since the assassin is dead, the girls will be okay. He can let the deputies get back to regular duty. We could use his help down in Mexico with the PFM."

****

It was evening when Antar stumbled into the residential area. He needed transportation. Staying in the shadows, he searched for a nondescript car he could hotwire and steal. On the street, he spotted the car. It was a white Ford Focus. Shortly after midnight as the lights in the neighborhood went out, Antar approached the vehicle. The car was unlocked, which made the job quick and easy. With the small car running, he slowly eased out of the development and headed for the apartment complex where his own car was parked. His next stop would be the vineyard in the Santa Ynez Valley.

****

Al-Hamaidi and Mohammed each flew separately to Riyadh, Saudi Arabi. They flew on the same day, but used different airlines. They had missed the Homeland Security watch notification by a matter of hours. A third cousin of King Salman bin Abdulaziz, Saleh Shamoun, had arranged their pick-up at the airport as well as accommodations in separate furnished apartments in one of Riyadh's newest and most plush apartment complexes. Being an extended part of the royal family, Shamoun was very wealthy. He had no part in governing and seldom associated with his distant cousins. In fact, he was considered to be one of the black sheep of the family and rarely, if ever, communicated with them, which was fine with Shamoun, given his radical tendencies. That said, Shamoun was starved for his family's respect. In his mind, he would finally achieve that by ordering the DC-10 to fly down the middle of Pennsylvania Avenue and release its deadly cargo. He was intent on killing as many as possible in Congress, not to mention the President. In turn, he was certain he would earn his family's approval.

Shamoun's home was gated, but nothing like the Al-Yamama Palace in Riyadh, home to King Salman bin Abdulaziz. Nevertheless, the ornate fixtures, gold trim, and structural details of the house dripped with wealth.

Mohammed and Al-Hamaidi sat on the sofa, while Shamoun and his assistant sat in side chairs across from them. The butler placed coffee and finger food on the table between them, then left the room, closing the tall double doors behind him.

Looking at the men in front of him, Shamoun ignored the coffee and leaned forward, his elbows on his knees. He asked, "Okay, where are we? We are ready to fly, are we not?"

Al-Hamaidi answered, "We did as we were instructed. The sarin crystals have been produced and delivered to the plane.

Once we were certain of the delivery, our part was complete. We know that Qasim modified the plane to fly remotely."

"Do you know why the pilot has not flown the mission? I am very concerned. I ordered my fixer, Antar, to accompany him everywhere. I have not heard from him and my calls have not been answered."

"We can only assume that he is waiting for the opportune time and place, away from authorities that have the potential to disrupt or terminate the plan," responded Mohammed.

"I can't imagine that he would wait any longer than necessary. Every minute the plane is on the ground increases the likelihood that the true nature of the cargo will be revealed," Al-Hamaidi replied.

"All right, then. We have no choice but to wait. My driver will take you back to your apartment. I am flying to the Maldives this afternoon. I'll phone you for updates. Qasim better complete the mission soon. Oh, and do not leave Riyadh," Shamoun said, turning to leave the room. "Good day, gentlemen."

****

Mike answered the phone after the first ring. "Bring me up to speed, Jason," he said.

"It's been a long day, Mike. The good news is that the assassin is dead. The bad news is that we've lost Qasim. We think he might be in Mexico. Are you up for a trip south of the border?"

"I'll pack my bag and be out of here within the hour," Mike said. "Where are you?"

"We're in Victorville. Head to Vladi's place in Dana Point

and we'll meet you first thing in the morning. Is everyone there okay?" asked Jason.

"Everyone's fine. They'll be relieved when I tell them the news. I'll see you in a few hours."

****

The large black sedan pulled up next to the gleaming white Gulfstream G550. The plane was big, with the capacity to carry four crew and 14 passengers. Designed as a business jet, it could fly fully loaded, 7,500 miles non-stop at an altitude of 51,000 feet. Shamoun and his entourage of six, including a secretary, executive assistant, and bodyguards were greeted by two pilots and a cabin steward. The worst seats on this aircraft were far better than any commercial first-class seat in the world. The passengers waited patiently with glasses of juice in hand while the ground crew stowed the luggage. Saudi Arabia adhered to the very strict tenants of Sharia Law, prohibiting the consumption of alcohol.

As soon as the cargo hold was secure, the pilot began to taxi. Given Shamoun's relationship to the royal family, his airplane was given a priority take off position and moved to the front of the line, passing ten planes queued for take-off. Within minutes, the two Rolls-Royce engines surged with power, flinging the jet down the runway into the air. As soon as the plane leveled off at altitude and passed out of Saudi airspace, Sharia Law went out the window; corks were popped and crystal flutes of champagne were distributed by the cabin steward. The five-hour flight to Malé would pass quickly.

****

It was three a.m. when Jason McClintock's phone rang. He jumped out of a deep sleep and answered, "What's up, Jack?"

"We have a hit! We've confirmed that Mohammed and Al-Hamaidi are in Saudi Arabia. One flew British Airways and the other, Emirates. We're trying to track them down now using CIA contacts in country," explained Schumacher. "Sorry to bother you so early in the morning, but I thought you should know. If I hear anything more, I'll call."

McClintock was sitting on the sofa and Petronovich was wide awake in a recliner in the corner. "Did you hear that?" asked Jason.

"I did and it's a concern. Why would the owners of AdvanChem leave the country without telling anyone?" Petronovich asked. "They're running. Whatever this group is doing, it involves Saudi Arabia in some way. Jason, do you remember Ivan Kamarov? He was at the Russian Embassy in Montevideo?"

"Sure. He helped us out last year, why?"

"I've kept in touch with him and he's been posted to the Embassy in Riyadh. It's three thirty now, what time is it in Riyadh?" asked Petronovich.

Jason Googled the question. "One thirty in the afternoon," he said.

"I think it's time to give him a call."

****

The sun was rising over the top of the mountains that ringed the Santa Ynez Valley. Antar sat on the rural road drinking a coffee purchased from the local gas station. He watched the home beyond the vineyard, anxious to see if anyone, especially the Russian, was present. There wasn't any activity on the road or at the house. But it was a school day, so he'd learn within the hour if anyone was home. Antar considered killing the women and the kids simply because they'd been a nuisance. He didn't want to, but if he had to, he would without thinking twice. It was the men he was after and he would do whatever was necessary to kill Petronovich and the McClintock brothers.

As he sat staring at the home, he failed to notice the police vehicle pull up behind him. The quick chirp of the siren startled Antar as he looked in the rearview mirror. The Santa Barbara County Sheriff Deputy was out of his car and walking toward his window.

"Is everything okay?" asked the Deputy as Antar rolled the window down.

"Yes, Officer, thank you. I was admiring the vineyard. I'm thinking about buying one or buying land and starting one from scratch," Antar replied, hoping he wouldn't be asked for ID and registration. He didn't want to kill the deputy.

"It's a pretty place, but you can't sit here. You need to move along. You might consider a real estate agent. Do you need one? I have a friend, Michael, his wife is pretty good," the officer replied.

"That would be great, sure," Antar said.

The deputy wrote the agent's name on a piece of paper and handed it to Antar. "Her name is Susan Beckmann. She's with Sotheby's here in the Valley, give her a call. She'll find what you're looking for. Have a nice day."

"I will, thank you, sir," said Antar as he put his coffee in the cupholder and started the engine.

The deputy got back into his car and waited for Antar to pull onto the pavement.

****

Qasim entered the lobby and noticed the concierge alone doing paperwork. "Good morning," said the young man, looking up from his work.

Qasim sat in one of the two chairs in front of concierge desk. "I have a special request," he said. "I need to make a purchase. A fairly significant purchase and I have lost my credit card." Qasim slipped a piece of paper toward the man.

The concierge looked at it. Qasim had listed the model number and price of the Zedasoft RPA console. "And you want me to do what with this?" the young man asked.

"If you could make the purchase using your name and credit card and have it delivered here, I would make it worth your while," answered Qasim.

The concierge looked down again. "This is the limit I have available on my card. I don't know if it would go through. And what do you mean it would be worth my while?"

"As you can see, the system costs $9,500 USD. That would be in addition to the delivery charge, whatever that is. I would give you an additional $1,500 for doing this," explained Qasim.

"This is legal, correct?" asked the concierge.

"Absolutely. You are simply helping me with the transaction," said Qasim as he pulled out the cash, counting out $12,000. "This should be more than enough to cover the unit cost, shipping, and your fee. The remaining difference is yours as well if you make the call now. The number is on the slip."

The concierge picked up the phone and dialed. Ten minutes later, the transaction was complete. The concierge discretely pocketed the cash. "The console should be here by the end of the week, Mr. Sarraf. I'll call when it is delivered, and have it brought to your suite."

Qasim shook his hand, "You've been very helpful."

****

That afternoon, Antar went to the local Ace Hardware in the small town of Santa Ynez. He purchased duct tape and rope as well as additional 9 mm ammunition for his handgun. His plan was to scout the house and determine the number of occupants after dark. If the men were there, his work would be done quickly, as he would kill everyone. If they were not and it was only the women and children present, he would decide on the fly how to handle the situation. It could be messy, but he had the duct tape and rope to keep things under control.

It was nine thirty in the evening when Antar parked the car on a dirt road adjacent to the vineyard. It was a vacant property of probably about 20 acres. His phone buzzed as he was about to get out of the car. Checking the number, he answered.

"Hello?"

"I've been trying to reach you. Where are you?" Shamoun asked.

"I'm in California, at the McClintock's house. I'm about to go in."

"I'm not happy with the way things are progressing with the mission. Tie up the loose ends with the McClintocks, then go to the Saudi Consulate in L.A. I have a suitcase there for you to pick up. Once you have it, call me and I'll give you further instructions. We are going to cause the Great Satan mass devastation one way or another."

"I understand. My business here shouldn't take long," Antar said. He terminated the call and moved away from the car toward the split rail fence marking the boundary of the property. The moonless night provided some semblance of cover.

Antar jumped the fence and moved through the vineyard, making his way between a long row of Syrah grape vines toward the house. When he came to the end of the row, there was a clearing leading to a lawn and a swing set. He could see lights on in the kitchen and another room beyond. Antar sprinted across the grass and moved to the house. He crouched below the kitchen window, then slowly rose high enough to peer inside. Beyond the kitchen he could see a show on the flat screen television in the family room. There was nobody in sight. *They must be in the bedrooms,* thought Antar, as he went around the house looking for a better view.

When Antar crossed the grass, he triggered a silent alarm that went to Julie's cell phone. Brenda grabbed her shotgun while Julie gathered the kids and dog. They ran to the walk-in closet in the master bedroom. At the far end was a wall with shelves of shoes. Julie pulled back on a pair of black high heels which caused the wall to slowly swing open leading to a safe room. Once inside, Julie pressed a button by the entrance, closing and locking the door, preventing access from the outside. The room was large enough to house them for a month, if need be. It had a pair of bunk beds, filtered air, running water, a stash of food, and an enclosed bathroom with a shower. They also had a small television and a case of DVDs for entertainment. The house could burn down around them, and they would be safe. The only drawback was the lack of cell service, because of the steel and cement that encased them.

After circling the home and seeing no signs of life, Antar grew concerned. He decided to check the interior. All doors and windows were locked. At the back door, he used his lock picks and expertly snapped the deadbolt into the unlocked position. He opened the door, waiting for the alarm to trigger. Nothing happened. With his handgun ready, Antar stepped inside and began to sweep the house, moving room to room. Something didn't feel right, though he appeared to be alone.

Inside the safe room, while the kids sat on one of the bunks, Brenda stood behind Julie as she viewed eight small screens on a console. They watched as the assassin moved through the house, searching for them. "I never thought we would need to use this room. But Mike, with his law enforcement background, insisted it be built," Julie said without taking her eyes off the screens.

"I'm glad he did," Brenda replied. "Now, what do we do? We have no way to communicate with the outside."

"He won't stay here for long, I'm sure," Julie said. "When he leaves, we'll run for the car and drive to the sheriff's station. For now, the only thing we can do is wait. We're safe. Kids, why don't you climb into a sleeping bag and we'll dim the lights? Zach, you take the top bunk and Sam can have the bottom."

Chapter 19

Kamarov was in his office reviewing reports that his secretary had brought in when his cell rang. Noticing the number, he said, "That will be all, Tanya, please close the door as you leave."

Petronovich waited, expecting the call to go to voice mail when he heard, "Vladimir, to what do I owe the honor of your call? Or should I say, what do you need now?" There was a slight chuckle. "Seriously, Vladi, is everything okay?"

"Ivan, I could use your help."

"This seems to be a regular event," Kamarov said. "How can I help?"

Petronovich explained the situation, ending with Abdullah Mohammed and Majid Al-Hamaidi, the two principals of AdvanChem. What is of concern, is that they too have left the country and their business without giving notice to anyone. We have confirmed that they are in Riyadh."

"What are you asking of me?" Kamarov asked.

"The FBI, with the help of the CIA are using Humint in Riyadh to try and locate Mohammed and Al-Hamaidi. I thought since you're there, you may be able to use your sources to find these two quicker than they can."

There was a pause on the other end. Finally, Kamarov responded, "Vladi, I am sorry for the two deaths. I really am, but why is it of such importance to you that these two be found? Are they directly connected to the murders or Qasim?"

"We have confirmation that Qasim has been in direct contact with AdvanChem. The evidence linking them to the murders is tangential. Ivan, you know me. And more importantly, you know my instincts. Need I remind you how many times I saved your ass when we worked together?"

"You saved me once, Vladimir, and I paid my debt in Uruguay last year if you recall?"

"That you did, Ivan, and I appreciate it. The bottom line is this: we believe that Qasim, Mohammed, Al-Hamaidi, and someone in the Saudi government – so someone in the royal family – have been radicalized. When you combine a very large UAV and people working with sarin, not to mention Saudi Arabia, you have the potential for very bad things to happen. Where did most of the 9/11 terrorists come from?"

"You've made your point, Vladi. We watch the royal family. I will make some inquiries there. I will also use my contacts and see if the immigration forms completed by Mohammed and Al-Hamaidi reveal where they are staying. Give me 24 hours and I'll call you back. If I'm able to come up with anything, you may have to fly here. We will not get involved in an American operation involving the royal family in Saudi Arabia."

"I understand, Ivan. I appreciate your help. I will have a bottle of Ciroc Vodka X for you the next time we meet," Petronovich promised.

"I will hold you to that," Kamarov said.

****

Antar turned off the lights in the house and waited, his gun ready. Sitting in a corner chair, facing the front door, looking out the picture window he could see anyone coming down the drive.

Three hours had passed since the family had entered the safe room. The kids were fast asleep. Julie sat at the console, keeping watch on the assassin, while Brenda dozed in a chair next to the beds. *This guy may not leave,* thought Julie. She'd had enough and turned off the light. Knowing they were safe, she slept.

****

When Vladi and Jason entered the Dana Point home, they found Mike packed and ready to go. He was on the phone with Schumacher, wrapping up a conversation. "Thanks, Jack, I'll be in touch when we get down there."

"What did Schumacher have to say?" Jason asked.

"The PFM in San Jose del Cabo are expecting us. He's texting me the contact information of an investigator that has been assigned to assist us," Mike answered. "When do we leave?'

"We have a direct flight out of John Wayne in three hours," Vladi said. "It's a 30-minute drive, so we should be going, get your bag."

****

The Gulfstream touched down with a slight screech as the tires connected with the cement runaway. The plane taxied to an area designated for private aircraft adjacent the commercial terminal. The passengers watched as the plane came to a stop and the ground crew placed orange cones on the ground at the tip of the jet's wings. Two stretch limousines pulled up just outside the barrier. The uniformed drivers stood next to the vehicles, waiting for the passengers to disembark and the luggage to be brought over. Saleh Shamoun was first to exit the plane, followed by his shapely secretary and the remaining passengers. Shamoun stood next to the open car door, "After you," he said to the secretary. The assistant and bodyguards got in the second limo.

The drive from the small island airport to the marina where they would be transported to Dhigu Island by speedboat was less than a mile away. Once on the boat, the trip to the Anantara Dhigu Maldives Resort would take about half an hour. With a temperature of 90 degrees and high humidity, the speed of the boat as it cut through the calm, turquoise sea provided a welcome breeze. An island appeared in the distance. The boat was kept at a constant speed until they were within a quarter mile of what appeared to be an entrance to a lagoon. The captain throttled back the power until there was no wake. He entered the lagoon through the center of a tight channel, nosing the large speedboat forward. As they turned the corner, a string of thatched roof huts sitting on stilts over the water came into view. There were nearly 40 huts, with almost twice that number of villas on the beach with lagoon front views. The boat eased into a marina slip where four deckhands stood ready to assist the passengers and offload luggage. Golf carts with Rolls Royce grills waited at the end of the pier to transport the guests to their quarters. Normal check-in procedures were waived, having been handled by Shamoun's assistant prior to arrival.

****

With the morning light peering through the windows, the assassin moved from room to room, his weapon ready, checking for any signs of the family. He would most likely have noticed them leave last night, but they didn't. If they were in a safe room, he may be able to locate it, but would probably not be able to penetrate it. He went through the house with the safe room in mind. He tapped walls and checked for hidden doors.

Julie and Brenda watched as the man moved through the house. They could see by the way he was acting that he was looking for their hidden location. The last room was the master bedroom. He quickly scanned the area and bathroom before moving into the closet. Shoving clothes aside, he checked the side walls for any sign of a door. At the far end, the shelves of shoes stood out. They didn't appear to be out of place, but at the same time, didn't quite fit. He began pulling shoes off the shelves and throwing them to the ground, until he came across the pair of black high heels that wouldn't move. Antar pulled on one. It lifted with slight click. He had found the false door. *Now what?* he thought. *I can't penetrate the room without the right equipment. Time to go.*

The two women looked on in silence as the assassin pulled on the high heels. Julie glanced at the door, confirming that it was locked and couldn't be breached. Nobody moved as they watched the man staring at the panel. He was within a few feet of them on the other side of the heavy steel door with a gun.

Julie and Brenda watched the screens as the cameras followed the assassin as he left the house. "He may be leaving," Julie whispered. "Let's wait a bit before going out, just to be sure."

"I'm in no hurry," Brenda replied.

Thirty minutes passed before Julie was finally able to breathe a sigh of relief. Looking at Brenda, she said, "You ready to do this? Let's get to the car and make a run for the sheriff's station."

"Ready when you are. I've got Zach," Brenda said, taking his hand.

Julie held on to Sam and opened the door. "Okay, guys, let's make this quick!"

Brenda hollered at Rosie, "Come on, girl!"

The family was out the kitchen door and in the car in less than two minutes. Julie fired up the engine, giving it more gas than she needed, and spinning the tires and kicking up gravel as she drove down the dirt driveway toward the road. She checked her rearview mirror and to her relief, saw no one following them. The sheriff's station was three miles away. They were safe.

****

The McClintocks and Petronovich were at the PFM headquarters before three. Prior to landing in San Jose del Cabo, Schumacher texted Mike and told him that Investigator Enrique Guzman would be waiting for him. When he walked into the waiting room, Guzman was not the picture of law enforcement. He was extremely thin and wiry, almost anorexic looking. The notion that he might not be able to provide the required assistance was quickly dispelled.

"Please, come into my office," Guzman said as he gestured through the door.

The three men walked in and sat down, while Guzman followed, pacing the room. "Every hotel and motel in San Jose as well as Cabo San Lucas are in our email blast system. After speaking to Jack Schumacher and learning the identity of the man you are looking for, Aaban Qasim, we sent an email to all establishments asking if they have a guest registered in that name. I didn't expect to have a positive return, but we had to eliminate the possibility that he might register with his real name. I followed with a second blast asking if there are any guests registered that appear to be of Middle Eastern descent. We received over a dozen positive responses. We sent those establishments a picture of Qasim that we received from Schumacher and are waiting for a possible match. Our investigators will follow up in person. Where will you be staying, do you know?"

"Can you suggest a place?" Jason asked. "We don't need anything fancy."

"When people come into town, we put them up at Hotel Posada Real. It's comfortable and you can probably get a room for about $55 USD."

"Sounds good," responded Jason.

"Okay, get checked in. Schumacher gave me your contact information. I'll be in touch. If Qasim is in town, it shouldn't take us long to locate him."

****

Petronovich walked into the room and threw his bag on the bed as his phone rang. "Hello?" he answered.

"Vladi, my sources have located Mohammed and Al-Hamaidi. Their visas indicate that they are in Riyadh on business, meeting with Saleh Shamoun. He is a member of the royal family. I have sources in Shamoun's office and after offering the secretary a significant bribe, we were given the men's location. They are staying in an upscale apartment complex near the center of town."

"Did the visa show their length of stay?" Petronovich asked.

"Yes, three weeks."

"Why would they be meeting with a member of the royal family?"

"Vladi, that is for you to determine. My direct work with this project is over. I will still help you when I can, but I suggest you get on a plane. Let me know your schedule and I will meet you at the airport," said Kamarov.

"I'll check flights, Ivan. I'm in San Jose del Cabo, so making the trip won't be as easy as leaving from LAX."

"I'll wait for your itinerary via text."

Petronovich went to McClintock's room. The door was open, so he knocked and walked in. Jason and Mike were sitting at the small table in the corner. "Kamarov located Mohammed and Al-Hamaidi," Petronovich said as he sat on the end of the bed. "It looks like I'll be going to Riyadh. Ivan said they're there to meet with someone from the royal family. This doesn't smell right."

"That was quick work on Kamarov's part, and you're right, why would these two be meeting with Saudi elites?" Jason asked.

"The GRU have their tentacles everywhere. It doesn't surprise me that they were easily found," said Petronovich. "I'm going to be on my way out of here as soon as possible. You two can handle Qasim when he turns up. I'll be in touch once I get to Riyadh."

****

After explaining what had happened to the Deputy on watch at the station, Brenda and Julie waited for a response.

"So, you waited in a safe room, watching screens with cameras while an intruder stalked you in your home?" Deputy Clagg asked.

"That's correct, Officer. He was in the house all night and left this morning once he found the safe room and realized it couldn't be penetrated," responded Julie.

"Do the cameras record the activity?"

"I believe Mike had the system wired so that once the room is entered and locked, the recording device is activated."

"Okay, I want those tapes. Let's head out to the vineyard. We'll keep a deputy on the premises 24/7 until we are certain the individual is no longer a problem."

Not a word was spoken during the short ride back to the house. The family was apprehensive about returning, but with the assurances of Deputy Clagg, they agreed to go. Clagg followed the McClintock family with a second sheriff's vehicle trailing them.

Julie emerged from the safe room with a disc and handed it to Clagg. "This is it. What are you going to do with it?" she asked.

"After what you've told me, I'll contact the FBI in Santa Barbara and see if they know who the guy on the tape is. I'll call with updates when I learn anything. In the meantime, we will have a deputy here day and night," Clagg said as he walked out the door to his car. He turned before leaving, "Mrs.

McClintock, have your husband call me. I want to update him personally."

****

Antar exited the 405 Freeway at Santa Monica Boulevard in L.A. The Saudi Consulate was located one block west on Sawtelle. He entered the small, secure garage for consulate employees. After flashing his ID to the parking attendant, he was allowed into the gated structure.

After passing through security screening, Antar was shown into a private office with a desk. "Please have a seat, someone will be with you shortly," said the woman in a loose-fitting pant suit and hijab.

Antar waited impatiently, wondering what the suitcase Shouman mentioned contained. A moment later, the same woman that had shown him to the office appeared at the door with the suitcase.

"I've been asked to give you this," she said. "We received it from the Saudi Embassy in Washington D.C. It was sent from Prince Shamoun and intended to be received by you. We have been instructed to give you privacy. As you can see, there is a combination lock. We have also been instructed to tell you to call the prince on his private line using our secure communication. The phone on the desk is yours to use to make that call. If you need anything, please let me know. Otherwise, after the call is made, you are free to go with the suitcase. Allah be with you."

Antar sat in the armchair, staring as the woman placed the suitcase by his side and closed the door. He slowly rose and walked toward the desk, uncertain about the call he was about to make.

****

Officer Clagg handed the disc off to the special agent in charge of the Santa Barbara FBI office. The agent stopped the camera and took a screen shot of the assassin's face, looking directly at the camera in the master bedroom closet. He ran it through the facial recognition database and almost immediately came up with a hit. Seeing that Jack Schumacher in the Los Angeles field office had posted the warrant, he called him.

"Jack, this is Russ Place in Santa Barbara. I'm sitting with a Santa Barbara county deputy. He's investigating a break-in at a home owned by Mike and Julie McClintock. I have a picture of the perp and it matches the one you recently posted. I just emailed it to you."

"I know Mike McClintock, he's in Cabo," Schumacher said.

"I'm putting us on speaker, Jack. This is Deputy Clagg with me. What is McClintock doing in Mexico?"

"The story is too long to tell, Russ. I told him to stay home, but he wouldn't listen," said Schumacher. "I just got the picture in my email. That guy has killed several people including one of our own, Kevin Mitchell, from the east coast. He's dangerous, Russ. Is the McClintock home protected?"

"Agent Schumacher, this is Brian Clagg. We have a deputy on site 24/7."

"Okay, that's a good start, but I think you should have at least two on the premises, three if possible. As I said, this guy is a professional killer."

"Understood, we'll get on it," Clagg replied.

"I'll call McClintock and explain what's happened. Russ, keep Deputy Clagg in the loop as we move forward. Thanks for the heads-up," said Schumacher as he ended the call.

****

Mohammed and Al-Hamaidi sat at a corner table in the coffee shop. After their drinks arrived, Mohammed leaned toward Al-Hamaidi. "I'm concerned," he said. "If Qasim doesn't fly the mission, I'm afraid our lives are in jeopardy."

"I have the same concerns. I've been thinking that it may be time to break with protocol and phone Qasim directly. Our phones will be monitored by the regime, but there is nothing we can do. If he has failed, we will need to act quickly. It won't be safe for us here. We will need to leave the country and go into hiding somewhere else in the world. If that happens, we will have two countries after us, the U.S. and Saudi Arabia. On the other hand, I pray to Allah this is the case. If Qasim is still on board, we can assure Shamoun that the plan is moving forward and our lives will be spared," Al-Hamaidi said.

"Spared for the time being. If he moves as planned but fails, we are still dead men," Mohammed added.

"You're right. For now, let's get back to the apartment and make the call," said Mohammed.

****

Kamarov met Petronovich at the airport. With nothing but a carry-on, Vladi was through customs and walking to the street before most of the other passengers. Kamarov couldn't miss Petronovich. He was big and still looked like someone you did not want to mess with. “I hope you have my bottle of Ciroc Vodka X,” Kamarov said as he squeezed Vladi’s shoulder.

“Had we been in Uruguay, I would have it,” Vladi said. “But I don’t think being incarcerated in a Muslim country because you broke Sharia Law is a smart move. Maybe next time.”

“I have a reservation for you at the Riyadh Airport Marriott, across the way. The car is waiting,” Kamarov explained.

“That will work. I’d like to get a little sleep before we approach Mohammed and Al-Hamaidi.”

“What do you mean by ‘we,’ Vladi? I told you, this is your op. I will help, but from a distance,” said Kamarov.

“I meant only that. Just point me in the right direction. I don’t intend to share the fun I will have when I waterboard these terrorists,” Petronovich stated bluntly.

“I’m glad we’re on the same page. Hop in,” Ivan said as he opened the car door.

****

Jason and Mike hadn’t heard from Guzman, so they called the department. When they reached him, Guzman explained that his investigators were following up with the hotels that had responded positively to their query about Middle Eastern guests. It was mid-day and they had not yet received a positive ID. “Gentlemen, we are working as fast as we can. If he is in town, I’m certain we will find him.”

“Inspector Guzman, we can’t just sit here. Let us help you,” Mike said. “As you know, I was with the FBI in the field for many years.”

"Mr. McClintock, Mike, you will not find any hotel front desk staff in Mexico that would release confidential guest registration information to you. This is not the United States and you have no authority here. They simply will not cooperate, nor should they. That said, I'm going out now. I need to stop at four hotels. I will pick you up on the way. Be ready in ten minutes."

Armed with a copy of the blast email and a picture of Qasim, Guzman approached the front desk at the first three hotels he had assigned himself. After speaking with front desk personnel, passing the picture around, and asking questions, he struck out.

The last hotel was the Hyatt Ziva. All three men approached the front desk and followed the same routine, passing the picture around, and asking questions. The concierge watched the commotion from across the room and approached. Having no success once again, Guzman and the McClintocks turned towards the lobby entrance and the car.

"Excuse me? May I see your picture?" the concierge asked.

Guzman stopped and turned, handing the picture to the concierge, "Have you seen this man?" he asked.

"His name is Sadik Sarraf. He is registered to stay one week," the concierge said. "I placed a substantial order for him two days ago by phone."

"What kind of order?" Jason asked.

"I don't know what it was. The firm is called Zedasoft," the concierge answered. "He paid me a fee to do this for him. He said he had lost his credit card."

"Do you know what Zedasoft produces?" Guzman asked, looking at Jason.

“They manufacture remotely piloted aircraft consoles for the public and military. When do you expect delivery of the merchandise?” asked Jason, looking at the concierge.

“He paid for express delivery and should receive the boxes in the next day or so. Given our location, sometimes express delivery is not as fast as advertised.”

“What is his suite number?” asked Guzman. The concierge walked back to his desk and punched the name into the hotel computer. “He is in 4124,” he said, writing the number down and handing the slip of paper to Guzman.

“Thank you very much. Do not, under any circumstance, alert Sarraf to our visit. When the packages arrive, call me immediately. Do you understand, my friend?” Guzman asked as he handed the concierge his card.

“Yes sir, absolutely,” the concierge said.

Guzman and the McClintocks turned and left for the station.

****

Qasim had finished his third Bombay Sapphire martini when his cell buzzed. *Who would be calling me?* He thought as he looked at the number. It was the area code for Orange County. The only people he knew there were Mohammed and Al-Hamaidi.

“Hello?” Qasim answered tentatively.

“Why haven’t you flown the mission? Our superiors are very concerned,” asked Mohammed.

“I had to relocate. We were being followed,” Qasim replied.

“Who is we?” Mohammed asked.

"Antar and I were at the hangar watching as the cargo was loaded. He checked the perimeter and went to the airport frontage road. I heard gunfire. I haven't seen him since. I left California and drove down the Baja peninsula to San Jose del Cabo, Mexico," Qasim explained. "Before I left, I made sure the plane was ready to be flown. I plan to fly the mission."

"Did you bring the console with you?" Mohammed asked.

"No, I ordered a new system. It should be here soon. Are you in Irvine?" Qasim asked.

"We are in Riyadh with the Prince, waiting for news of the attack. I pray to Allah you are successful. If not, we are all dead men, Qasim. You do understand?"

"Our mission is pure of heart. With Allah's guidance, we will succeed. I hope your crystals are as potent as you portrayed them to be," Qasim replied.

"The strength of our sarin crystals is the least of your concerns, Qasim. Stay focused on the mission. You better be successful, or we are dead."

****

Petronovich concealed his weapon along with a pocket full of zip ties. He was given the address for both Mohammed and Al-Hamaidi and decided to start with the latter. After scouting the residences of both, he confirmed that they were home. It was eight p.m. when the fun began.

Petronovich tapped lightly on the condo's front door, then stood out of view of the peep hole. He waited until the door opened slightly, then rushed in and subdued the scientist with a sleeper choke hold. Al-Hamaidi was out in two seconds. Petronovich eased the body to the ground, then quickly retrieved a dining room chair and brought it into the bathroom. He went back into the family room and, as if swinging a large sack of potatoes, swung Al-Hamaidi over his shoulders and carried him to the chair. After strapping his arms and legs down, Vladi stuffed a washcloth in the man's mouth and secured it with duct tape. He grabbed the hand towel by the sink. This condominium had a handheld shower head, which would make Petronovich's job much easier. Al-Hamaidi began to come around. When he realized his head was leaning over the rim of the bathtub, he instinctively knew what was coming and began to panic.

Petronovich controlled the writhing and soaked the towel. He placed it over the mouth and nose of the groaning Al-Hamaidi. Turning on the water, he let the spray rain over the man's face. Al-Hamiadi passed out and Petronovich dropped the spray into the tub. He lifted the towel, but before removing the duct tape and wash cloth from the man's mouth, he said, "If you scream, we will do this one more time. I want answers and you are going to give them to me, agreed?"

Al-Hamaidi nodded and Petronovich removed the tape and cloth. A-Hamaidi was wide eyed as Vladi spoke, "Tell me what your connection is to Qasim."

"I don't know who you are talking about," Al-Hamaidi replied.

With the speed of a biting snake, Vladi threw the man back and secured his mouth. The cloth went over his face and the water streamed down as the man shook with terror. This time, Vladi went ten seconds longer. When his KGB comrades experienced this interrogation technique while training, the average time they lasted before giving in was 14 seconds. Al-Hamaidi made it to 30 seconds before Petronovich stopped.

Again, the terrorist had passed out. After rousing him, Vladi asked, "I'll ask one more time, and if you don't answer, you will die. What is your relationship to Qasim?"

"He is a pilot," panted Al-Hamaidi as he turned his head away from Petronovich and threw up into the tub.

"Why do you need a pilot?" Petronovich asked.

"We didn't hire him, someone else did," Al-Hamaidi answered.

"Who hired him and why? Be truthful and you may live."

"Saleh Shamoun hired him to fly a mission," panted the sweating terrorist.

"We're getting somewhere," Petronovich said. "What mission?"

Al-Hamaidi hesitated, then began to ramble when he saw Petronovich lift the duct tape and cloth, "A mission to attack the United States."

"What kind of mission, you piece of shit?"

"If I tell you, you will kill me. Just kill me now!" demanded the terrorist.

Petronovich stopped, smiled, and withdrew his Glock with the attached suppressor. He threw Al-Hamaidi backwards into the tub and placed one 9 mm round between his eyes. It was time to pay Mohammed a visit. The time was eight thirty, ten thirty in the morning in California, one thirty p.m. in Washington, D.C.

****

It was five o'clock when Jason and Mike arrived at their hotel. Guzman turned in the driver's seat, facing them before they got out. "I'm going back to the office," he said. "We are going to put together a team to confront Qasim after the equipment is delivered. We have no reason to arrest him now. Being in possession of such sophisticated equipment will give us probable cause that something very suspicious is going on. At least, that's what we'll plead. At that point, if we can get him to talk, he may reveal something solid we can hold him on. If he does, as I mentioned to Schumacher, we will allow the U.S. to extradite. I'll phone tomorrow morning with an update."

"I don't understand why we don't do this now, Inspector," Mike said. "We have confirmation that the man is at the Ziva."

"Mr. McClintock, the FBI has its way of doing things, as does the PFM. I need to get this operation cleared with my superiors before we go. It won't be long. Nothing is going to happen between now and when the equipment arrives, I assure you."

"If something does happen, Guzman, it's on your head," Jason interjected.

"Mr. McClintock, I don't like your tone. Remember, you are guests here. If you want this man, you need my help. If I decline to help, you won't get him, and I will have you on the next plane out of Mexico. So if I were you, I'd tread lightly. Do I make myself clear?"

"Perfectly, but if we don't act the minute that equipment hits his suite, we'll take care of this business our way," Jason responded as he got out of the car and slammed the door behind him.

****

The lights were off in Mohammed's apartment. Petronovich looked both ways before taking his lock picks out of his pocket and quietly unlocking the door. Stepping into the threshold, he could see the bedroom light emanating into the hall. Petronovich drew his gun and stepped toward the open door. The shock was immediate as Mohammed looked up from his book and saw the Russian standing in the doorway.

"Do not make a sound. If you do, you'll be dead in an instant, just like your colleague," Petronovich whispered. "We can do this the easy way or the hard way. The easy way is I ask a question and you answer. You've already experienced the hard way. Which is it?" he asked.

Mohammed softly spoke, "The easy way."

"Smart decision, Mohammed. We'll begin where Al-Hamaidi left off. I know you plan to attack the United States using the DC-10 and Qasim as the pilot. What kind of attack are you planning and when will it take place?"

Mohammed hesitated, but began talking as Petronovich leveled the weapon at him. "The plan is to attack a major city. Only Qasim knows which one," Mohammed lied, hoping the Russian would believe him.

"Is the aircraft equipped with a nuclear device?" Petronovich asked, growing impatient.

Mohammed saw the look in Petronovich's eyes and knew he had to tell the truth, at least partially, "No, no nuclear device."

"Then what?"

"Sarin. We made sarin crystals. They were placed in the tanks of the DC-10. Water was added to dissolve them."

"That's why you had the industrial equipment," Vladi said.

"Yes."

"So, the liquid is released into the atmosphere over a

populated area and as the water evaporates, the sarin crystals are dispersed. Anyone breathing the substance dies."

"Essentially, yes," Mohammed said, his voice shaking.

"Was this the plan of the Saudi royal family?"

"One member, Saleh Shamoun, the King's cousin."

Petronovich knew the terrorist was telling the truth, at least about the aircraft's payload. "When is this attack supposed to happen?"

"Qasim is responsible for the attack. Shamoun left the timing to him since he is flying the plane."

Petronovich took a step forward, the gun pointed at Mohammed's head, "Now you will tell me where the attack is to take place."

"I've told you the truth, please let me live," Mohammed pleaded.

"Answer my question. Where?" demanded Petronovich.

"Allah, be with me, I do not know, I swear!"

"Fuck your Allah, you can join him in Hell," whispered Petronovich as the "pfft" of the bullet exiting the suppressor filled the quiet room. Mohammed's lifeless eyes stared at Vladi as he holstered the weapon and left the room.

****

In his apartment, Petronovich would have liked a stiff vodka. Instead, he opted for a cigar as he dialed Jason. It was nine thirty p.m. in Saudi Arabia, twelve thirty in Cabo, and two thirty p.m. on the east coast as Jason's phone buzzed. "Vladi, what's going on?" he asked.

"Jason, listen to me. I have neutralized the two AdvanChem scientists. The information I have is that Qasim's

DC-10 is loaded with sarin crystals that have been dissolved in water. He plans to drop the load over a major population center. He's got to be stopped before it happens."

"Do you know who's behind this?" Jason asked.

"A cousin of the Saudi king. His name is Saleh Shamoun. I don't think any other members of the royal family are involved. I'm going to use my contacts here to find Shamoun and put an end to this. Jason, do whatever it takes to stop Qasim. The attack could take place at any time."

"We know where he's located, but he doesn't have the ability to fly the plane yet. I'll contact the authorities and let them know what we suspect the cargo is," Jason responded. "We'll be in touch."

Chapter 20

Shamoun sat on the deck of the bungalow next to his private pool and half-naked secretary, who was basking on a chaise lounge in the sun. He was anxious about the mission. If the attack had occurred, it would have been all over the news, so it was obvious that it hadn't. The question was why? He dialed Mohammed without success, then Al-Hamaidi with the same result. The next call he made was to his office. He demanded that one of his security detail personnel physically check on the two scientists to be sure they were still in town.

At 6'2" and 270 pounds, the security guard was larger than life. In a suit and dark glasses, he approached Al-Hamaidi's apartment and tapped on the door. After waiting a moment, he rang the doorbell and knocked more forcefully. Getting no response, he turned the door handle and the door swung open. With his hand inside his coat on the handle of his weapon, he entered. Nothing in the small family room or kitchen seemed disturbed as he walked toward the hallway and bedroom. The bed didn't look as though it had been slept in as he approached the master bath. Turning the corner, he gasped and stopped. The sight was one he had never seen. A kitchen chair lay on its side next to the tub. Al-Hamaidi's legs hung over the side of the tub while his torso and arms were splayed out inside, exposing half a skull, grey matter, and blood. His eyes were open and he appeared to be in shock. The bodyguard opened the toilet lid and threw up what remained of the lunch he'd had several hours earlier. His concern now was Mohammed.

The bodyguard had his gun ready. He didn't bother to knock and opened Mohammed's unlocked door, stepping quickly inside. The family room was empty, but the bedroom was a mess. Mohammed had a book by his side and he sat on the sofa, staring with lifeless eyes at the ceiling. The pool of blood coagulated around his head. The guard shook his head, locked the front door, and made his way back to the office. He had an unpleasant call to make to Shamoun.

In a private office, away from staff, he dialed. "What did you find?" Shamoun asked.

"Both men have been executed. It was a professional hit," said the guard.

The silence on the other end seemed to last for minutes. Finally, Shamoun responded, "We've been compromised. Send the staff home until further notice. Keep the security detail in place on high alert. I'll be in touch."

****

Kamarov was at his desk when his phone buzzed. Recognizing the cell number, he answered, "I trust you were as successful with your current targets, as you've been in the past working for Mother Russia?"

"I'd like to discuss this with you on Russian soil. Can we meet at your office in the embassy for a glass or two of vodka?" Vladi asked. "I don't suppose you have Ciroc X?"

"Grey Goose will have to do," Kamarov said. "I already have it on ice. It'll be ready when you arrive."

****

Kamarov handed Petronovich a tumbler filled to the brim with the clear, ice-cold liquid. He sat next to Vladi and raised his glass, "Na Zdorovie! Now tell me about your mission!"

"Both jihadists were terminated. That is why we must talk. There is one more that needs to die. In fact, the most important one and you know who that is, my friend."

"Vladi, I told you that Russia could not be involved in what you are about to do. I have helped you too much as it is, and you know it," Kamarov explained. "To kill two unknown scientists is one thing, but to kill a Saudi Prince is something else entirely."

"Ivan, if these dogs will do this to the U.S., don't you think they would do the same at some point to our country? I'm not asking you for anything but Shamoun's location. Where is he?" Vladi drained his glass and held it up for more.

Kamarov rose from the chair and walked to the bar. He stood for a moment as if in thought, then grasped the bottle of Grey Goose, brought it over to Petronovich, and poured. "All right, Vladi. I will help you one more time, no more. Do you understand?"

"I do, and I am grateful, Ivan."

"Good, that's settled. We watch many of the royal family as you know and have recently placed Shamoun under surveillance because of his involvement with Al-Hamaidi and Mohammed. I will get his location and call you. In the meantime, drink up! You don't have many opportunities to enjoy this beverage while in Saudi Arabia."

"You are absolutely correct, my friend," Petronovich said

as he sipped, relaxing in a thoughtful mood. "Let me ask you a question, Ivan."

"Go ahead."

"Do you remember when Reagan gave the speech at the wall in Berlin?"

"Yes, it was June of 1987, I believe. You and I were covertly working in Western Berlin. Why?"

"When I heard that speech, I knew it was only a matter of time before the wall would come down and the Soviet Union as we knew it would come apart."

"I remember having that conversation. It was the furthest thing from my mind. I thought you were crazy until it happened. I will never forget your prophesy," Kamarov said.

"When we were approached in 1989, after the fall of the wall, why didn't you accept the offer?" Vladi asked.

"Vladi, we were 25 years old. George Bush was head of the CIA when he began to recruit. Our circumstances were different. I had family and friends that I couldn't leave. My parents needed my help and support. You, on the other hand, had no siblings and your parents had recently passed. I have never begrudged the decision you made in accepting the offer to go to the United States. You know that, right?"

"Of course, I do, Ivan. I'm fortunate to be able to call you as a friend after all these years," replied Vladi, as he reached for the bottle to top off his drink. "Can you believe that it has been 32 years since I made that move?"

****

Shamoun paced the length of the suite and back again, trying to digest what he'd been told. *How could anyone know about the two scientists from America?* he thought. *They were placed under supervision immediately!* Shamoun was afraid. If what he had done became known and was tied to the royal family, he would be killed. He stopped pacing when his phone buzzed. It was Antar. "Do you have the suitcase?" he asked.

"I do," Antar replied.

"You will notice the case has a combination lock. Write this down. The numbers left to right are 01399358. I repeat 01399358. This will activate the device."

"What kind of device?" Antar asked.

"Let's just say once activated, you will have 30 minutes to get as far away as possible, at least five miles and not downwind. Do you understand what I have said?"

"I do. What do you want me to do with it?"

"Today is Friday. On Monday at about noon, I want you to take the suitcase to One Wilshire Boulevard at Wilshire and Grand. Place it in the lobby where it won't be noticed. Activate the device and leave the area. There will be buses coming and going and should allow you ample time to get away."

"I am not comfortable with the short window of time I have to leave. If Allah wills it though, I will survive. If not, I will die knowing I did the right thing fighting the Great Satan."

"You are a true and faithful warrior," Shamoun replied, "Allah Akbar."

****

It had been a long night. Petronovich and Kamarov reminisced about their experiences in the old KGB for hours. After finishing the bottle of Grey Goose, they both stumbled out of the embassy into waiting cabs, ready to shuttle them home.

Petronovich hadn't had that much to drink in years and he knew he was going to pay the price in the morning. He dropped his clothes on the floor and tumbled into bed, out cold before his head hit the pillow.

He dreamt someone was buzzing his door. The sound wouldn't stop. Finally, Vladi stirred and turned toward the nightstand. With one eye barely open, he saw his phone lit up and buzzing. He grabbed the device and whispered, "Hello?"

"Vladi, are you awake?" Kamarov asked, sounding as chipper and alive as a kid in his thirties.

"Ivan, what did you do to me?"

"You're a grown man, Vladimir, I did nothing but provide you with a little of the best vodka this world has to offer in this Godforsaken teetotalling country. Wake up! Get a pen and paper. I have the information you requested."

"Give me a minute, I'm putting the phone down," Petronovich said as he slowly rose from bed, holding his hand to his throbbing forehead. With pen and paper, he sat back down, prepared to write the information down. "Go ahead."

"Shamoun is in the Maldives on Dhigu Island. He's staying at the Anantara Dhigu Maldives Resort. He normally travels with two, sometimes three armed security personnel, so be forewarned. We have a contact that will help you with supplies you may need. He owns and operates the Trident Dive Shop on the island. His name is Vasily Volkov. He will be expecting you. When do you plan on leaving, Vladi?"

"I'll try to get the next plane out and plan on staying at the same resort. Thanks for your help, Ivan. I hope the supplies you mentioned include a 9 mm?" Petronovich asked.

"I'm certain it does, Vladi, be safe," Kamarov said and hung up.

Chapter 21

Petronovich exited the Emirates flight and passed quickly through customs. Having only one carry-on, he proceeded to the water taxi that would take him from Malé International and the island of Hulhule to Dhigu Island and the Antanara Resort. He could have waited for the resort's own transportation, but then he would have had to wait for other passengers. He was in a hurry so he opted for the private boat. The young man in charge of the vessel looked to be in his late twenties and was more talkative than Petronovich would have liked.

"How was your flight?" asked the boat captain.

"Fine, thank you," Petronovich replied.

"You're in luck. The monsoons aren't scheduled to hit for another couple of weeks."

"That's good."

"How long are you here for?"

Realizing he was not going to get out of this conversation, Vladi ignored the question and asked his own. "Do you know the Trident Dive Shop?"

"Of course, everyone who loves the water and that's most people here, know the dive shop. It operates out of the marina where we dock. If you like, I can show you where it is located, once we arrive."

"That would be great, thank you," Vladi replied as he looked off into the distance hoping to see Dhigu Island and further praying the roar of the engine would stifle the conversation.

A half hour later, the young captain offered his hand to Petronovich after he'd tied the speed boat to the pier. He helped the Russian onto the dock, then pointed, "The dive shop you are looking for is at the end of the pier."

Petronovich peeled off cash for the fare plus a hefty tip for the assistance. "I appreciate your help. Here's a little extra for a beer after work," he said.

"Thank you, sir, but a soda will do. We are a Muslim country and do not drink alcohol." Looking at the wad of cash he said, "You are very generous." He pocketed the money, then waited while another fare boarded the boat for the trip back to the airport.

Petronovich hefted his carry-on over his shoulder and made his way up the pier toward the dive shop. In the distance, he could see a group of young women in bathing suits sitting at a picnic table with a man, probably in his early forties, with long blonde hair and a dark tan. They were laughing and animated in their discussion. *That guy looks like he belongs on the beach in Dana Point*, Petronovich thought. As Vladi approached, the conversation died down and the laughter stopped.

The man at the table looked up. "Would you like to rent dive gear?" he asked. His accent was thick, obviously Russian.

"No. A friend asked me to look up Vasily Volkov," Vladi said. "Would you know where I might be able to find him?"

"Girls, it's time for me to get back to work, let's talk later tonight," the man said. With that, the group got up and left the dock.

"I am Vasily, who sent you?" he asked, not standing or

offering his hand.

"Ivan Kamarov suggested you would be able to assist me in securing supplies."

"Ah, yes. You must be Petronovich," Volkov replied, standing and walking past Vladi toward the shop. "Come with me."

Vasily led Petronovich through the shop to the back office. After closing and locking the door, he pointed to a chair, "Have a seat."

Petronovich set his bag down next to the chair and sat. He watched as Vasily opened a closet door and pulled out a canvas bag. "This is for you," he said as he handed the rucksack to Vladi. Vladi took the bag and opened it.

"I took the liberty of including items I thought might be helpful. Inside, you will find a set of lock picks, nylon cord, duct tape, latex gloves, 9 mm hollow points, a suppressor, and Glock 17."

Petronovich pulled out the final item in the bag, a quart bottle of vodka. "Oh, yes," Vasily said. "The vodka. The resorts here sell alcohol to their guests, but at a premium. I thought you might like it."

"You've thought of everything," Vladi said. "How much do I owe you?"

"Nothing," he said, waving off the question. "Ivan told me to tell you it's on the house. Where are you staying?" he asked.

"At the Anantara Dhigu."

"Very nice. You can walk from here. It's maybe a quarter of a mile, if that. If you need anything else, you know where to find me. I hope you are successful with whatever you are doing." Vasily opened the door for Petronovich.

"Thank you, Vasily. I shouldn't need to trouble you

again," Petronovich said, as he walked out of the shop.

****

Petronovich checked into the resort and was escorted to a beach-front room steps from the lagoon. After unpacking what little he had and storing his weapon in the room's safe, he decided to stroll the grounds. If Shamoun had security with him as Kamarov suggested he would, his location should be relatively easy to spot. Vladi was certain the prince would be in one of the over-water bungalows. Approaching them on the walkway without being noticed was impossible. However, swimming in and around the suites while snorkeling was doable, and something many of the vacationers did.

After purchasing swim trunks at the gift shop, Vladi headed to the activity shack on the beach. Donning a mask, snorkel, and fins, he headed out for the reef. The fish were abundant and colorful. For a brief moment, Petronovich was mesmerized and spent some time taking in the sheer beauty beneath the crystal clear waters. He slowly made his way to the pylons rising in a long row from the ocean floor. He approached the over-water bungalows.

As he neared, he noted one set that jutted farther out into the lagoon, set apart from the others by a significant distance. *I'd bet anything that's a VIP accommodation,* Petronovich thought. He surfaced briefly to get a better look and saw that he was at the rear of the unit. He swam around the side until he could see the entrance. A man in slacks, a white shirt, a jacket, and sunglasses sat in a chair next to the door. *Bingo*! he thought. To confirm, Petronovich swam out past the unit, hoping to get a look at the suite's back deck and anyone who might be there. The deck faced the lagoon with the open ocean in the distance. So as not to appear obvious, he swam out and away from the unit, positioning himself about 150 yards from the suite. When he looked up, he determined that he was far enough away not to attract attention but close enough to see two people, one male and one female, lounging in the sun. The man had an obvious Arabic look and from the photos Kamarov had shared, was most likely his target. *Time to head back to shore,* Petronovich thought.

****

The guard noticed the man snorkeling. After the swimmer moved on, he entered the suite and made his way towards the back deck. With binoculars from inside the unit, he followed the snorkeler. The guard was relieved when he saw him swimming away. However, his relief was short-lived when the man stopped and turned around to stare at the deck. The hair on the guard's neck rose as he realized the prince was being watched. "Your Highness, we must talk," he whispered out the sliding glass door.

The prince turned. "What do you need, Wasem?"

"Please come inside," the guard asked.

The prince set his drink on the table and walked into the unit. "Yes?"

"I believe we are being watched. A swimmer has been paying far too much attention to this villa. I'm going to follow him and try to determine his identity. After what just happened in Riyadh with the scientists, we cannot take any chances. Botros and Najjar will remain with you here."

"Very good, Wasem, go," Shamoun replied.

Wasem moved quickly down the walkway, keeping an eye on Petronovich as he swam slowly to shore. The guard stayed well off the beach, being careful not to be noticed, even though his jacket in the temperature and humidity made him conspicuous. But this was the only way to conceal his weapon.

Petronovich sloshed out of the surf carrying his flippers in one hand and the mask and snorkel in the other. The activity shack was only twenty yards away. He set the gear on the counter and the attendant looked up and smiled. "How was the water?"

"Very nice. My name is Petronovich, room 122."

"Yes, Mr. Petronovich, have a nice evening," she said as she crossed off Vladi's name, noting that he had returned the snorkeling equipment.

"Thank you," replied Petronovich as he turned toward the pathway back to his room.

Wasem saw the swimmer had finished his business at the activity shack. He stepped into one of the many restaurants lining the beach and waited out of sight until Petronovich passed, then walked to the shack. The attendant looked up just as Wasem placed 1,545 Maldivian Ryfiyaa (the equivalent of $100 USD) on the counter. "Tell me the name and room number of the man who just dropped off the mask and snorkel," he said.

The attendant took the money and turned the sheet toward Wasem. Without saying a word, she pointed at the name that had been crossed out. Wasem snapped a picture with his phone and left.

****

After taking a quick shower and changing, Petronovich went down to the palapa beach bar. He selected a corner table and sat in the chair with his back to one of the three walls. The fourth side was open to the beach. From where he sat, he could see the water and he watched as the sun began to set. Young men in slacks and white coats lit tiki torches up and down the various pathways. The resort was almost mystical in its serenity. Soft background music played and combined with the hum of conversation. No one seemed eager to disturb the ambiance.

A young waitress, wearing a red and white flower-patterned dress stopped by his table as he scanned the horizon. "Beautiful, isn't it?" she asked.

Petronovich startled, looked up. "Yes, stunning," he said.

"I'm sorry I surprised you, can I get you something to drink?" asked the young brunette.

"Yes, I'd like a double Grey Goose, rocks, and what might you suggest for an appetizer?"

The waitress thought for a moment. "I think you might like our Bis Keemiya. It's like a spring roll but pastry filled with tuna, hard-boiled egg, onion, and sautéed, shredded cabbage. How does that sound?"

"Fantastic, let's do it," Petronovich said, his mouth watering at the thought.

She smiled, "I'll be right back with your drink."

Petronovich watched as she moved gracefully away, her dress swaying with the breeze. *I could enjoy this place if I didn't have a job to do,* he thought. *How do I get Shamoun?*

From a distance, Wasem and Najjar, one of the other guards, kept watch on Petronovich. They planned to follow him to his room to try to determine why he was so interested in the prince. Both men were skilled in security and willing to die for the royal family.

Petronovich finished his first drink and halfway through the appetizer, which was large enough to be dinner, ordered a second. The sun had set, and the stars were beginning to light up the sky. Vladi finished his second drink, paid the bill leaving a generous tip, and began to make his way back to his beach-front room. Though the path was lit, it was still dark. Wasem and his partner followed far enough away so as not to be noticed. Pertronovich had no idea he was being followed. Every room had its own private walkway that branched off the main path. A short, three-foot high post with illuminated white numbers identified each unit. Vladi passed 121, the unit before his own. The jungle foliage on either side of the walkway was thick. When Petronovich turned toward his room, Wasem and his partner moved quickly to cover the distance between them and their target. The Arabs were no less than three feet away when two soft "pffts" were heard. Even though the noise was very quiet, Petronivich heard it and knew instinctively what it was. He dropped to the ground and watched as one of the men fell. The other, though hit, swung around, raising his weapon to fire as a third "pfft" rang out and he collapsed. One small crimson hole appeared in the forehead of the first dead guard, while the second sported two in his torso. Petronovich waited, listening for movement. Finally, out of the thick jungle, Vasily Volkov emerged.

"Quickly, help me," Vasily whispered. They couldn't be seen from the main walkway, but they had to hide the bodies.

"What have you done?" Petronovich asked.

"Look at their hands. They were ready to kill you. You need to brush up on your skills. Now, help me move these two thugs into the brush."

Petronovich took the legs of one of the men, while Vasiliy dragged the other. They would be hidden for the night, but once morning light came, the flies, insects, and jungle land crabs would give away the location of the bodies.

"Come inside, Vasily," Petronovich said as he unlocked the door and stepped into his room, holding it open for the Russian.

"Petronovich, whatever you are doing, you need to get it done tonight. You must be off the island before morning. I can take you to Malé by boat where you can catch a plane. I was told not to get involved, but I think that ship has sailed. Now, what do you want me to do?"

Vladi took two tumblers from the bar and poured the vodka. "Have a seat. Why were you out there?" he asked as he handed one glass to Volkov.

"Kamarov asked me to keep an eye on you. When I realized you were being watched, then followed, I couldn't let them out of my sight. When they pulled their guns and ran towards you, I had no choice but to shoot. Good thing for you, I think," Volkov said with a smile, raising his glass. "Na Zdorovie."

****

Antar sat on the bed in his room at the Motel 6 in Anaheim. It was twelve thirty and the fog was just beginning to clear. He stared at the suitcase he had picked up at the embassy; it sat on the floor next to the three-drawer dresser. The room was sparsely decorated. Though it was chilly outside, Antar had turned the air conditioner to high, but he was still sweating.

Finally, he phoned Shamoun. After two rings, the prince answered, "Is everything all right?" he asked.

"I'm not sure I can activate the device," Antar said.

Silence lingered on the other end. Finally, Shamoun said, "This is the moment you have been waiting for all of your life. The souls that have been martyred before you in paradise have eyes upon you and will help you through. You know you can do this, Antar."

Antar lowered his eyes, took a deep breath, and agreed, "Yes, you are right. I only needed to hear that what I am about to do is Allah's will. I will not bother you again."

The line went dead. Shamoun placed the phone next to the table on the back deck. *Wasem and Najjar should be back soon,* he thought.

****

At the Russian Embassy in Riyadh, the analyst recorded the conversation. After listening to it twice, he decided to call Kamarov and let him know what he'd heard. Kamarov was awake and at his desk when he took the call. "You said there was reference to a device being activated?" he asked.

"Yes, sir. The subject's name is Antar, and he seemed very agitated, at least initially."

"Do you have this Antar's location?" Kamarov asked.

"He is in California."

"We must determine what kind of device he means to activate," Kamarov said. "I have some calls to make. Thank you for the information. I'll be back in the office in a few hours." Kamarov thought for a moment. *The two scientists were from Southern California as well. There is no such thing as a coincidence like this. Antar is part of the equation involving Shamoun. Time to call Petronovich.*

****

Vladi's phone buzzed. "Ivan," he answered. "Why are you calling so late? Is everything okay?"

Kamarov told Vladi what he'd learned. "Vladi, this guy, Antar, didn't mention the type of device to be activated, or when it will occur. Shamoun will have the details. It is vital you get this information from him."

"We were just leaving to pay Shamoun a visit."

"Who is we?"

"Your friend Vasily saved my life tonight. It's a long story, I will tell you about it later. But suffice to say he is all in at this point. Thank you for posting him as a look out."

"I had hoped he wouldn't be necessary, but he has the skill and youth to be of help. I'm glad he is there. I will let you go. Call as soon as you learn about the device."

Petronovich and Volkov slipped into the water off the pier next to the dive shop with mask, fins, and scuba tank. Each carried a small submersible dry bag with tools, including a handgun with suppressor. Volkov's training in the GRU left Petronovich with the feeling that he could trust the man, especially after what he had done to save his life a few hours earlier. According to Volkov, with two guards down, there was only one left, plus the secretary and Shamoun. They had decided to try and keep the secretary alive. However, if she should see them, that changed things. It was a moonless night and the swim was short. There was a water ladder positioned on each side of the over-water deck. Petrononvich swam to the far side. Volkov waited for Vladi to flash his light under the water twice before withdrawing his weapon from the pack and ascending the ladder. Both men were quiet, but quick. The lights in the unit were off. They assumed the remaining guard was in front waiting for the other men to return.

Volkov put a finger to his lips, withdrew his knife, and moved through the living room to the front door. He opened it slightly to find the guard in a chair next to the door, his head slumped over and his chin resting on his chest. Volkov doused the exterior light, then grabbed the guard by the chin and in one motion, lifted him out of the chair and attempted to slit his carotid artery. The guard struggled briefly, then, his eyes wide open, he realized he was about to die as the knife slid swiftly across his neck. Volkov dragged the body inside and dropped him by the front door. Petronovich remained by what they assumed was the door to the master bedroom. Before leaving the dive shop, they had decided that Volkov would neutralize the secretary and Petronovich would subdue Shamoun. Vladi wanted the terrorist to himself.

The men stood on either side of the closed doorway. Vladi, using his fingers, gave the signal one, two, three, then nodded and opened the door. Volkov stepped in first, grabbed a pillow and placed it quickly over the secretary's face. She couldn't see or breathe. Petronovich lifted Shamoun by his hair and gave him two quick punches to the face, knocking him unconscious. Volkov took long strips of duct tape and secured them over the secretary's eyes and mouth. He carried her to a side chair in the dining room and taped her securely to it, her legs and arms bound tightly. He returned to the bedroom to find Shamoun with his arms and legs splayed out wide and secured to the bed posts with rope. As the man came to, he started to scream when Petronovich hit him again. This time, he remained conscious.

"I'm going to ask you a question and you will answer me," Vladi said. "You will die tonight; that's a fact. How you die will be up to you. It can be quick or very slow and painful. Now," he said, making sure that Shamoun was paying attention, "you received a call tonight from a man named Antar. He has a device he is going to activate. What kind of device is it? Where is it? And when is he going to activate it?" Petronovich watched the man's expression. It was obvious he was surprised.

"I don't know what you are talking about!" he slurred, through the blood dripping from his swelling lips.

Petronovich didn't hesitate. He raised the gun and with a "pfft," placed a bullet into the terrorist's left foot. The man screamed. "I'll ask you one more time: what kind of device, when, and where?"

Shamoun shook his head, tears running down his face. "Pfft," the suppressed shot from the 9 mm hit the top of the other foot. Volkov had placed duct tape over the man's mouth to hold back the scream. Shamoun shook his head. Volkov lifted the tape.

"He has a suitcase bomb, uranium-233," Shamoun said. "He is placing it in the lobby at One Wilshire Boulevard in Los Angeles on Monday." He closed his eyes, knowing what was coming.

Petronovich didn't hesitate. He placed the 9 mm hollow point between the terrorist's two closed eyes. It was time to go.

****

Before leaving his unit, Vladi packed his carry-on bag, bringing it with him to the dive shop, anticipating a quick exit. They had left the squirming secretary tied to the chair with duct tape over her mouth and eyes. She was innocent; there was no need to kill her. Housekeeping would find her and the other two soon enough.

After a quick change of clothes, Volkov and Petronovich boarded one of several power boats used for diving and motored slowly out of the atoll into open ocean. As they increased speed, Vladi called Jason, hoping he would be able to connect before losing his signal. It was two thirty in the morning in the Maldives, five thirty in the afternoon in San Jose del Cabo. Mike was checking his emails while Jason paced the room. Jason's cell buzzed. He answered immediately, "Vladi, glad you called, where are you?"

"On my way to the Malé airport. We may lose our signal, but if I do, I'll call as soon as I get one. Jason, a nuclear device in a suitcase is going to be placed in the lobby at One Wilshire Boulevard by the assassin on Monday. His name is Antar."

"How do you know this?" Jason asked.

"Shamoun told me before I killed him. He had no reason to lie, Jason. Kamarov's people have been monitoring his calls and they taped a call from Antar to Shamoun this evening. He's detonating the bomb on Monday."

"What happened to Mohammed and Al-Hamaidi?" Jason asked.

"They've been dispatched. Did you stop Qasim?"

"Not yet. The PFM won't act until they have evidence that Qasim is planning an attack. They want to wait until the equipment he ordered to fly the aircraft arrives at his suite. I thought the sarin was our primary concern! Now we have this to deal with. We need to contact Schumacher." The line went dead.

****

Mike put his phone on speaker and dialed Schumacher's cell. "What do you have, Mike?" Schumacher asked.

"Jack, we just got off the phone with Petronovich. We're facing a Threat Level 2 involving a WMD in Southern California."

"Are you certain this is a credible threat? What are you basing this assessment on?" asked Schumacher. Mike told Schumacher everything Petronovich had said.

"Where are you?" followed Schumacher.

"Still in San Jose. We may be here a couple more days. The bomb issue is going to be yours to deal with. Petronovich is on his way back from the Maldives. He should be in L.A. late tomorrow afternoon."

"Good. Have Petronovich call me as soon as he gets in. His sources may be able to track this guy."

Chapter 22

Volkov eased the boat into the marina near Malé International Airport. The runway lights could be seen from the boat slip. Sunrise was about two hours away and the terminal would most likely be empty. Petronovich shook Volkov's hand, "Thank you for all you've done, Vasiliy. I hope we meet again under more relaxed circumstances."

"The pleasure was mine. I was getting a little bored hanging out at the dive shop. This got me back into the game, even if it was only for an evening. I'm certain Dhigu Island will be buzzing with excitement once the bodies are found. You must be on an airplane and out of the Maldives before sunrise. Understand, brother?"

"I'll be safe, take care," Petronovich said as he walked away from the dock toward the terminal. The streets were empty and the walk would only take 10 minutes.

Inside the terminal, he found a seat and accessed his travel app. He wanted to book the first flight out which was a Sri Lankan Air flight to Singapore then on to LAX. The flight would be a little out of the way and would take 24 hours, but it was better than going back to the U.S. through Riyadh. The further away he was from the Middle East, the better. The flight left at eight a.m. Housekeeping wouldn't be bothering patrons until nine or ten, if that, especially with a "do not disturb" sign hanging from the room door.

With his flight reservation made, Petronovich phoned Jason who was sitting at the small table in his hotel room when his cell buzzed. "It's Vladi again," he said to Mike.

"Good, put him on speaker," Mike said, as he sat on the edge of the bed.

"Vladi, Mike is here with me. I want to conference in Agent Jack Schumacher. He has some questions regarding the bomb. Give him as much detail as you can," Jason said as he placed his cell phone in the middle of the desk and called Schumacher.

Schumacher answered immediately. "Mr. Petronovich," he said, "where are you?"

"Malé International. I'm leaving in 90 minutes for Singapore, then LAX," Petronovich replied.

"How did you learn about the nuclear device?"

"I have contacts in the GRU that informed me of a bomb. They taped a conversation between one of the Saudi family members, Prince Shamoun, and a man in Southern California named Antar. The conversation didn't reveal the type of bomb. I secured that information directly from Shamoun about two hours ago. It's a suitcase bomb containing Uranium-233."

"Can you allow us access to the taped conversation?"

"Given the seriousness of the situation, I can probably arrange some sort of accommodation. The Russian government will probably not want to be involved directly, but my contact knows Jason. He could be the conduit."

"That will work. Put your contact in touch with McClintock immediately. Do you know if they are able to track Antar through his cell phone?"

"I don't know. But I'll call him right now and have him call Jason. You can determine how best to handle the situation," Petronovich said as he cut the call short and dialed Kamarov.

Kamarov answered, "Fill me in, Vladi."

"The bomb is nuclear. It's uranium-233 in a suitcase. They plan on detonating it in a high-rise office building on one of the busiest streets in Los Angeles. The FBI needs your help. Jason can act as an intermediary if you don't want to be directly involved."

"I spoke with headquarters, and given our tenuous position in Saudi Arabia, we cannot be seen helping the U.S. directly. Our surveillance methods and intel networks could be compromised and that cannot happen. I'll work through McClintock," Kamarov replied.

Petronovich gave the Russian McClintock's contact information, "Call or text Jason as soon as you can, Ivan. He's waiting, and so is the FBI. Good luck, I'll phone when I land."

****

Twenty minutes after Mike hung up with Schumacher, Jason's cell buzzed. "It's out of country," he said looking at Mike. "This is McClintock."

"Jason, Ivan Kamarov here. I want to help you as much as possible without being directly involved."

"Thank you for your call, Ivan. Can I put you on speaker?" asked Jason as he motioned to Mike.

"Yes, by all means," replied Kamarov.

"Ivan Kamarov, I'd like to introduce you to my brother, Mike, formerly of the FBI."

"Mr. Kamarov, we understand through Vladimir Petronovich that you intercepted a call between Prince

Shamoun and somebody by the name of Antar, is that correct?" asked Mike.

Kamarov reiterated what he knew, ending with, "They plan to detonate the device around noon, placing it in the building's lobby."

"Yes, we just heard that. Do you have the ability to track this Antar and provide his current location?" Mike asked.

"Yes, I believe we can pinpoint his location through his cell phone," said Kamarov.

"He's got to be in the Los Angeles area. That gives us only 48 hours to find him and the device. We must get him before he's able to activate the bomb. Mr. Kamarov, we need you to identify his location immediately. Our government owes you a tremendous debt for the help you have given us."

"I'll do what I can and I'll speak with you soon," Kamarov said as the line went dead.

****

It was five thirty in the evening and Antar felt the motel walls close in on him. He decided to go for a drive. He had missed the Jummah, which was the day of gathering every Friday, a little after noon, but he could make the Isha, or nightly prayer if he could find a mosque nearby. Before leaving the motel room, he searched for the closest mosque. It was the Islamic Center of Anaheim on Brookhurst, five to ten minutes away, depending on traffic. He felt he needed to pray, and Allah was his strength.

****

Schumacher was finishing the call with the head of the energy department when he asked, "If this suitcase device blows at One Wilshire, what kind of damage can we expect?"

There was silence at the other end of the line as he waited for a reply. "Jack, One Wilshire is downtown L.A. in the business district. If that thing goes off, 90% of the population within a quarter mile radius of the blast will die immediately. 70% will perish within a half mile. The percentage goes down the further out you go. At lunch hour, we're talking hundreds of thousands of casualties. In addition to the deaths, serious injuries will be substantial, with everything from major lacerations caused by flying debris to broken bones and third-degree burns. Our medical facilities from San Francisco to San Diego will be overwhelmed. Many people that could have survived will die because of a lack of timely medical care. One more thing, Jack: One Wilshire is one of the top three telecommunications centers in the world. It's the most highly connected internet point in the Western U.S., with submarine communication cables allowing one third of the internet traffic from the U.S. to Asia to pass through the building. The internet would go down for a long time, impacting a good part of the world. I'm not that concerned about us or our kids having internet access on our iPads or laptops as much as I am with our military operations being compromised. You get the point. You've got to get this asshole."

"I get it. Have the bomb disposal unit here as soon as you can. We're going to need them," Schumacher replied, ready for the next call to DEST, the Domestic Emergency Support Team.

****

The sun was setting in the Santa Ynez Valley. Zach and Sam were in the back yard playing on the swing set while Julie stirred the sauce, waiting for the pasta water to boil. Brenda sat at the counter with a glass of Syrah, both she and Julie content and relieved that the drama of the past few weeks was finally coming to an end. Brenda looked down at her phone as it vibrated on the counter. "This is my Aunt Helen," she said. "I'll take it outside." Brenda walked out of the kitchen onto the front porch.

Fifteen minutes passed, and dinner was nearly ready. Julie poked her head around the corner, trying to see if Brenda was still on the call. She could see Brenda sitting on one of the porch chairs. She was leaning forward with her hands covering her face, rocking back and forth, sobbing.

Julie dropped the spoon on the counter and hurried outside, "Brenda, what happened?"

"My aunt has been trying to reach Dad," Brenda said through sobs, tears running down her cheeks. "He never answered, so she drove over to his place to check on him. He was murdered, Julie! Auntie said he was tortured first, then killed. That's how the killer knew we were at Roosevelt Lake! My dad told him. Oh my God, what have I done?" she whimpered.

Julie bent over Brenda, wrapping her in her arms, "Oh, Brenda, I'm so sorry."

****

Antar placed the skullcap on his head before exiting his car. As he approached the mosque, the main door opened, and he was greeted by a short imam. "Peace be unto you," the man said.

"Unto you, peace," Antar responded with a bow as he entered. The nightly prayer was about to start, and the room was half full with men. The women were in a separate location. Antar removed his shoes and walked around the communal rug to the other side of the room apart from the main body of worshipers. His dress and manners indicated that he was not American. This piqued the interest of one of the men in the room.

After the service, the man approached Antar. "Welcome, my friend. You are new to the area?" The man extended his hand.

"Yes, I'm passing through," Antar replied.

"May I introduce myself? My name is Fahad Obeid. And you are?"

"Omar Antar."

"If you have time, we have a community hall that is serving tea. We can sit for a bit and enjoy the refreshment," suggested Obeid.

Antar thought for a moment, considering the confines of his small motel room. He accepted the invitation. "Sure, thank you," he said.

The two men walked into the hall and with tea in hand, selected a table in the corner of the room. "So, what brings you to Southern California?" Obeid asked.

"Work," Antar responded without explanation.

"What kind of work is it that you do, if I might ask?"

Antar hesitated, "Odd jobs."

"From your accent I would guess you to be from Saudi Arabia. My family immigrated from there about ten years ago.

You are Sunni?" asked Obeid.

"Yes Sunni, from Riyadh. You are good," Antar said as he sipped the tea and wondered how long he was going to let the inquisition continue.

Obeid smiled. "I was a child when we moved. I miss the old country. I miss the community. It is difficult to fit in here, especially with a culture that is totally bereft of the tenets of Islam. The people have no dignity or shame. They truly are infidels."

Antar thought for a minute, "You believe this?"

"Of course! There is a group of us here that would give our lives to fight and bring justice to these infidels."

"How many?" Antar asked.

"We have a core group of five. Where is your allegiance?" Obeid asked, sensing he already knew the answer.

"My allegiance is and always will be to Allah. I work for him and him alone," said Antar.

Obeid stared at Antar, then put his cup of tea down and leaned forward. "I sense that you are in this country for reasons other than simply odd jobs. Am I right, my friend?"

"If I were to answer yes, how would you feel?" Antar responded, waiting.

"I believe that my small group would want to assist you in any way we can. That is how I feel," answered Obeid. "What is this odd job you are here to accomplish?"

At that moment, Antar realized that it might be beneficial to have some help. If he were being followed, though he had no reason to believe he was, this group could be instrumental in ensuring the success of the attack on Monday. "When can you get your group together?" Antar asked.

"They are here, across the room," Obeid answered as he

nodded in the direction of four men. Obeid motioned for them to join them.

****

Kamarov checked with the analyst who had intercepted the call. After accessing the specialized computer, the analyst was able to track and locate Antar. He gave the information to Kamarov, who immediately dialed Jason McClintock.

Jason answered after the first ring, "Ivan?"

"As of ten minutes ago, Antar was at 1136 N. Brookhurst, in the city of Anaheim. We will continue to monitor him. If he moves, I will call. You must get the FBI on this as quickly as possible." Kamarov hung up.

Jason dialed Schumacher who answered immediately, "I'm listening."

McClintock relayed the information he had been given. "How quickly can you act, Jack?"

"We can be there within a half hour. I've got to go."

"I'll call if Antar moves," Jason said before the line dropped.

****

Obeid introduced Antar to his team. He quickly forgot their names, focusing instead on how best to use them. After hearing that Antar was from Riyadh, one of the men asked, "Did you see the evening news? Prince Shamoun was found murdered at a resort in the Maldives."

Antar looked up, his jaw dropping in shock. It was as though he had been kicked in the gut. "Where did you get this information?" he asked.

"There was a short segment on the news tonight," responded the other man.

Realizing he may be in danger, Antar had to act, and quickly. He felt providence had brought these men to him. It was the will of Allah and he had no doubt that he trusted them. Antar looked around the table and spoke quietly, "I was working for Prince Shamoun. His death changes everything and I will need your help in completing the mission I was entrusted to perform. You must understand that if you choose to help, it may be dangerous."

"We are committed and willing to help however we can," Obeid said. The other men at the table nodded in agreement.

"I believe I may now be a target with the U.S. Government after me. I have a suitcase in my car I am going to leave in your possession. It is to be taken to One Wilshire Boulevard on Monday at noon and placed in the lobby of the building, out of the way, so as not to attract attention. I'll try to be with you." On a napkin, he wrote the combination to the lock and slid it across the table to Obeid. "If I'm not able to make it, before you set the suitcase in the lobby, activate the code. Do not, under any circumstance, try to open the case. Can you do this?"

"Is that all you ask? This will not be difficult," Obeid responded.

"It may not appear so, but it is most important," replied Antar. He looked at Obeid. "Walk with me to my car so that I might give you the suitcase," he said.

The two men walked outside together. It was a dark, moonless night. The parking lot was illuminated by several lights. Antar unlocked his car trunk and pulled out the bulky case. He handed it to Obeid. “Keep this safe. I must be going.”

“We will not let you down, Omar,” Obeid said. “What is in the suitcase?” he asked.

“If you must know, it is a bomb that will take down the office building,” Antar said, not being entirely truthful. “I must go. Keep the suitcase out of sight until Monday. I will meet you here on Monday morning at nine a.m. If I don’t show by nine fifteen, go without me and carry out the mission.”

Antar got into his car and drove back to the motel. He was relieved to be rid of the bomb and believed the assignment would be carried out as intended, with or without him. *Allah Akbar*!

****

Kamarov received the update from the analyst. He was told that the terrorist had moved and seemed to be stationary at an address in Anaheim. Kamarov dialed McClintock. He spoke with a sense of urgency, “Jason, Antar is no longer at the address I gave. He is at 100 West Disney Way, which is a Motel 6 across the street from the main gate of Disneyland. I’ll get off the line so you can call Schumacher.”

Jason didn’t hesitate. Schumacher was in route to the Brookhurst Street address when he received the call. After listening to Jason, he informed all units of the address change and ordered that the approach be silent, with all units parking off the motel property. Once onsite, he would determine Antar’s room number and only at that time would he approach the subject, the FBI SWAT team taking the lead.

It was close to eight p.m. when Schumacher entered the motel lobby. The young lady at the front desk looked up and smiled as he approached. "Hi, would you like a room?" she asked.

Schumacher held up his badge for her to see. "I'm looking for a specific individual and believe he's here," he said. He opened the pictures app on his phone and showed her a head shot of Antar. "Do you recognize this man?"

The clerk looked closely and responded, "Yes, he registered this afternoon. I believe I know the room, but let me check my records to be sure. I'll give you a passkey." The clerk studied her computer, tapped several keys, and responded, "He's in room 135, first floor, at the end."

"We're going to cordon off the area, don't leave the lobby," Schumacher said. "I'll let you know when it's safe to come out."

Outside the lobby and off to the side of the building, Schumacher consulted with the Special Agent in Charge of the SWAT team. It was imperative that the suspect be taken alive, a point he stressed with the SAC. Five minutes later, the SAC team moved into position.

****

Antar sat in the dark. The small table and chair were positioned next to the door. He had dozed off for maybe fifteen minutes, but he woke with a start when he realized there was no traffic noise coming from Disney Way, a street that was packed with cars most hours of the day. He got up abruptly and peered out the window, parting the curtains slightly. There were no cars in sight. The hair on the back of Antar's neck rose as he backed away from the window and door, grabbing the handgun off the nightstand. He faced the doorway, the gun raised as he backed slowly into the small bathroom. His instincts were normally accurate and right now, they were screaming for him to run, but he had nowhere to go. The next minute seemed to go by in slow motion. The window next to the door exploded as a flash bang grenade was hurled into the room, bouncing off the bed and exploding in mid-air. The sound was oppressive but was tempered slightly by the bathroom wall. Antar knew that within seconds, the door would open and he would face an overwhelming assault by the U.S. government. As the door opened, Antar raised the gun to his head, screamed "Allah Akbar!" and pulled the trigger.

Chapter 23

Petronovich rented a car and drove from LAX to the FBI offices in downtown L.A. Schumacher's office was empty except for the secretary who directed Vladi to the "war room" in the basement. Federal Agency personnel, from the WMD Coordinator to the Counterterrorism Division leader to State and local law enforcement were meeting to prepare for the worse case scenario. They were there to do whatever was necessary to apprehend the terrorists and prevent the nuclear device from detonating. Schumacher, surrounded by a dozen other people, looked up from the map of downtown Los Angeles on the table and saw Petronovich in the doorway. He motioned for Petronovich to follow him to a private office.

Once inside, Schumacher closed the door. "I don't have time to give you all the details, but the bottom line is that we don't have the bomb. Antar killed himself before we could get to him. We believe he was working with someone at the Islamic Center of Anaheim on Brookhurst. We questioned the imam, but he was uncooperative. We have only 24 hours before the device is supposed to be detonated and we're developing a plan to intercept anyone trying to plant the bomb. We have agents at One Wilshire and the surrounding buildings right now," Schumacher explained.

"The Islamic Center is the key," Petronovich said. "Can't you pressure them in some way?"

"We've done everything we can within the limits of the law. We have agents watching and able to follow the cleric if necessary, but so far, nothing has come up."

"Let me see what I can do," Petronovich said.

"Leave it to us, Petronovich," Schumacher said. "Let me be perfectly clear. You are unauthorized to interfere in this investigation in any way. Do you understand me?"

"Perfectly," replied Petronovich as he opened the door and walked out.

Schumacher watched as Vladi left the basement, taking the stairs two at a time. Schumacher dialed his phone, speaking to one of the agents assigned to follow Vladi, he said, "If Petronovich approaches the Islamic Center, do not apprehend him. I repeat, do not interfere with anything he does."

****

Even though it was late afternoon on a Sunday, packages were still being delivered. The delivery person carted them into the lobby where they were stacked near the concierge's desk. The concierge noticed the Zedasoft label and phoned Sarraf. There was no answer, so the concierge directed the bellhop to deliver the boxes to the suite. He dialed Guzman to inform him of the delivery.

Later that evening, when Qasim entered his suite, he saw the boxes in the living room area. He opened each one and began the assembly process. It went more quickly than it had the first time, but it still took longer than expected. He powered up the console and inserted the flash drive. The screens lit up as the program began to download. Qasim sat and watched as computer code breezed across the monitors. After twenty minutes, the system stopped humming and the DC-10 console appeared in shutdown mode. He was able to look out the cockpit windows, seeing nothing but a dark hangar. *Praise Allah, it worked,* thought Qasim as he shut down the system and made a call to the Victorville airport. After instructing the ground crew to have the plane gassed up and on the apron by five a.m., he sighed in relief and went to his bar for a drink. The moon was rising over the Sea of Cortez and he sat listening to the crash of the surf from his balcony. *Life is good,* thought Qasim, *soon I will make history.*

****

Petronovich entered the Islamic Center and noticed the office door to the right. Without knocking, he entered and closed the door behind him. The sound of the lock being engaged caused the imam to look up from his desk. Petronovich pulled a chair out and took a seat without being offered.

"I need information," he said. "And you will give it to me. If you don't do as I ask, I assure you, you will regret it." Petronovich spoke in an even tone, his eyes cold and hard.

The imam nodded but did not speak. He had never been more afraid for his life.

"You have a group of radicalized Muslims at this center," Petronovich said. "I want the names and contact information for every one of them. I don't care how many there are." He gestured to the cleric. "Now. I will wait."

The cleric rose from his desk and went to the file cabinet. He opened one drawer and rifled through several files, before pulling out a manila envelope and handing it to Petronovich. "This is what you want," he said. "There is one page for each individual. I've tried to provide pictures as well. The data, as far as I know, is current. I try to keep radical elements from spreading their hate, but I can't control their thoughts or actions. We are a peace-loving congregation."

Petronovich skimmed the list, "Except for these five."

"Yes, except for them," the imam replied.

"Why didn't you give this to the FBI?" Petronovich asked.

"I didn't want any trouble. I would have given it to them if a warrant had been presented. I gave it to you because you would have killed me otherwise."

"That's very astute," Peetronovich said. "Don't tell any of these men about our meeting." He stood.

"Never," the cleric said as Vladi heard the door close behind him.

****

The FBI agents had a clear view of Petronovich as he walked from the mosque to his car. One of the men phoned Schumacher, "Petronovich left the mosque carrying a large manila envelope."

"He's got something. Follow him, but be warned, he's a professional and will spot you if you're not careful."

Petronovich sat in his car and put the first address into his phone's GPS. After a twenty-minute drive, he found himself in front of a vacant lot in an industrial area. *So this is the way it's going to be,* he thought as he input the second address and drove away. Four hours later, Petronovich returned to the Islamic Center and parked one block away with a clear view of the main door and parking lot. Each of the four remaining addresses had been the same; a park, retail shopping center, skating rink, and marina. He had only the suspect's pictures to go by, so he prepared for a stake-out. On the front seat, all five photos were laid out along with his 144x Hammacher Schlemmer binoculars.

****

Qasim couldn't sleep. At four a.m. he was at his computer checking weather and filing a flight plan from the Victorville Airport to Reagan National, three miles from Washington D.C. By five a.m. he was pacing back and forth across the family room. After ordering coffee, he settled on the balcony and watched as the moonless night turned to dawn. The DC-10 would be ready to fly at five a.m. California time, seven local. Qasim was ready and anxious.

At six forty-five, he was at the console with his headset on, watching the ground crew as they secured the pushback tug to the aircraft and pulled it out of the hangar onto the tarmac. They disengaged the tug, moving it out of the way in preparation for engine startup. Qasim began the startup sequence sending compressed air to the engines and spinning the turbines before the igniters started firing. There was a light pop as a puff of smoke blew from the rear of the engines when fuel was added. Qasim increased the fuel flow, spinning the engines up, then bringing them back down in preparation for clearance to taxi. The tower delivered their instructions as Qasim moved the aircraft into position for takeoff. He was so engrossed in the details that he felt he was in the cockpit, second in line for takeoff, even though he was sitting at the RPA console in a suite at the Hyatt Ziva in San Jose del Cabo, Mexico.

Several minutes later, the large DC-10 shuddered as Qasim gave the aircraft maximum power, then released the brakes and hurtled down the runway. The plane took off, leaving Victorville behind. Qasim checked the time. It was seven fifteen. The estimated time to target was four hours and fifty minutes, placing them in the Washington D.C. area at 1.05 p.m., or eleven a.m. in Los Cabos.

****

Jason phoned Guzman at nine forty-five a.m. "The package has to have been delivered, Inspector. We are not waiting much longer. If you aren't ready to go within the hour, Mike and I will go alone."

Guzman listened to McClintock, then cut him off, "I have confirmation that the equipment was delivered. We will be leaving the precinct by ten. Be outside and ready, we'll be there about 10.10."

With the McClintocks, the three unmarked law enforcement vehicles raced through town toward the Zona Hotelera and the strip of luxury hotels lining the beach.

****

Petronovich watched through his binoculars as the cars pulled into the parking lot near the rear of the Islamic Center. The men congregated next to a car that was driven by a man who, according to the pictures, was Fahad Obeid. Obeid motioned the other four men to the back of the car where he opened the trunk and pointed at something within. Petronovich couldn't see what they saw. Obeid closed the trunk, looked at his watch, and said something.

While Petronovich was intent on observing the five Muslims, the FBI agents kept close watch on him. They saw the men pile into Obeid's car and knew that Petronovich would be on the move shortly.

****

The DC-10, inbound for DCA Reagan National, was 40 minutes out and beginning its descent into the Washington area. Qasim followed the vectors given by air traffic control. His plan was to veer off the flight path at the very last moment, then fly down Pennsylvania Avenue and drop the load. There would be no time for military aircraft to intercept and destroy the plane, given the elevation, glide slope, and proximity to the city. *I'm almost there,* Qasim thought as the plane slowly descended from 30,000 feet.

****

The three vans came to an abrupt stop, tires screeching in front of the stairs leading to the open-air lobby at the Hyatt Ziva. The men, their weapons ready, entered and waited while Guzman approached the manager. The manager led the men through the hotel grounds, past the bank of elevators to the stairs. The lobby was on level three, so they had only one flight to climb. Qasim's suite was three doors down from the stairwell. With the men ready and their guns raised, Guzman nodded at the manager. "Open it," he said.

****

Obeid handed the keys to one of the men and took the front passenger seat. The others got in without saying a word. Once inside, Obeid spoke, "We are changing the plan, but only slightly."

One of the men responded, "But our instructions were…!"

"Stop! I am in charge. Just listen. We were given instructions by our brother, Antar to go to One Wilshire. He believed that he was being followed and he did not show this morning. He might have been compromised and if so, the building might be under surveillance. As a precautionary measure, our new target will be only half a mile away at the Wilshire Grand Center. If Antar's objective was to cause great devastation, this will be as good, if not better, a target. One Wilshire has only 30 floors. The Wilshire Grand Center has 73. A good part of it is the Intercontinental Hotel. I made reservations there for myself today, which will provide me good cover for the suitcase. Does that make sense?"

The men nodded in agreement as they merged onto I-105 West for the one-hour and fifteen-minute drive.

****

Qasim veered abruptly off course as he descended through 3,000 feet on final approach. He ignored the frantic calls from the tower and directed the aircraft towards the white Capital building in the distance. He anticipated dropping the load at about 800 feet, maintaining that elevation all the way to the White House. He had perhaps three or four minutes max before reaching the drop elevation, opening the payload doors, and releasing the deadly contents.

The door to the hotel room was flung open and agents raced in. Qasim wasn't in the living or dining room. A humming noise could be heard coming from the second bedroom. The men turned saw Qasim's back to them as he sat at a console, staring at three monitors. He had a headset on, so he didn't hear the commotion of the entry. Guzman flashed his badge in front of Qasim's face. Qasim jumped and moved to open the plane's bay doors and drop the load.

"Stop!" hollered Guzman, as one of his agents fired a single shot, dropping Qasim to the floor. They pulled him aside just as Jason and Mike entered the room. Jason pushed past everyone and sat down at the console. "I don't have a pilot's license, but I have soloed. I think I might be able to control this," he said, as he donned the flight headset.

Air traffic control was threatening military interception if Qasim didn't acknowledge and change course back toward DCA. Jason ignored the tower and said, "Tower, I'm declaring an in-flight emergency and taking this plane toward the Chesapeake Bay and the open ocean." The plane was dropping fast. McClintock gave the aircraft more power to gain elevation. He rose past 900 then 1,000 feet before making the slight turn toward the bay in the distance.

"What is the nature of your emergency?" asked the controller.

"The aircraft is carrying a weapon of mass destruction, specifically a nerve agent and needs to be clear of any populated area," Jason replied. "Do not have this plane shot down. If you do, you could kill thousands."

"I'm directing military aircraft to escort you to Andrews Air Force Base," said the controller.

"That won't happen, tower," said Jason.

"What do you mean?" asked the controller.

"I can't land this plane, I'm not a pilot."

"You're going to kill yourself?"

"I'm flying the aircraft remotely," Jason said evenly.

"Oh my God," replied the controller.

"Say a prayer, tower," Jason said.

Guzman and the other agents stood mesmerized as they listened to Jason and watched the screens on the RPA console while the DC-10 changed direction.

Jason levelled the aircraft off at 7,500 feet. Within minutes, he had two F-16 fighters from Andrews AFB on either wing. It was obvious they'd been told the DC-10 was unmanned, but to let the pilots know he'd seen them, Jason rocked the plane's wings back and forth. Jason maintained communication with the tower at Reagan National.

"The airspace is cleared for you to take the aircraft down the bay into open ocean," the tower said. "Fly at least twenty miles offshore before ditching it. The Coast Guard has been notified and are keeping all boat traffic away."

"Got it, tower. Let me know when my distance is good to take it down. I don't want the plane to break up. I'll try a water landing, so the plane sinks intact, without releasing the nerve agent into the air," Jason said.

"Understood. What's your name, pilot?"

"McClintock. Jason McClintock. I've got to concentrate, tower. Let me know when I'm cleared to take her down."

"Will do. Good luck, McClintock."

Jason stared intently at the console, keeping a close eye on the plane's speed and altitude. Without looking up, he asked, "Mike, I'm not that familiar with the east coast. Google the distance from D.C. to the ocean, heading down the bay. I want to keep this aircraft away from any populated areas."

Mike opened his phone and tapped in the question. "It looks like it's about 160 miles. How fast are you flying?"

"I'm at 250 knots. If my math is correct, that should put us at the coast and open water in about 34 minutes."

"I think that's about right," Mike said as he accessed his phone's calculator and punched in the numbers to confirm.

****

Petronovich followed the car onto the 105-West freeway. *They're heading downtown,* he thought. The FBI stayed well back from Petronovich, keeping no less than four cars between them. One agent drove while the other acted as spotter and gave directions.

****

Schumacher's team consisted of several hundred people, including FBI agents, DEA, and state/local law enforcement. Most, except for a few city and county officers, were in plain clothes. At least 30% of the people inside the lobby of One Wilshire were law enforcement.

The nuclear weapons experts from the Department of Energy were in the building, protected, and would be on scene within minutes of the weapon being apprehended. Tensions were high as the noon hour approached.

Schumacher's cell buzzed. He took the call in a private office just outside the lobby, "Schumacher."

"Petronovich is following the suspects and we're behind him, traveling west on the 105. Looks like we're coming your way. I'll call when we exit the freeway and have a better idea of the direction we're headed," said the agent.

"Did you just get on the freeway?" asked Schumacher.

"Yes, sir. If they're going to One Wilshire, we should be about an hour out," responded the agent.

"Keep me posted," Schumacher replied and terminated the call.

****

Guzman's men had moved Qasim to the dining room. The bullet had hit the center mass, most likely hitting a lung and, judging by the loss of blood, a major artery or vein. The men packed the wound and waited for an ambulance to arrive, though they were certain it wouldn't be needed.

"What's going to happen to me?" Qasim whispered, barely audible.

"With any luck, you'll die a slow death here," said one of the guards.

Qasim began to shake with fear as his eyes started to glaze over. "It can't end like this," he slurred softly, exhaling his last breath.

Guzman stood next to Mike as they watched Jason fly the plane. He appeared to know what he was doing. Once he figured out the controls, it wasn't that difficult. The hard part, and the most dangerous, was thc landing. He hoped for a glassy sea with few waves but he knew that was unlikely. You could have cut the tension in the room with a knife.

"McClintock, at your current speed, you have five minutes until you will be cleared to ditch the plane," said air traffic control.

"Understood, tower, five until cleared to take her down," Jason responded, as he took the aircraft down to 5,000 feet. "Level at 5,000, maintaining 250 knots." The mouth of the bay was in sight. White caps could be seen in the distance. The fighter escort had maintained altitude at 7,500 feet, but dropped their speed to 225 knots. If the DC-10 broke up, they didn't want to fly through a mist of sarin gas. The two fighters held back and watched as the aircraft began to lose altitude.

"You are now cleared to take her down. The Coast Guard has confirmed that the area is clear of watercraft."

"Copy that, tower, here we go," Jason said softly as he concentrated on the controls and the monitors. He continued to drop altitude and after lowering the flaps, began to reduce air speed. Jason was descending at close to 600 feet per minute with a reduced speed of 115 knots. The landing gear remained up and locked. The room was quiet as Jason brought the aircraft down. He figured impact to be about eight minutes away. The ocean swells were not nearly as bad as they could have been, but the sea was by no means flat. *This is going to be tricky,* thought Jason as he took a deep breath and exhaled slowly. In the distance, he could recognize the white Coast Guard cutter, with large red and thin blue stripe on the bow. They were well clear of his approach. The ocean white caps were more pronounced the lower he dropped. Talking to himself, he said, "500 feet, 400, 300, 200…nose up and, impact."

The plane hit the water, spraying ocean widely as the nose and wings cut through the surf. One large swell bounced the plane into the air. The right wing came down unevenly and dug into the next swell. The plane cartwheeled, flipping two times before resting upside down in the ocean. It did not break apart, but it quickly began taking on water. "Tower, the aircraft is down and seems to be in one piece."

"Good job, Jason," Mike said as he patted his brother on the shoulder.

"It could have been much worse," Jason responded with a sigh of relief.

Chapter 24

Obeid's driver took the 6th street exit off the 110 north toward L.A. They had no idea that Petronovich was behind them. After half a mile, the driver turned right on Grand. The FBI agents called Schumacher and alerted him that they were close. There was only one car between them and Petronovich. Obeid's car approached One Wilshire and passed it without slowing down. Petronovich was perplexed. *What the fuck?* he thought.

The agent phoned Schumacher in a panic, "He passed One Wilshire! We're following Petronovich and they're turning left on San Francisco. Oh crap! They're pulling into the Wilshire Grand Center! That's the target."

"We don't have boots on the ground there, so it's going to be up to you to stop this guy," Schumacher said. "I'll redirect assets immediately."

"Yes, sir," replied the agent as they continued toward the Wilshire Grand following Petronovich.

Obeid's driver pulled to the curb in front of the valet parking service. Obeid got out and waived off the attendant as the driver popped the trunk. He grabbed the heavy bag and rolled it toward the doors of the massive building looming above him. The building's design was meant to emulate Yosemite's Half Dome, with the sloping roof above. The lobby for the Intercontinental was on the 70th floor. The hotel space included all floors between the 37 and 73. As Obeid entered the atrium, he walked to the bank of high-speed elevators that would take him directly to hotel registration, bypassing the retail stores, restaurants, and offices occupying the floors below 37.

Petronovich slid to the curb after Obeid's car departed. He handed the keys to the valet and quickly followed Obeid into the massive building, keeping him in sight as Obeid got in one of the elevators. Petronovich caught the next elevator up to the 70th floor. Several additional passengers entered, including one of the FBI agents dressed like an unassuming businessman. Vladi used the 40-second ride to breathe deeply and compose himself. *I can't handle this shit,* he thought.

****

Outside the building, the streets were blocked off and a swarm of law enforcement vehicles, both marked and unmarked, swept into the area. Men and women with guns were everywhere. Helicopters circled above; one landed on the rooftop helipad, allowing an FBI SWAT team entrance from the top.

Obeid was at the registration counter checking in when Petronovich's elevator opened to the lobby. Obeid appeared nervous. Instead of focusing on the desk clerk, he was glancing around the room. He looked left, then right, then back again. On the last sweep, he picked up Petronovich standing in the corner. The two men locked eyes and Petronovich began walking toward him. On the other side of the room, the agent in the suit witnessed the subtle confrontation and made his move toward the registration counter. Obied bent over the suitcase and as he did, Petronovich and the agent began to sprint toward him. Obeid input the code just as Petronovich dove through the air, hitting Obeid with such force that he was slammed against the registration counter and knocked out. The agent shoved Petronovich out of the way. He rolled the limp suspect onto his stomach. With one knee in the small of Obeid's back, the agent pulled both arms back toward him and secured the handcuffs.

Petronovich jumped to his feet. "Who the hell are you?" he asked.

"My name is Jacobs, FBI. I was sent by Schumacher to follow and assist you if needed," he replied.

Petronovich bent down to inspect the luggage, "This isn't luggage. You know that, right?"

"That's why I'm here," he said as he dialed Schumacher.

"Jacobs, this suitcase is ticking! We've got to get it out of here! Now!" Petronovich yelled.

Schumacher told Jacobs that a helicopter was on top of the building waiting to take the suitcase away from downtown. Petronovich sprinted to the stairs, taking them two at a time until he reached the emergency exit. He slammed through the door and saw the helicopter waiting, its rotors spinning. Petronovich jumped into the open door, throwing the heavy suitcase onto the seat next to him. The pilot didn't wait for Petronovich to shut his door before lifting off.

****

Mike and Jason were checking in for their flight back to LAX from San Jose del Cabo when Mike phoned Schumacher. He had tried minutes after Jason had taken down the DC-10, but there had been no answer. It was past noon in Los Angeles and the McClintock brothers kept looking at their phones for any information of a bomb being detonated in Southern California. So far, they assumed no news was good news.

"I'm surprised we haven't heard from Vladi," Jason said.

"The fact that we've confirmed that his plane landed and that he hasn't answered is a concern," Mike said. "I wouldn't be surprised if he's up to his neck in what's happening there."

"We leave in an hour," Jason said. "I say we go through security and grab a margarita or two."

"I'm up for that, let's do it."

****

The pilot turned the helicopter west toward the ocean. Speaking into the headset to his co-pilot and Petronovich, he said, "I'm going off the coast about twenty miles before we dump the suitcase into the ocean. I know it's a gamble, but I want to be as far away from the coast as possible."

"We don't know how much time we have before this thing blows," Petronovich said. "If there's an air burst, with the winds blowing west to east, hundreds of thousands of people would be impacted. I say we go out ten miles. The continental shelf drops off rapidly here, so there's deep water that far out. If this bomb is deep when it explodes, damage to human life will be minimal."

The pilot looked at the co-pilot and shrugged. "I'm good with that. I'd like to see my daughter's soccer game tonight."

****

Schumacher was holding Obeid in a private office within minutes of his apprehension. It didn't take him long before he had the names and contact information of the other four men involved. Four separate FBI teams were sent to arrest the suspects. Within an hour, all the roads surrounding the Wilshire Grand were open and traffic was moving as though nothing had happened. *The public will never know how close we came to a disaster today,* thought Schumacher as he walked to his car and waited for news that the bomb had been destroyed.

****

"We're approaching the drop zone. Make sure you're strapped in, then open the door," the pilot said to Petronovich. "I'm bringing the helicopter to a hover just above the waves. When I give the word, drop the device into the water."

"I'm ready when you are," yelled Petronovich into the mic as the wind tore through the helicopter's open door.

"Okay, do it!" commanded the pilot as he watched Petronovich over his shoulder. The Russian shoved the suitcase out the door.

"All right, let's get the hell out of here," said the pilot as he swung the bird toward the coast, giving the aircraft full power, its nose tilted down, skimming 200 feet above the surface of the water.

The co-pilot phoned Schumacher. "The bomb is in deep water," he said. "We're safe."

"Thank God! I'll meet you at the office when you land. Good job! Tell Petronovich that I'll have a bottle of Ciroc Vodka X waiting for him. That's the least the U.S. government can do."

The co-pilot relayed the information. Petronovich smiled, closed his eyes, and rested his head against the back of the seat. He was suddenly exhausted.

Chapter 25

After landing at LAX, Mike drove directly to FBI headquarters. When he and Jason entered Schumacher's office, they found Schumacher and Petronovich sitting on the sofa, the distinct blue bottle of Ciroc Vodka X and a tall green bottle of Glenfiddich on the coffee table between them. Schumacher stood and pulled two leather chairs away from his desk and positioned them opposite the sofa.

"Have a seat, gentlemen. I think we've earned the right to a little libation," Schumacher said as he placed two more glasses on the table.

Jason reached for the single malt while Mike opted for the vodka. Jason raised his glass, "Here's to Kevin Mitchell, our friend and colleague. He gave his life for our country, and for that, we are forever grateful."

Petronovich dropped his head, then looked up and raised his glass. "And here's to my friend Marina. If not for her exposing AdvanChem, we could have had one of the most devastating attacks this country has ever seen."

"I want to thank the three of you for what you have done not only here in the United States, but also in Mexico and the Middle East. Without your help, we could have fallen short of stopping these attacks." Schumacher raised his glass and sipped the vodka.

After a half hour, Mike looked at his watch. Schumacher

spoke, "You guys have family you need to see. You'd better take off. We'll be in touch regarding the formal debrief in the next few days."

"I can't speak for Mike, Jack, but I'm heading back to Montana soon," Jason said. "The debrief will need to be by Skype."

"Same for me," Mike said. "I've got several weeks of work on the vineyard that need my attention."

"I'm sure we can arrange something. Be safe," Schumacher said as he stood and shook each man's hand.

****

The Los Angeles traffic on the 101 was heavy but moving. After Ventura, it lightened up considerably. Barring any unforeseen incidents, the McClintocks would be back in the Valley by seven. The usual brotherly banter was nonexistent, as each man was lost in thought. With a sigh of relief, Mike said, "Almost home."

They turned off Highway 246 onto Refugio Road. There was only a mile to go. The driveway was dark, but the house and perimeter were lit up. Two Sheriff's vehicles were parked in plain sight.

"I think we're safe letting these guys get back to their regular duties," Jason said as they pulled in.

"Why don't you two go inside while I thank the deputies for their help," Mike replied as he parked next to one of the patrol vehicles.

When Jason and Vladi entered the house, it was eerily quiet. The kids were in their room with the doors closed and Brenda was sitting on a sofa in the family room, staring out the picture window. She had clearly been crying; her eyes were red and bloodshot. She looked up as Jason walked in the door and smiled weakly.

"What happened, Brenda?" Jason asked in a whisper as he knelt down beside her chair.

"Daddy's dead, Jason. He was killed, most likely by the killer that followed us. My aunt called about an hour ago."

"I'm so sorry," said Jason as he took a seat beside her and pulled her close.

Hearing talk in the other room, Julie poked her head out of the kitchen. "Oh, I'm so glad you're home," she said. "Where's Mike?"

"He'll be in in a minute," Jason explained. "He's talking with the deputies and thanking them for keeping watch."

"Are you sure it's safe?" Brenda asked through sniffles, as she dabbed her nose with a tissue.

"Yes, positive. The killer is dead. But there's a story to tell, once Mike comes in and we get a drink," Jason said as he rose and walked into the kitchen for glasses and liquor from the cabinet. He returned with two wine glasses filled to the brim with Syrah for Julie and Brenda, then made a second trip with three glasses of ice as well as a bottle each of Glenfiddich and Grey Goose. Mike walked through the door as Jason placed each glass on a coaster.

Mike gave Julie a hug then sat and sipped the scotch. "It sure is quiet around here. Where are the kids?" he asked.

"They're in the bedroom watching a movie," said Julie. "What happened in Mexico?"

Mike looked at Jason, "Let's just say that Jason had a flying lesson in a DC-10 down the Chesapeake Bay."

"I thought you were in Mexico! You don't know how to

fly!" said Brenda.

Jason and Mike filled in the details, then deferred to Petronovich and the Maldives island of Dhigu. "It was there that Vladi confronted Shamoun and learned the critical news," said Jason.

"Which is what?" Brenda asked.

Jason took a long sip of his drink, refilled the glass and handed the bottle to Mike. "The killer's name was Antar. He was in southern California. Vladi here was told by Shamoun that Antar had a small nuclear bomb in a suitcase and had been instructed to set it off around noon today in the Los Angeles business district."

"A small nuke? You guys were dealing with a nuclear device? That could have been devastating!" Julie said, looking back and forth between the three men.

"In a busy area like downtown L.A., especially at lunchtime, it would have been catastrophic," Jason replied. "Vladi was the guy that dealt with the bomb, not us."

"So, what happened?" asked Brenda.

Petronovich shrugged. "We were lucky. With the FBI's help, we located the guy with the bomb. We took it out to sea and dropped it in deep water. Nobody was hurt. That's the end of the story. Now, what's for dinner?" He smiled. "After that, I'd like a good night's sleep. Jason, don't we have a mine in Montana that needs tending?"

"We do indeed," Jason replied smiling, as the bedroom door opened and Sam, Zach, and Rosie bounded into the room, greeting the three men.